Obsession

Aspen Wolff and Arianna Courson

Published by Aspen Wolff, 2024.

OBSESSION

First edition. December 15, 2024.

Copyright © 2024 Aspen Wolff and Arianna Courson.

ISBN: 979-8230745495

Written by Aspen Wolff and Arianna Courson.

Also by Aspen Wolff

Obsession

Also by Arianna Courson

Chronicles of the Enchanted
The Silent Kiss
The Silent Kiss
Lullaby: A Book of Enchanted Shorts

The Bane Saga
Alpha Bane

The Chained Saga
Quiet, Now
Quiet, Now
Be Still
Be Still

The Crave Saga
Crave

Chains
Secrets
Bloodless: The Entire Crave Saga

The Fallen Shadow Saga
Lily's Fallen Shadow
Jason's Angel of Storms
Silence Me
Silence Me

The Switched Chronicles
Switched
Twisted
Deviant
Hush, Little Angel: The Entire Switched Chronicles

The Vendetta Saga
The Demon's Duchess
The Shattered Carnival
City of the Dead
The Wonderland Show
A Song of Darkness
Duchess of Death
Vendetta

Table of Contents

To you, my readers.

I hope you are willing to read books in the future

PARIS'S NOTE

This is a story about a beautiful girl who'd been trauma-tized by the death of people she loved, the same girl who was afraid to love after being hurt.

The same girl who always hid her internal desires and was never able to satisfy herself.

Because she wanted to be normal.

But "normal" is overrated, isn't it?

No matter how much she shoved down all the things she did at night, she couldn't keep it from me. And no matter how "normal" she tried to act, she would never satisfy the burn.

That was...

Until I corrupted her all over again.

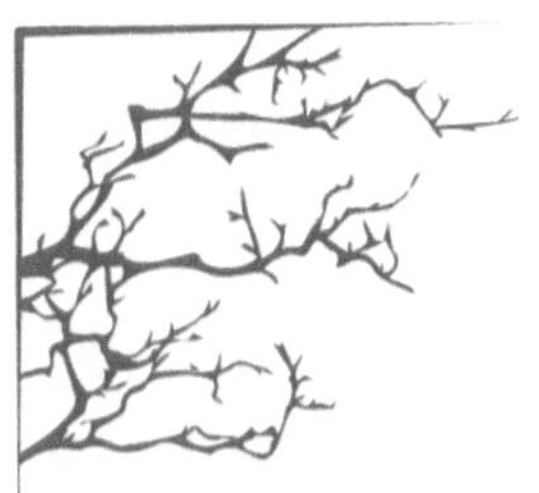

1

Riley

" *'The New York Police are still attempting to solve the murder of Bella Swines,'* " the news reporter said on the TV. " *'The death of the freshman at Manhattan High School still shakes the community of the Manhattan homes. Officer Jonah states that currently, the police have not placed the death of the student a murder, because there is evidence suggesting manslaughter or suicide. Fellow officers urge parents to keep their teens safe and to not step outside your houses after ten pm.'* "

I sat on the floor of my living room, staring at the TV blankly for the last ten minutes. My spoon was halfway up to my mouth, the milk dripping off the edge and into my cereal.

"Riley," a girl said, catching my attention and I dropped my spoon into the bowl. When I gazed up, I saw my mother standing there with her brown hair curled around her shoulders. "You should really stop watching this stuff," Violet told me.

I looked back to the TV. "I want to see if they figure out what happened."

"They took your statement," Violet said, kneeling down beside me as I leveled my eyes on the floor boards. "There's nothing else you can do, Riley."

"I watched her die..." I whispered. "I knew something was off by the way she was acting and...."

"It's alright," Violet whispered, pressing my head to her chest and drew back. "There was nothing you could do, Honey. Seriously, you shouldn't blame yourself."

I only stared back at the TV. "I know what's happening. I know she was murdered. I told the police that, and they still don't believe me."

"They have to find evidence," Violet explained, "that suggests that there was a murder."

I stared back at the TV. "I want to know what happens."

"And I know you do," Violet said, "but it's not good for you if you're staring at the TV for twelve hours watching the news about it."

"I want her to have closure. I know she's dead, but she deserves it. Her spirit deserves it."

"Riley," Violet said, "you have your therapy in thirty minutes. Let's go now, okay?"

I stared at the TV blankly for a moment before turning it off and standing, glancing over at my mom before making my way to the front door, where the shoes were.

"Riley," mom whispered, "I know you're not the average teen and you won't run from these situations until you find the culprit, but you have to let this go."

"I found who killed dad and now that person is in jail for the rest of his life," I stated. "And I'll find out who killed my best friend."

"How was therapy?" Ryan said as both he and I sat on my bed, me twiddling my thumbs on my lap.

"Good," I answered.

"You dodged all the questions," Ryan said, eyes dimming, "didn't you?"

"I don't have time for *therapy*," I said cynically. "I want to know who killed Bella."

"You can't solve all murders, Riley," Ryan stated. "I'm serious, you're going to go crazy. You're a nineteen-year-old high-schooler, not a fucking detective."

"I'm not a normal teen," I stated, "you know that. I'm not saying I have special magic powers that somehow make me emotionless, but I can control myself."

"Don't you consider this an unhealthy obsession?" Ryan questioned. "Because that's what this is, you're obsessing."

I glared at him, then. "You think wanting to know *who murdered my best friend* is considered an *obsession*?" My eyes dimmed. "You don't know me Ryan," I stated. "That's why I decided to dump you when we were dating."

He flinched as if my words were knives, and gazed back at me. "We left on good terms," he stated. "Why are you still angry with me?"

"I'm not," I answered, standing up and stepping over to my desk, sitting in the chair while twirling around until I faced him. "I'm irritated because everybody is telling me to chill out about this. Bella and I were close, you have no idea."

"You don't know if it was a murder," Ryan stated. "The police found evidence that stated otherwise."

"I *know* it was a murder," I told him. "She would *never* kill herself, and there were no signs of minor injuries indicating manslaughter. If she was murdered on accident, there wouldn't have been so many injuries, Ryan. I know my friend, you *don't*."

He was silent for a moment, eyeing me. "You know what you're doing to yourself is dangerous, Riley."

"I know what I know," I answered, eyes narrowing. "And I don't need you judging my opinions. Another reason why you're not boyfriend material, Ryan; you judge everything I do."

"Still thought good terms," he stated, crossing his arms over his chest. "Now I suspect you have some kind of grudge on me, Riley."

I rolled my eyes and looked back to my desk, getting to work on my drawing.

"Wow," he said, "now you're ignoring me? At this rate you could just tell me to piss off and slam the door in my face."

I waved to my bedroom door. "You're free to leave whenever you want, Ryan. I didn't chain you to the bed."

I heard him slouch back on the mattress.

"Ah," he said, "no, I'm good right now, Riley. I'm not leaving you alone." He threw his hands up. "Who knows? Maybe you'll accept me for who I am and let us move forward."

"For the hundredth time," I growled. "I'm not having sex with you, Ryan."

He sat up on my bed. "Why not, huh? Why? What's it about me that you don't like?" He paused. "Are you listening?"

"I'm trying not to."

"Fuck, Riley," he said, glaring at me, "you're being a bitch right now, I think you should know."

"That's nothing new," I told him cynically.

"When I kiss you, you always draw away."

"Because I'm not in the mood, and when you keep pushing, I'm *more* not in the mood."

He sighed, lying back down on the bed. "I'm not leaving without a goodbye kiss. One on the throat for a full minute, Kay?"

"That's called sexual assault and breaking and entering."

"Is it?" he said then. "It's not assault if you want it, and *you* let me in the house."

"For one, I don't want you to kiss me, so yes, that's assault. And two? You barged in here without my permission—I did *not* let you in—so yes, that's breaking and entering."

"Stop playing hard to get and come over here already."

I spun around to snap at him, but paused, staring down at the floor next to my window.

"What?" Ryan said, sitting up on my bed with his shirt slightly exposing his stomach.

There was something clearly seductive about his pose.

I got up off my desk chair then, stepping carefully over to the window and kneeled down to the floor, picking up a black feather that lay on the floor before me.

"A feather?" Ryan said. "Really? Now are you suddenly distracted like a fucking dog or what?"

"Where did it come from?" I said more to myself, standing and leaning out the window, my brown hair blowing gently in the breeze as it curled in the humidity.

But when I looked down to the ground below, I saw a figure there, clothes covered in shadows as the cloak he wore waved around him in the wind.

But... what...?

I narrowed my eyes, staring down at his face that was half-masked in shadows.

But... he was wearing something on his eyes... and there was a feather attached to it, and both sides of his head consisted of horns.

My breath caught, eyes widening.

He was wearing a masquerade mask, one that looked like a demon, but it had beautiful golden embroidery and a crown centered at the top.

But who was he...? And why was he dressed like that?

When I opened my mouth to question him, he pressed his finger to his lips, telling me to be silent.

He pointed to the roof, and when I gazed at one of the tiles, there was a piece of paper flapping in the wind, and I reached out to grab it, currently forgetting about Ryan.

When I gazed back up at the mysterious guy, he pressed his finger to his lips again and stepped back into the shadows.

I leaned back over the window, searching the darkness for him, but he was gone.

The feather must've been from his mask.

But who was he…?

"What was that about?" Ryan questioned from behind me, and I nearly jumped. His hands snaked around my waist and threaded through the fabric of my shirt. "You want everyone to watch?"

"Nothing happened," I answered, pushing the paper and the feather into my pocket and turned, throwing his hands off me. "And don't touch me."

Ryan eyed me suspiciously for a moment. "You're *really* good at playing hard to get, aren't you?"

"Back off." I brushed past him.

He rolled his eyes, and glared at me. "When are you going to ease up around me?"

"When you stop emitting *rapist* vibes," I answered.

His glare sharpened, and he stepped out of my room. "Whatever, it's late and we have school tomorrow. Night."

"Night," I said as he left my room, then muttered to myself, "Thank fucking god. He finally left."

After a couple seconds of hearing the front door close, I shut my bedroom door and shuffled the paper out of my pocket.

It was a note, and I blinked in confusion for a moment before I opened the folded paper, gazing curiously down at the writing seconds later.

Meet me at the bridge on Coal Street. If you don't feel safe alone, bring a friend, but don't bring your boyfriend. I am here to answer your questions about recent events.

I squinted down at the paper.

Huh?

Who was my boyfriend? This was news to me.

I looked down at the signature down at the paper, eyeing it curiously for a moment.

P.

So his name started with the letter P... Was it Perry? Peach? Patrick?

Or was it a girl?

I shook my head, pulling my phone out of my pocket. No, he gave me the option to bring a friend, so this was worth something. He didn't have any red flags...

Well... major ones.

And a part of me pleaded to see him.

He must've had answers about Bella's death. He must've.

Meet me at the park on Summit Road, I texted my friend.

Uh, why? she texted back.

Just do it, I answered, *trust me.*

Okay, see you in five.

I smiled at her lack of questioning.

So I grabbed my phone and stuffed it in my purse, throwing it over my shoulder as I darted down the stairs to find my mom there, typing frantically on her work computer.

"Hey, mom!" I said, Violet looking up at my voice.

"Oh," she answered, "hey, Honey. Going somewhere?"

She probably noticed my purse and jacket were on.

"Yeah," I responded, "I'm meeting my friend."

"Just be careful," Violet said a little sternly. "You have your taser?"

I nodded.

"Okay, go on," she said. "And remember, any *slight* trouble and you text the code word to me. What is it? Do you remember?"

I nodded. "'*Peanut butter.*'"

Violet smiled. "Be back before ten."

"Thanks, mom." And I darted out the front door.

"**O**kay, what the hell are we doing here?" Claire, my best friend, questioned. "And why now? It's almost eight and it's kind of dark out here, not gonna lie."

I was in a small friend group in my high school, Manhattan. The group consisted of Claire, Ryan, Bella, and me, and everyone was very close despite previous broken off relationships.

Bella died many months ago, almost a year ago, and Claire as well as Ryan slowly got out of the grieving process after the first eight months, but I never really had closure knowing that my best friend's killer was still out there somewhere.

I was the one who found her body, anyway.

Claire was the average teen girl, though she never really died her hair blonde like Bella did; she had long, black locks that fell past her shoulders.

Bella—on the other hand—had straight, blonde hair that she curled at the ends every morning, and after the recent pandemic across the entire world, she was one of the select teens who wore pajamas to school.

Ryan was the average jock, though he was silently nerdy. I never really understood how he had straight A's whereas the rest of my classes who played sports their whole lives had B's or below. Ryan had brown hair, though it was pretty dark so some thought it might've been black, and he had those odd brown eyes that also had specks of black in them.

I—on the other hand—was the mixed race teen in the group; I had dark brown curly hair that—for some reason—decided to be wavy some days. I straightened it most of the time, and of course curled it at the ends. I honestly hated how it looked naturally, and I had to buy expensive hair stuff in order to get those coils I really liked. My skin was a very light brown, so light that some considered me tan. I had beautiful silver eyes, as my mother once said; the eyes I got from my ancestors. And my average day-to-day clothes were skirts and a T-shirt, or jeans and a sweatshirt.

If I wore skirts, it was usually worn with leggings. I honestly didn't like showing off my body like other girls did.

"Earth to Riley," Claire said, waving a hand in front of my face. "We've been standing here for ten minutes, and it's getting kind of chilly. What's happening, girl?"

"Ryan was in my bedroom earlier," I explained, "and as I was shoving him out the door, I found a feather in my room."

"So, we looking for a bird, or...."

"No," I answered shortly, "I looked out the window and saw a guy out there."

Claire raised her brows. "Secret boyfriend?"

"No, I don't even know him," I said. "And can you please let me speak? Thanks." I stared off into the distance for a moment. "He was wearing a masquerade mask, and it had like these weird horns and feathers attached to the sides, but when I was going to ask him who he was, he told me to be silent."

"That's creepy."

"He pointed to the roof of my house," I said, pulling out a note from my pocket, "and I found this."

Claire read the lines of the note before pulling back. "Riley, if you get us killed, I *swear* to God."

"We're going to be fine," I answered. "He told us to meet him here and he mentioned that I could bring a friend if I felt unsafe alone. So that's a good sign, right?"

"Or because he has an entire group of strong ass men with him so they can mug us and dump us in the river." Claire put her thumbs up. "Great job, Riley. We're dying tonight."

I just stared off in the distance for a moment. "I don't know why... but I have a feeling he's going to help us."

"Why do you have this feeling? Did he say something about it?" Claire questioned.

I didn't know why, but when I found the feather from his mask that flew in my window, I got a sudden assurance that I was safe... Mainly because I found the same dark feather at my father's grave, and the other at Bella's.

It was highly possible that this guy was the murderer... but something told me...

He was someone else.

But I didn't know if he was harmful or helpful.

Not yet.

Claire bumped my shoulder suddenly, and nodded to the alley ahead of us when I glanced at her.

"Is that him?" she whispered.

I squinted my eyes, noticing a dark figure standing in the shadows of the alleyway, the same cloak waving around him like tides in an ocean, and the same black mask covering him from his eyes up.

The hood was always drawn over his hair, so I couldn't see it's color or style.

I took one step up to the man, watching to see if he stiffened or gave any signs of excitement or nervousness.

He gave off nothing, and instead, just stood there.

So I stepped up to him faster, Claire whispering in protest, "Riley!" but I heard her follow seconds later.

I slowed when the mysterious boy put his hand out, indicating for me to stop.

And I did.

But Claire was far behind, and when I narrowed my eyes to watch the boy's blue gaze, I whispered, "You look young."

"Riley," he whispered menacingly, making me stare up at him when he shielded his voice with the quiet one, "you're entering dangerous waters. You need to tread more carefully."

"What are you talking about?" I questioned him.

"Girl, you run too fast!" Claire said, gasping as she continued to run to me.

"Riley," he said, leveling his blue eyes with mine, "you're in danger. I don't think you understand that. You need to stop searching for the culprit."

"How the hell did you know I was searching for the culprit?" I questioned suspiciously. "How do you know my name? How did you know where I live? And how do you know so much about me?"

"You won't understand," the man told me. "You're completely arrogant, for one. And you must give up the curiosity and the guilt, for two. This obsession to find the killer is not how the grieving process works. It's dangerous, what you're doing. There are dangerous men wanting to hurt you, so stop being a moron and back off. That's the police's job for a reason, you idiot."

"Stop being a dick, emo boy," I said at his name-calling. "Also, why does everyone call it an *obsession*?" I questioned angrily. "And why doesn't anyone understand that I can take care of myself? I have training for these situations."

"Karate won't be the only thing that could protect you from a gun to your head, Riley," he stated coldly. "And the fact that you have such confidence in these things without proper training is dangerous. Stay away from the searching. The police will find the culprit."

"You seem like you know *everything*!" I said to him, Claire stopping at the mouth of the alley and gasping. "Why can't you run to the police and tell them everything you know, huh? Let them capture the killer! Who's the moron now, huh?"

The boy's eyes grew darker. "You're such an idiot."

"*What*?" I questioned.

"I'm not on good terms with the police, Riley. Clearly—with the mask? In fact, I'm wanted across the entire state, but they don't know what I look like. I just wear this as a precaution."

My eyes grew. "What did you do?"

He sighed, shaking his head. "Stay away from this, Riley. And you'll live; life is precious. I only take it when it's needed. Goodbye."

"Stop," I stated, catching his arm to prevent him from leaving, "did you kill her? Did you kill Bella?"

"No," he answered shortly.

"What did you do?" I questioned. "Should I trust you or run from you?"

He was giving off mixed signs.

"I'm dangerous," he answered vaguely. "But I am your ally."

"How dangerous?" I continued. "Did you kill anyone? Hurt them?"

He never responded.

I let go of his arm then, eyes widening when I backed away.

He just stood there, watching my next move.

I caught Claire's arm.

"Ow!" she said, clearly taken off guard. "What's going on? What the hell?"

"You're staying at my house tonight," I told her as I continued to stare at the boy. "No fighting, got it?"

"Uh, okay," she said.

I started backing out of the alleyway, keeping my eyes on the boy as I pulled Claire along with me.

My best friend just seemed to glance around nervously. "Are we in danger?"

"I don't know," I answered, "but let's go home. Now."

We both ran out of the alleyway, me pulling my phone out of my pocket and dialing 9-1-1.

"9-1-1, what's your emergency?"

"I think I found a killer," I said, "I'm safe, but I last saw him at an alleyway behind a brewery on Coal Street. I'm not sure if he's still there. He wears a masquerade mask and a black cloak, he told me he's on the run from the police."

"Okay, police are on their way, can I catch your nam—"

I hung up on them, pushing my phone into my pocket.

"Why did you do that?" Claire questioned. "It would help them protect you."

"I can't trust anyone I don't know," I answered. "It's too dangerous."

And we ran back home seconds later.

I had been staring at the ceiling in my room for almost half an hour, Claire asleep in the guest room across from my space.

I couldn't sleep for the life of me... everything seemed so scary and nerve racking... The eyes of the boy looked so dark... like the ocean at night, but he seemed so young and kind.

But he also seemed so scary and intimidating.

Could he have been the killer? Was he the bad guy?

I couldn't really tell... It was horrible, not knowing. Everything seemed so off and confusing, and I intended to get an answer.

My father was murdered when I was around eight years old, and I'd been traumatized since.

When I was fourteen, I managed to start looking for the killer, and I found him.

It was some mugger... but he didn't really mean to kill my father; it was an accident.

I found evidence at a young age, and I managed to figure out who killed him within a week. When I told the police about him, they looked him up and found he had a major history of robbing and theft, and they caught him off guard.

He was in jail now, and I felt safer.

Until Bella's death.

Honestly, I felt like I was in one of those TV shows on that channel; the one that played murder mysteries and romances. Like the author in, *Murder She Wrote,* or the baker in, *Murder She Baked,* and the librarian in that other show, *Aurora Teagarden Mysteries.* They didn't need training to find the culprit, did they? Then why did I?

It's fiction, Riley, a part of me said. *Seriously, are you going insane?*

Probably.

Honestly, I felt like I was unsafe all the time. Every homeless person a murderer, every pedestrian a mugger; I never felt safe alone.

Could the boy in the mask know that?

Why else would he tell me if I *"wasn't safe to bring a friend?"*

Also, who was this *boyfriend* he was talking about? I didn't have one. Was there another guy stalking me?

Wow... my brain wouldn't shut off... I wasn't going to sleep, was I?

Well... that was nothing new.

All the sudden there was a tap on my window, and I nearly jumped off my bed before I saw a shadow out there.

He waved to me and pointed to another piece of paper attached to the window, jumping off the roof seconds later.

I shot up from my bed and threw the window open, scanning the ground for him, but...

He was gone.

Huh...?

I grabbed the paper and closed the window, opening the note and aiming the writing under the moonlight so I could see better.

Wow... called the police on me? That's rude, you know. You don't even know me, Riley.

Whatever, I get it. I know I'm hiding things that you can sense, and I get your fear, Riley. I get it.

I've done bad things, I think you should know. And I can't tell you those things I did because I know you won't understand. Not yet.

Just know this, my intent is to help not harm, I swear it. You won't know me for a while, but you will eventually. I swear, I mean you no harm, okay?

You just have to trust me.

P.

I stared down at the paper for a moment, going back to my window to gaze down at the trees where I saw him earlier.

He was there again... gazing up at my room with his blue eyes glowing in the darkness.

I opened my window, putting my hand out to gesture for him to stay, and I took the paper he left, turning it over and scraping a note back to him.

If you want me to trust you, tell me your name.

And I released it into the night, the wind blowing it down to him and he caught it, staring down at the paper for a moment before gazing up at me.

I watched in awe as he used the American Sign Language to spell it, and I grabbed the pen I was using and wrote the letters down on my arm.

P. A. R. I. S.

Paris? As in the capital of France?

I looked down at him, seeing his blue eyes reflecting my image even far below.

I knew learning how to spell in sign language would come in handy some day, and I signed back:

T. H. A. N. K. S.

He nodded in response, signing:

G.O.O.D. N.I.G.H.T.

I nodded, closing my window.

Paris... *Paris*... Paris who?

I knew he wasn't going to tell me that yet, and that name he gave me was probably a fake one; or one that he went by.

I already called the police on him, why wouldn't he expect I'd call them again and tell them his name?

Oh, well... It was something, at the very least.

I looked back to my window, eyes dimming.

I wanted to ask him a million questions, a *million*; why he was so interested in me, what horrible things he had done, who he was, how he knew about my interests, and what he knew about the murder of my best friend.

I ran over to the window, throwing it open to the cool, night air.

"Paris!" I called into the darkness. "Paris!"

There was no response.

My eyes stung with tears. Could I trust him...?

"Paris!"

Silence.

And I called one last time, "*Paris*!"

No response.

So I closed the window, sighing into my drafty room and stepped over to my bed, getting under the covers seconds later.

After switching off my light, I eased into my mattress, feeling a sudden cold consume me and I attempted to drape more blankets over myself, but it never left.

So I curled up under the sheets and held myself as my eyes stung.

Sometimes I wished I never broke off with Ryan... Because on nights like these—when I felt cold and icy and my skin stung with sorrow—I just needed someone to hold... and I got rid of all my teddy bears when I was fifteen; I was too old for them, anyway.

Everyone told me I was trying to grow up too fast, but I knew if I stayed a child, I'd be dead right now.

Bella was gone... all gone... my father, too.

Sometimes it felt like there was someone after me, intending to cause me immense pain.

What did I do to deserve this? Why did this have to happen?

Hot tears slid into the pillowcase, and I clutched the pillow, beginning to cry.

"Hey," a voice said into my room.

I cried out, shooting up from the bed and scrambled to the headboard, covering myself with a blanket despite me showing no skin.

There was a shadow at the foot of my bed, and I breathed shallowly as he eyed me through the familiar mask.

Paris.

Though when I dropped the sheet as an attempt to scramble for something on my nightstand, I noticed his eyes travel to my chest, and then down further, until they drifted back up to my lips, then finally my eyes.

Why was something pooling in my belly with his stare?

This only happened at night... when I was in the mood to touch myself, but I shoved the thought away.

"How did you..." I said, voice shaking, "get in here...?"

"The window," he responded, nodding to it.

My eyes moved to the window and then back to him, widening when I realized he used his normal voice.

His tone was soft, but somewhat deep; it was a mixture between dark and soothing.

The pool inside me was getting hotter; I was nearly sweating.

I backed myself against the headboard when he stepped further to me and he stopped.

"You were calling me," he stated, "what did you need?"

When I was silent, he stepped further to me and I pushed myself further to the headboard.

"You're... crying..." he said then.

I pushed a finger to my eye and drew back, seeing the tip of my finger glisten with the leftover tears from my cheek.

I wiped my eyes almost violently before drawing back, gazing up at him with my eyes still glistening.

"Your friend..." he said softly, making me clutch my comforter tighter. "Her death was a while ago... but it's still fresh to you, isn't it?"

I gazed down at my bed, rubbing my arms uncomfortably.

"Are you cold?" he said, making his way over to the window and shutting it. "Is that better?"

But I continued to notice his gaze trailing my form.

My eyes shot up to him, and they dimmed in concern. "Who are you?"

"I gave you my name," he stated, looking at me now. "That is all I can give you, Riley."

"Paris..." I said, "is it fake or real?"

"It's what I go by."

Right, as I thought.

"What do you want from me?" I asked him.

He was silent for a moment. "You won't understand."

I gazed up at him then. "Give me a reason to trust you. A valid one."

His eyes dimmed. "I can't. You'll have to learn."

"I can't tell what you want," I told him, trying to understand this fluttering feeling he was giving me. "I can't tell what your intent is. If you want to kill me, then you're probably luring me somewhere. If you want to kill me, you would've already. I don't understand your motive. If you really want to protect me, why? Why me, huh? It's concerning."

He was silent.

My brows drew together. "Who are you, Paris? What are you to me...?"

"I know you," he stated. "You sort of know me."

"Paris..." I asked him, sitting up now, "will I see you again soon?"

He nodded. "You know me at school. You've seen me multiple times. And I'm in some of your classes."

"So I'll see you? Tomorrow?"

He nodded. "Yeah, and just so you know, I won't show myself to you until you recognize me. Only then will you know me," his eyes pierced into mine, "and you'll *have* to keep me a secret."

"How do you know I will?" I questioned more out of curiosity.

His eyes locked on mine. "Or you'll be punished."

"What does *that* mean?" I questioned.

"You know what it means, Riley," he stated.

My breaths quickened.

"I have to go now," he told me. "Stay here tonight. Don't leave the house until morning, got it?"

I nodded numbly, still questioning whether or not he was the killer.

"Riley," he said then, "everything will be okay. So don't cry, alright?"

I pressed my finger to my eyes, feeling my cheeks dampen suddenly.

I didn't even realize I was crying.

He started to the window, and stopped, clearly hesitating.

When he turned to look at me, his eyes were dark enough to look like the night sky. "Riley..." he whispered, clearly not wanting to leave me alone, "I'm sorry. I really am. I know you don't understand, but I just need you to know that everything will be okay."

"At least tell me one thing," I whispered, and when he looked up, I continued, "who's next...?"

His eyes darkened, but he sighed, hands twitching at his sides as if it was a nervous tick. "Claire..." he whispered, "Claire is next."

I almost screamed, but swallowed the urge down. "Who's the killer?"

"I..." he sighed, "I don't know, but I have a suspicion."

"How could you know she was next and not know who the killer is?"

He gazed at me. "I heard someone *say* it," he said irritably, "and I don't know who that person was."

My brows drew together.

It seemed legit... so why did I suspect he was lying...?

"Riley..." he whispered gently, "just trust me this once. I think you'll recognize me at school. So I'll see you then, yeah?"

I nodded, and he turned back to the window, hopping back onto the window sill and disappeared into the night.

I got off my bed and closed the window.

"Paris…" I whispered to myself, trying to remember, "blue eyes… white skin… Paris.…"

I stared off into the night. "Why can't I place you…?"

But I shook my head, getting under the covers and pulling the comforter up to my shoulders.

"I'll find you…" I said to myself, snuggling into the mattress, "I'll find you, Paris."

2

Riley

"**S**eriously," Ryan said, leaning against a pile of lockers while I shut my own, "what's going on, babe? You've been quiet all day."

What was going *on* was that I was already half-way through the day, and I still wasn't placing Paris anywhere. Some guys had a similar voice as him, but none had his eye color or his skin color or his... *build* for that matter.

"Riley," Ryan pressed, "are we not on speaking terms now?"

"We are," I told him, rolling my eyes. "Stop being so over dramatic."

"Me?" he said, clearly offended. "*I'm* over dramatic?"

"Yep," I responded shortly, "you're calling *me* obsessive? Then why are you so keen on finding out if I'm upset when I'm not? You've never acted that way, so now I suspect you're trying another way to get into my pants."

"More like panties," he commented.

I shot him a look.

Ryan rolled his eyes and walked off into the other direction without another word.

I exhaled a soft sigh.

Finally... a moment of peace. God, I hated him.

I didn't like thinking that, but I really didn't like Ryan. He was a jerk, a user, and a manipulator; not in a bad way, of course. He never assaulted me or hurt me in any way.

Even though he tried to get on me multiple times.

He was just... very, *very* possessive, and I hated it. Many girls would squeal over his possessiveness, but it took a while for me to get over the squeal and realize that it was all selfish.

Ryan never liked me, he just liked getting the attention from dating a writer.

And also the fact that he could have me help him with his essay; if by "help" you mean "write it for him."

Ryan was a smart guy, per say. He was good at math and science and knew many pointless facts, but he was really lazy when it came to certain assignments; ones that I specialized in.

Yes, he was good at Math and Science, but I never asked him to do my homework for me or to give me the answers on the next unit test.

He did the opposite, though, and as hard as it was to re-alize the relationship was all based on his ego, I broke it off.

I sighed and pressed my forehead to my locker, deciding to take a deep breath before running off to my Health Education class.

But right as I exhaled, something caught me off guard.

"Paris!" someone yelled, making my eyes shoot open. "Ma' man! Yo! What's up?"

I started breathing shallowly, waiting for him to respond.

"Eh," his familiar voice said, "nothing much. Got some-where to be, though. Mind letting go?"

I remained in the same position as I heard the boy's arm ruffle against Paris's clothes when he let go.

"What class you got?" the boy said.

"Health Education," Paris responded, making me still.

"Oh, I heard that class sucks."

"It's not bad."

Hold up... Paris was in my next class...?

Who was he?

I turned then, daring enough to lock my eyes on him.

My breath caught, eyes taking in his familiar sandy-blonde hair and white skin, but I could tell from his ocean blue eyes that it was him.

He was the boy in the mask.

How did I not recognize him before? I could've sworn that I never heard his name in this entire school... so...

Hold on...

I squinted my eyes at him.

He was that quiet boy in the class; the one my teacher always called "Lucan" because it was his last name. He very rarely spoke, and he never really seemed shy or anything; he seemed almost moody.

But as I watched him, I placed him in other classes.

He... was in my Biology class... English, too... and my Algebra class...

What the hell?

And he was somewhere else, too... Somewhere I went quite frequently.

And it slapped me in the face.

Oh, Jesus... He was the waiter at my favorite restaurant.

The one that was very short staffed.

My breaths came shorter.

I always thought he was cute, but... never really knew him that well...

I always thought he was moody and angsty.

He wasn't cute... he was *hot*... Jesus Christ, fucking *steaming*.

My eyes trailed his body, figuring that since he was paying attention to his friends, I could eye-fuck him a little.

I had a bad mouth—a bad mind, honestly. I cussed mainly on joke-full occasions but rarely did I do it out of anger.

But really—how I was taking in all of him—this was the exact definition of eye-fucking.

Because I was invading *everywhere*.

"You know it's rude to stare, Riley," Paris said, and I shot up from my position, startled.

His blue eyes looked somewhat warm but also cold, and he smirked at my reddened cheeks, and I stared at the floor then, hoping to get out of this embarrassing situation.

How was that possible? What was he thinking?

Did he get this fluttery-hot feeling, too?

The bell rattled my ears, making me jump, and I realized the halls were empty apart from me and him.

I was late to class, too.

Paris nodded down the hall, still smirking. "Come, walk with me. We can go to class together."

He started down the hall, and I stumbled over my own feet until I followed behind him.

"Paris?" I clarified.

"Yep."

"As in… the Paris who came into my bedroom last night?"

He gave me a side glance, and smiled. "Yeah, I guess. Although, the way you put that sounds kind of creepy."

"It was creepy," I countered.

He shrugged. "I didn't think so, you *were* calling me, Riley."

I was silent then, noticing the way he walked.

He strolled coolly down the hall as if nothing weighed his body at all; his muscles were relaxed, and he seemed as if he was always at ease.

"Paris…?" I said as we passed the science hall.

"Yes?"

"Are you okay?" I said automatically.

He gave me a side glance. "Do I *not* look okay?"

"No, I mean, *yes*, but… With everything you know, with your secret life, it sounds kind of… nerve racking."

He laughed, though silently, and gazed back at me in amusement. "'*Secret life*?' You make that sound like I'm a superhero or something."

"You kind of are," I answered. "You know… with your mask and everything. But what I don't know… is who you're trying to save."

He stopped then, and I nearly stumbled when I slowed, as well. When I looked back at him, his eyes were dark, and he shook his head.

"Riley, Riley, Riley," he said, exasperated, then looked at me, "seriously. Stop asking questions. You need to let this go, okay?"

"Why?" I questioned. "Why do I need to let this go?"

He gave me a sad look. "You're endangering yourself."

"But you don't know the murderer, right?" I said. "You can give me answers, right?"

"No," he said, "I can't. Because if I do, you'll know the answers, and you'll be next."

"How is that possible?" I questioned him. "How? You know the answers, don't you? So why is that a problem? You clearly haven't been targeted yet."

He gave me a bored look. "Riley, I'm very stealthy, okay? I grew up in a dangerous family, and I know my way around things like this."

"What do you mean?" I said, stomach coiling. "Dangerous? How dangerous?"

"You see?" Paris said. "Now you're asking me about *my* past, and that's none of your concern. I'm not the bad guy, Riley. And you need to stop looking for them."

"But I need to find who killed—"

I suddenly found myself pressed harshly to the lockers with Paris in front of me, breath heating my cheeks.

"Riley," Paris said, tone sharpening, "enough. I don't care what you say, you're obsessing, got it?"

"I am *not* obsessing," I snapped. "Why does everyone say that?"

He shoved me harder to the wall, making me suck in a breath when his knee brushed a little spot in between my legs.

"Because you are," he responded, and I forced myself to glare at him despite this making the heat in my belly worse, "you are obsessing, Riley, and you are putting yourself in danger." He paused when he noticed something in my eyes flicker. "Do you..." he said, studying me, "you *know* you're putting yourself in danger, don't you?" And he leaned further into me, his knee brushing farther as I winced. "You don't care, though."

I moved my eyes to the wall behind him, avoiding eye contact.

"Look," Paris said, standing back up but I didn't move from my position, "I know it's hard to do this, Riley, but you need to let this go."

What were we talking about again?

Oh, right. Murder.

"I can't," I said, slightly breathless.

"Why?" he countered. "Why can't you?"

"Because..." I said, "if I don't stop him... Then I'll be all alone."

Paris was silent then, watching my stiff stance.

"You're not alone," he said.

"I will be," I retorted, "I need to find him. Or my mom'll be gone, and Claire and everyone I care for, too."

Paris watched me for a moment. "This has happened before..." he said, "hasn't it?"

I sniffled, wiping my eyes that started stinging. "Yeah, but it was an accident."

My father.

"You don't think it was," he said, "do you?"

I looked to him. "I don't feel like talking about this, Paris, alright?"

"What's his name?" he questioned before I could walk off.

"Who?" I said.

"Your boyfriend," Paris said as if I were dumb. "His name?"

My brows drew together. "I don't know what you're talking about, honestly. I don't have a boyfriend."

He paused. "Yeah, you do."

"No," I said, "I don't. All alone, and I like it that way."

"The dude," Paris explained despite me countering my previous comment of loneliness, "the dude with the brown hair and brown eyes. Nerdy as hell."

I rolled my irises in response. "I think you mean Ryan," I stated. "And no, he's not my boyfriend, I broke it off because he's an ass."

"Why is he always at your house then?" Paris questioned.

"One, you're a stalker, you gotta stop doing that, and two, he comes in uninvited."

"So, you're calling *me* a stalker when your *ex* comes in by breaking and entering without your permission."

"Yep."

Paris sighed, shaking his head.

"I don't know why you're so interested in my love life," I stated, "but stop it. It's creepy." I turned. "I don't care if your repeat yourself ten thousand times, I'm not letting this go."

And I walked off to my Health class.

"Alright, class," Ms. Johnson said. "Ten pushups!"

The whole student body groaned in annoyance.

"Why are you all complaining?" she said, throwing her hands up. "We just spent half of the ninety minute block learning about *baby making*. Is this really a problem?"

I heard Paris chuckle from behind me.

"Alright," the teacher stated, shrugging. "Do what you will, kids. Twenty pushups, and grab a partner, too, they'll spot you."

The class exhaled another sigh at the increased number of push-ups.

But I knew by now they secretly liked having partners so they could mess around.

Ms. Johnson knew, too.

"Ah—ah," she stated, "I wasn't finished, *I'm* picking the partners, my friends."

Another groan.

"Yep, sucks, doesn't it?" She pointed to me, making me still. "Riley, you're with Paris."

"Wait—" I said.

"No arguments," Johnson said, shaking her head. "Johnathan, you're with Alex."

I took a glance at Paris behind me while the teacher continued to talk, and he smiled back at me.

Though, not kindly.

I stared back forward.

So this was how my day was going to go? Great.

"Alright!" Johnson said, clapping her hands and earning a couple gasps. "Let's get to work, kids! Twenty push-ups and your partner has to spot you!"

"Ladies first," Paris said, smiling when I shot him a look. "Wow," he commented, "that was nasty, you might want to glare sharper, though." He then whispered, "It's more menacing."

I shook my head and dropped to the ground, Paris remaining in a standing position and leaning lazily against the bleachers as I started doing my pushups.

"Your back's not straight," he commented, "you're arching it."

"Shut up," I said, breathless.

"I'm your spotter, remember?" he commented. "So you listen to me."

"Why do we even *need* a spotter?" I questioned cynically. "It's pushups, it's not like we're lifting hundred pound weights or something."

Paris chuckled from above me. "You complain a *lot*."

"And you're irritating *a lot*," I snapped back, "but do I mention it? No."

"You just did," he said.

I finished my last pushup and stood, glaring at him with sweat sliding down my temples. "I hate you so much."

"You barely even know me, and I could argue that you hate everyone, Riley."

I rolled my eyes, staring back at the floor seconds later. "Yes, I have trust issues, but there's reasons, okay? Now get on the ground and drop twenty."

He smirked. "Yes, ma'am." And he dropped down, starting his pushups.

My eyes rounded at how fast he did them, it was two pushups per second, and he didn't seem to be straining or hurting at all.

My arms, on the other hand, were screaming in agony.

He stood after about ten seconds, stretching out his arms as if he just woke up and shook off his body, gazing at me seconds later.

"What?" he said. "You're staring."

"What are you?" I questioned. "A *robot*?"

He chuckled. "Does it seem that way?"

"Yeah," I said as if he was stupid. "Either that or you've worked out since you were a toddler."

Paris shrugged. "My father always taught me to protect myself, Riley."

"From who?"

He stopped, and stared at me, blue eyes suddenly cold. "The police."

My heart stopped.

"Okay, kids!" Johnson said. "Let's end class with a little kick ball, huh?"

"Thank you," one of the popular girls muttered sarcastically.

"Alright, let's get into our formation!" Ms. Johnson said. "Go! Go! Go!"

All the kids ran all over the gym, but I kept my eyes fixed on the bleachers behind Paris.

"Paris..." I whispered, "what are you to me? Are you dangerous?"

"Yes," he responded shortly, making my heart stop, "but not to you. Everyone but you."

I backed away from him and shook my head. "I don't know how I can trust you...."

"You'll have to learn," he responded. "Trust takes time, but I'm warning you," he leaned forward, "your time is running out."

And he walked off, leaving me standing alone in the now empty gym; everyone already gone through the doors to the other one.

Was he bad... or was he good?

Either way, if I told the police who he was, they would take him, and whether he had followers or the fact that someone was after him.

Paris was right with what he told me last night.

I had to keep his identity a secret.

Everyone's lives in this school depended on it.

"'*And the fifth girl who was murdered at Manhattan High School was found in the basement of an abandoned church,*'" the news reporter said, "'*though the police are still attempting to find the time of death of this girl, but two of the other girls they found passed about one to two years ago. Manhattan is still deciding whether or not they are going to shut down the school, but for now, tomorrow's the last day.*'"

I stared at the TV in horror.

There were *five* girls now? Who would even think to kill this many people? And if it was a student, how would they do it so many times without getting caught? Wouldn't they falter at some point?

But all the sudden, the TV drained to black, and I looked around for a second to realize that the power was still on in the house, and I glanced up to find mom standing above me, a hand on her hip as she held the remote.

A slight annoyance passed over me at mom's horrible timing.

"Stop watching this stuff," she said a little sharply. "It's corrupting you."

And she walked off with the remote.

I sighed and decided to go straight to my bedroom, flipping on the lights and sat in my desk chair.

When I realized I couldn't draw or write, I stood and paced the room impatiently, rambling to myself with inaudible dialogue that was clearly gibberish.

I was trying to figure out what was going on... What was happening.

But I stopped, looking at the floor below my window.

And what sat there, was another black, shiny feather.

I stepped over to it, picking it up and ran my fingers down the edge, but then opened my window and gazed down onto the streets.

He was there again, Paris.

He still had the mask and the cloak, but I knew it was him.

He waved at me, mouth curving into a smile.

Did he honestly leave the feathers there knowing I'd find it and open the window?

It was his way of playing a boom box outside my window and stuff, wasn't it?

I rolled my eyes and walked off into my room, leaving the window open for him to enter, though I didn't really know why.

While I waited for him to hop up on the roof and climb through, I decided to do something useful and pulled out my notebook and worksheet, getting to work on my Algebra homework.

Paris came through the window seconds later, brushing off his pants that had grime from the roof on them.

He still had the mask and the cloak, and I would've studied him harder if I wasn't doing my homework right now.

Like I always said: business before pleasure.

In this case the pleasure was the urge for me to grab him right now and wait for him to slip his hand—

No, bad, Riley. Bad.

Think not sinful thoughts.

Paris walked over to me and leaned down to see my paper.

His familiar ocean scent washed over me, but I chose to ignore it.

"What are you doing?" he asked me.

"Studying."

"Ah," he said, sitting on the desk beside me, "can I watch?"

I gave him a concerned look. "Um, okay? It's pretty boring to watch, though."

He was silent, and I continued my homework, feeling his eyes burn me more as he watched me write.

Almost twenty minutes passed, feeling like seconds, and Paris finally broke the silence. "Your hand writing's really nice," he commented.

I cast him a look before going back to what I was doing. "Uh, thanks?"

We were silent for another moment, and Paris finally focused his attention on my room.

Why was he so curious? I honestly didn't understand.

He gazed around, eyes scanning my bare walls and bedsheets, and I glanced to see what he was looking at.

His expression seemed very cautious.

"What's this?" he said, lifting something pink in his hand.

It only took me a moment to realize what it was.

I shot up from my chair and launched over to him, about to grab the object in his hand when he raised it out of my reach, making me grunt in frustration.

"Give it!" I said, jumping for it but he was too tall.

"What is it, Riley?" he said.

I tried to grab it, but he pulled it out of my reach more.

"Riley," he sang, "is this a *vibrator*?"

"Give it back to me!" I yelled.

"When do you use it?" he questioned, eyeing it while I continued attempting to grab it but failed. "Every day? Every other day?"

Something inside me started burning. "Paris, give it back."

"How does it feel?" he asked curiously. "Inside you?"

I froze, taken aback by the question. "Why?"

His eyes raked me through the mask. "Just curious."

"You can ask every other girl or go onto a porn site to figure it out, now give me the fucking thing."

"But porn isn't real," he said, not listening, "and I don't know any other girls as interesting as you."

I drew back in surprise.

"Is there more where this came from?" he asked me, and started shuffling through my drawer.

"Fucking God, Paris!" I yelled, pulling at his arm. "Stop! Get out of there!"

But when I heard the bottom of the drawer shift, I exhaled a curse.

"Ooh," he said, "what have we here?"

"Get the *fuck* out of my drawer," I growled.

"You have a bad mouth," he commented, shuffling through it. "Eggs, dildos," he drew back in surprise, "*clit vibrator*? Wow. You have everything."

"Paris," I warned.

"Which one's your favorite?" Paris said, making my insides catch fire. "I bet you like the pink dildo, don't you? And then you add the little clit brush on top, huh?"

"That's not—"

"No?" He stepped a little closer, making my heart race. "Then why were they the only ones not buried, huh?"

His hot stare made me break a sweat.

"Which one's your favorite?" he repeated.

"What are you doing?" I questioned silently, but for some reason didn't shy away.

"Testing you," he answered, making my stomach swell with heat.

"Testing me on what?" I said then.

"How worked up you get when you're attracted so someone."

"*What?*"

I was *not* attracted to him. I barely even *knew* him.

Even *I* knew it was a lie.

"It's a sickness," I stated, rubbing my stomach as an indication. "Just feeling a little queasy."

"You sure it's not anxiety?" he asked me.

My eyes rounded slightly. "Why are you saying all these things?"

"Because..." he responded, "you make me curious."

"Why me?"

"Because you don't run away from danger."

I paused. "So... talking to me about my sexual desires is considered dangerous territory? I can assure you that sex and murder are two different things, Paris."

He just watched me through the mask.

"What?" I said then.

"What you just did," Paris responded, "when you talk to Ryan about these things... you shy away like a terrified puppy, and then when he pushes you, you get angry and defensive. But I'm doing the same thing and you're not considering this dangerous territory."

Oh, God. He was right.

Why was he right?

My heart beat quickened when he stepped closer, whispering in my ear, "You, Riley, are a very intriguing person."

He watched me for a moment when he pulled away.

"Riley?" Violet called from the door, making me almost jump.

Paris didn't look as if he cared, and I was tempted to shove him in the closet or tell him to hide, but I didn't want this moment to be a cliché, so I let him do what he wanted.

"Yeah?" I said back, glancing to find Paris going back to shuffling through the drawer.

He honestly couldn't care less, could he?

Violet could walk in any moment and find him shuffling through my... *toy* drawer.

"They'll be here in two minutes!" Violet said.

"Thanks!"

And mom's footsteps padded away in the opposite direction.

"Who?" Paris pressed carefully, standing up now while closing the drawer. "Ryan?"

"No," I responded, "and stop obsessing about him. If you want to fuck him, go right ahead. I won't stop you. He's horny as hell."

Paris gave me an annoyed look, and I saw it from the corner of my eye and smiled.

Two minutes later, Paris and I heard loud patting footsteps echoing from the halls, and the door threw open, a tiny little girl running in seconds later.

She jumped at me—somewhat startling Paris—and I caught her when the little girl giggled excitedly.

"Riley! Riley!" she said. "Yaaaay!"

"Julie," I greeted, hugging her back as I said in a silly voice, "Hi."

Julie glanced over at Paris, tipping her head to the side. "Who's he?"

"My friend," I answered, "he likes cosplaying."

Paris glared at me through his mask.

"Anyway," I said, setting the girl on the floor, "well, do you want to read more of that book?"

The young girl jumped. "Yes! Yes!"

I stepped over to my bookshelf and shuffled through it when I pulled out a small little novel titled, "Black Magic," and handed it to the girl. She happily took it and ran off.

"You're really good with kids," Paris told me, and I glanced at him before blushing slightly.

"Thanks." My voice was quiet.

"Riley," he said with urgency in his tone.

I gazed over at him. "Yeah?"

His eyes shone with something dark; as if he knew something was going on inside me. "You're safe," he promised.

I gazed at my door, eyes darkening.

I then shook my head. "No," I said, "no, I'm not."

And I walked out of the room, not caring that he would probably raid through my stuff.

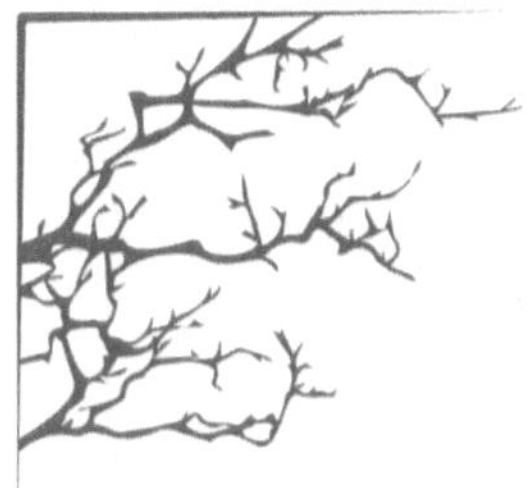

3

Riley

"We have a problem," Paris said as he and I sat next to each other in Biology.

My week was going *great*. First the police haven't ruled out murder for my friend's death, and then I found there was a guy in a masquerade mask stalking me, and he was giving me a weird feeling in my belly that I hated, and now the teachers were miraculously putting us both together.

Great, right?

"We have a problem," Paris repeated when I didn't answer.

"Let me guess," I responded back while taking notes, "you caused it?"

He was silent, but I felt him glaring at me.

"Would shooting you fix this problem?" I asked him. "No? Then leave me alone."

His eyes raked me head-to-toe, but he still said, "Meet me outside during lunch."

Lunch? That was after this class, and I had no classes after that. I usually just went home after hanging with Ryan and Claire.

"No," I responded.

"You have to," he stated.

"No," I responded harshly, "I don't. I'm my own independent person and you don't control me, Paris."

"Riley," the teacher said when I felt Paris glaring at me again. "Are you paying attention?"

"Yep," I said. "Paris and I are having a conversation about how squids spray ink at other animals to catch them off guard and then eat them in their most vulnerable moment."

Paris rolled his eyes at the metaphor I used, and also the reason that it wasn't factually correct.

"Uh," the teacher responded, "okay. I guess we're talking about squids, yeah. But we aren't on the whole 'what they eat' thing yet."

And she continued talking to the class.

"Riley," Paris said in a lower tone; probably so we wouldn't get caught again.

"*Paris*," I said sharply, still taking notes.

"You need to listen to me," he said.

"Or what?" I countered. "You'd kill me? Let me finish my Algebra homework first so at least that's complete."

"I'm not going to *kill* you," he said.

I never responded.

"Riley," he pressed.

"I'm *busy*."

"Can you listen to me for *one* second?" he snapped.

"Nope," I said back, "I'm physically incapable."

He sighed, shaking his head. "Riley."

I was silent.

"Riley."

A sudden irritation washed through me like fire and I snapped my head to him, hissing through gritted teeth, "*What*?"

"Meet me outside at lunch," he repeated, "got it? And fix that tone or I'll *teach* you to fix it."

"*Fine*," I said despite his threat, "now let me work."

He smiled in satisfaction.

I t was lunch time now, and I snuck out to my car without Paris knowing and drove home.

The teacher let us out two minutes early and I slinked through the crowd of students, and since Claire was gone today due to some kind of appointment—and that I hated Ryan—I was able to go home now.

I always got a chai latè from one of my favorite places on my way home, so I stopped at the shop and got out of my car, going up to the door seconds later.

This area was oddly quiet; usually the outside of the café was full of people chattering and some kind of animal making noises.

But it was quiet...

Almost *deathly* silent.

I stopped at the front door, narrowing my eyes at a note on it when I realized the door was locked.

Family Emergency, we're closed for the rest of the day, 05-10-2023.

Wow, this was *not* my week, was it?

I was about to walk to my car and passed an alleyway when I crossed the street.

But a sudden, "*Riley*!" caught my attention.

I stopped, scanning the silent parking lot.

"*Riley*!" they said again. "*Help*!"

Was that...?

"Claire?" I called. "Is that you?"

"*RILEY*! The *alley! The alley! Hurry*!"

I darted down the alleyway then, scanning the shadows as my heart pounded wildly against my chest.

"Where are you?" I questioned.

"Behind the trash!" Claire said, voice cracking with a hint of pain.

I ran behind the bins.

And my heart stopped.

Claire was slouched back onto the building, clutching her T-shirt while sweat stuck her black hair to her temples.

But there was blood everywhere.

Red staining her hands, feet, legs, shirt.

Oh, God... it smelt horrible.

Like rotten meat and copper and metal.

I felt my heart pound faster, and tears blurred my vision but I blinked them away.

I had to help; now wasn't the best time to cry.

Something cold consumed me.

The same feeling when dad died; the same when Bella died.

No... no... not again...

I won't let you leave me, too.

So I kneeled by Claire, heart shattering and pulled a cell-phone out of my pocket, dialing 9-1-1 with my trembling hands.

"9-1-1, what's your emergency?"

"Yeah," I said, voice shaking as I pulled off my jacket, "I have a friend on Summit Boulevard and in the alleyway right next to *Coffee Coffee Café*. The right one."

"Emergency is on their way. Are you safe?"

"Yes," I stated. "Yes, I think so."

"What's her name?"

"Claire," I said, voice cracking, "Claire Nightingale."

"Is she conscious?" the operator said.

I choked down sobs, every part of me hurting.

I didn't want to lose her.

Why did this keep happening?

"Ma'am," she said, "I need you to stay calm. The police are on the way. Is she conscious?"

"Y—yes."

"What happened?"

"I think she was stabbed," I said, trying to breathe but my throat constricted. "There's—there's a lot of blood. Oh, G—god...."

"Ma'am, what's your name?"

"I'm Riley... Riley Princes. And—and I'm her best friend."

"Okay, Riley," the operator said, "do you have a jacket? We need to stop the bleeding."

"I took it off," I said, voice shaking, "I don't know what to do with it."

"Press the cloth on the wound," she said, "and put pressure. It will hurt, but you need to ignore her pain and hold pressure, okay?"

"Claire," I said, catching my jacket tighter, "move your hand." When she listened, I placed my jacket on the wound and pressed down, Claire crying out and catching my wrist.

"I know..." I whispered gently despite Claire's nails digging into my skin. "I know... I'm sorry."

"Is the perpetrator in the area?" the operator said.

"I—I don't think so. It's very quiet. And it's just us."

"Okay, put pressure. The police are almost there."

Sirens wailed distantly from a couple miles away.

Claire started sobbing, scratching my arms as she fought the pressure and making me wince.

I could barely feel the pain, though...

"I'm sorry, Claire," I said, stomach twisting as my voice shook. "I have to stop the bleeding. I can't have another death happening again, okay?"

Hide it... hide the pain. Don't make Claire worried...

"Is she still conscious?" the operator said.

"Yes," I responded, eyes stinging with tears. "Fighting like a mother."

"That's good," the operator said. "That's a good sign, just keep pressure."

"Alright," I said, skin slick with sweat.

"Riley..." Claire whimpered, the sirens getting louder as my heart shattered to pieces. "Riley, stop. It hurts."

"I have to," I responded, eyes blurring again but I blinked the tears away. "I know it hurts, I'm so sorry."

I can't lose you. I need you, please don't leave me like Bella did; like my dad did.

The sounds grew deafening, and two ambulances as well as three police cars screeched to a stop at the mouth of the alley, and ten medics came running out, surrounding us.

I couldn't think... It hurt. This hurt so much. It was agonizing.

I couldn't breathe.

"Ma'am," one of the officers said, "we'll take care of her, it's time to get up now."

When I never responded, tears slipped down my cheeks.

Just the thought of releasing her terrified me.

I didn't want to lose her.

Not again.

Not again.

Two officers caught my arms and I cried out, both men prying me off and I kicked and screamed as many medics surrounded Claire and started attending to her wounds.

"No!" I cried, fighting them. "NO! Claire! CLAIRE!"

It had been about thirty minutes since the police came, and I stared off into the distance as I sat on the back of an ambulance, a single medic taking care of the wounds on my arms; the ones that developed by Claire's nails.

The police had already gotten my statement, and when they found out that I was very quiet and not completely honest as to my past, they called my mother before they asked me what happened.

Violet got off work two hours early when she heard what happened, and was now frantically speaking to an officer, but I couldn't hear anything that was happening; couldn't feel the pain of the medic rubbing alcohol in my wounds.

It hurt... It hurt.

I wanted to cry, and I wanted to scream.

This wouldn't stop, would it? Was I cursed?

"The operator told us that she heard you say 'not again,'" the police said about twenty minutes ago, "has this happened before?"

I was silent.

"Riley, I need to know what happened. Has this happened to Claire before?"

"No," Violet cut in, "not to Claire. Can I talk to you in private?"

They walked off, but I could still hear them speak.

"It's happened to her father," Violet told the officer, "her father was murdered by a mugger, and her other best friend, Bella Swines, was murdered about a year ago."

"Oh, Jesus," one of the officers said. "That's a lot to handle."

Violet looked to me. "Yes, it is."

"There," the medic said, "you should be fine now. Do you need anything?"

I was silent.

"Okay..." he sounded slightly defeated, "if you need anything, I'll be around the corner."

And I was left alone.

Claire was already on her way to the hospital, and I distantly remembered holding her hand while they rolled her to the ambulance on a stretcher; there was an oxygen mask covering her mouth, and Claire's cheeks were drenched in tears.

I stared off into the distance, entire body going numb.

It hurt... It hurt so much.

Make it stop. I want it to stop.

Make it stop, please. I can't handle this anymore.

"Riley," Violet said, making me slowly move my eyes up to her, "she's there. Let's go. I'll drive you."

I blinked slowly.

Violet kneeled before me. "It's alright, Honey. They're done with the statements for now. Let's go take care of your friend, okay?"

"**R**iley," someone said, their voice drowned out like I was sinking in water. "Riley," he said again, voice clearer. "*Riley.*"

I looked up as if I'd been asleep for the past hour, and saw Ryan sitting next to me. "Huh?"

I wasn't asleep, I was spacing out and recalling memories I never wanted to think of again.

"You okay...?" he said cautiously, drawing back when he noticed there was tears in my eyes.

I blinked them away and nodded, looking down to my hands that were cracking at the fingers. "Yeah."

Ryan eyed me with a look I always hated.

Even in desperate situations, he was being an absolute self-serving dickwad.

He still wanted what he wanted, but I wasn't ever in the mood, so he decided to *eye-fuck* me instead. Great, right?

I was sick of this.

"Riley," the doctor said, "right?"

I nodded. "My mom's in the bathroom."

"It's alright, I just wanted to tell you what's happening." This doctor had brown hair and bright green eyes, but he still seemed pretty nice unlike Ryan.

I stood suddenly, but Ryan remained seated.

"Is she okay?" I said quickly.

The doctor hesitated, making something cold wash over me.

"What...?" I said, voice breaking. "Is she...?"

"No," the doctor said, "she's alright, in a way. She lost a lot of blood and her organs were failing, but there's a chance we can get them working with blood transfusions. We're doing it now."

My heart stopped despite the light of hope he gave me.

"There's still hope," the doctor said at my grim expression, "but she won't be the same. She's paralyzed from he waist down. When she was stabbed, the knife hit her spine, so...." He sighed. "I'm not really supposed to be telling you this, but I thought you should know. Does she have parents?"

"Her mom's on a business trip," Ryan said. "And her dad's passed away years ago."

"The police will have this sorted out, Riley," the doctor promised me, Ryan's brows raising when he noticed me shaking heavily.

"I want to see her," I told him.

Two minutes later, I walked into a hospital room. My eyes stung when I noticed all the blood packs scattered all over the room, and my heart wrenched in my chest when my eyes landed on Claire.

She was asleep on the hospital bed; patches from the heart machines pasted all over her chest, the low beeping echoing through the room.

Her heart was beating normally... I hoped.

But there were also needles sticking into her skin, blood and saline packs gently bleeding into her veins.

I stepped over to her numbly, chest caving as all the numbness vanished, the guilt coming back like a tidal wave.

I collapsed next to the bed and caught Claire's hand, sobbing into her skin as all sorrow crashed into me.

"I'm sorry!" I cried. "I'm so sorry! This is all my fault! I'm sorry!"

My tears warmed my cheeks, and every part of me hurt.

Everything—hurt.

Everything.

Ryan sighed and shook his head, leaving the room seconds later.

And I was all alone, knowing the doctor left to care for other patients.

All alone.

If this was my future, I hated it.

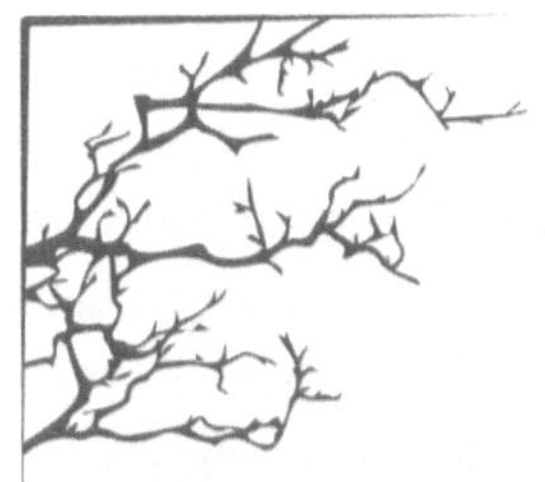

4

Paris

It was almost two in the morning when I walked in the hospital room, shooting my gaze around before they settled on Riley.

She was sound asleep on the armchair, curled up like a tiny kitten.

I sighed, stepping out of the room.

"Nurse!" I called.

A singular girl came running toward me. "Is everything okay?"

"Yes," I responded, "I just wanted to know where her mother was."

"Oh, she's on vacation."

"No," I said before she could walk away, "the other girl, Riley."

"Oh, her friend? Her mom went home, I think. She told the doctors it was okay for her to sleep with her friend tonight." The nurse looked back to Riley. "After what happened, I don't think I'd want to leave my friend either."

"What happened?" I pressed.

The nurse gazed up at me. "Are you a family member?"

"Yes," I lied, "yes, I am."

She eyed me curiously for a moment before shrugging, clearly thinking this was none of her business.

"Well... I think that girl on the couch there found the other one in an alley. She was critically injured. The girl who was injured almost died, but we actually saved her, she'll be okay in a couple weeks. But she was stabbed and lost a lot of blood. The stores of where the alley she was in were both closed due to family emergencies; she was very lucky that Riley found her. If it was minutes later, she'd be dead."

I looked to Riley through the room's window and my eyes darkened.

Jesus... whoever was up to this was playing her sanity like a game.

I gazed back at the nurse before she walked away. "Ma'am, can we get a second bed in here?"

She nodded. "Yeah." And walked off.

Almost twenty minutes later, there was a bed rolled in by two nurses.

One of them gazed up at me with a slight shock. "Oh!" he said. "You're the volunteer, Paris, right?"

I nodded.

"Do you know them?" he said, the other nurse rolling her eyes and walking off.

"Yeah," I responded.

"Did you hear what happened?" he questioned. "Poor thing," he looked down to Riley, "that girl on the couch found her friend here."

I guessed that the news was going around the entire hospital; that's how they worked, anyway; all of them gossiping like teenagers.

"Yeah," I said, "I heard."

"Well…" the nurse said then, "we're supposed to be monitoring her, so…."

"Yeah," I said, "I'll stay. I know what to report and stuff."

"Thanks, Paris," he said. "We need the extra help. We're very packed and short staffed. So you being here is a saint."

He walked off seconds later.

They weren't really supposed to do that due to "conflict of interest," but whatever, I wanted to be near Riley anyway.

"Wow…" I commented to myself, staring after the nurse, "they really don't know I don't have a college degree, do they? That sucks."

I gazed down at Riley on the couch seconds later, sighing heavily.

And then I stepped over to her, pulling her arm so it wrapped around my neck and lifted her seconds later.

She groaned in annoyance, shifting in my grip.

"I know, I know," I said, holding her tighter. "I'm disturbing your precious beauty sleep, but I don't really care, so stop complaining."

I lay her down on the bed, feeling her ease into the mattress when I gently draped the covers over her.

She shifted to her side, snuggling up with herself under the covers.

I smiled and stepped over to the couch, settling down on it seconds later.

I was going to be here for a while, but I didn't really care.

This was my job, after all.

"Riley..." I whispered, shaking her slightly. "Riiiiley."

She groaned in annoyance, shifting to her side.

"Wake up," I pressed, shaking her still, "come on."

"Leave me alone, Paris..." she muttered.

She was silent then, and her eyes shot open as she turned to look at me, seeming slightly concerned. "Wait... what are you doing here?"

"Look," I told her, gesturing to the other side of the room.

Riley rolled over a little, pressing her hands to the bed as she sat slightly up.

Claire was on the other side of the room, pushing herself over to us in a wheelchair.

She clearly was coming back from the bathroom.

She was still in a hospital gown, but I knew the wound was still open.

"Claire..." Riley whispered, and her friend looked up at her voice.

"Sorry," Claire commented, "still getting used to this thing."

Riley shot up from the bed at an instant and tackled her best friend, but still was gentle because of her open wound.

She apologized a million more times, but she stopped clearly because didn't want Claire to feel bad with her own guilt, so she just held her tighter.

"How are you paralyzed...?" Riley said silently, clearly trying not to cry. "Did it go that deep...?"

"No," Claire responded, "he got me from behind first and then got me in front."

"Who...?" Riley whispered.

"I can't really remember," Claire said. "It's all... *blurry*, but the doctors said it'll come back. I'm staying here for a week anyway." She glanced behind Riley then. "Who's that guy? He's been watching over you all night."

Riley cast a look behind her to me.

My face was expressionless, but I still shrugged.

Her mouth twisted slightly in annoyance because of me not giving away any emotion.

I was good at that, too.

I could tell she wasn't sure if I was a bad guy or not.

Even though I've given her reasons to trust me.

"He's nice..." Claire said. "Every time you started having a nightmare, he'd walk over and calm you back down."

Riley gazed over at me again, confused.

This time a smile barely peaked through my lips.

Her cheeks reddened slightly, and she looked to the wall, avoiding eye-contact.

"Claire..." Riley whispered then, "if you don't want me to leave, then—"

"Yes, Riley," she promised. "Go, it's okay. I know what today is. I have police outside the door, and they're planning on putting me under protective custody. I'll be fine."

"Are you sure?" Riley pressed.

She nodded.

"What's today?" I asked then.

Claire hesitated, and Riley's fists clenched.

"Alright," Riley said, voice touched with something dark, "well, I'm going."

She caught her purse and walked out the door seconds later, nodding to the police officers outside Claire's room to assure them she wasn't being suspicious.

I looked at Claire after Riley left. "What's today?" I said.

She looked at me then, slightly concerned. "I thought Riley told you."

She probably thought because of my "kindness" this whole night that we were close.

"No," I said, "she never tells me anything."

Claire looked out the door, sighing. "I can't tell you because I promised her I wouldn't speak of it to anyone, but I can loophole it and say, *1924 West Third Street.* The number of the stone is a hundred-thirty."

"Oh..." I said, slightly confused but shook it off, "thanks."

She nodded.

I walked out of the room after Riley, nodding to the officers, too.

They nodded back, and I ran off, determined to find the address of which Claire gave me.

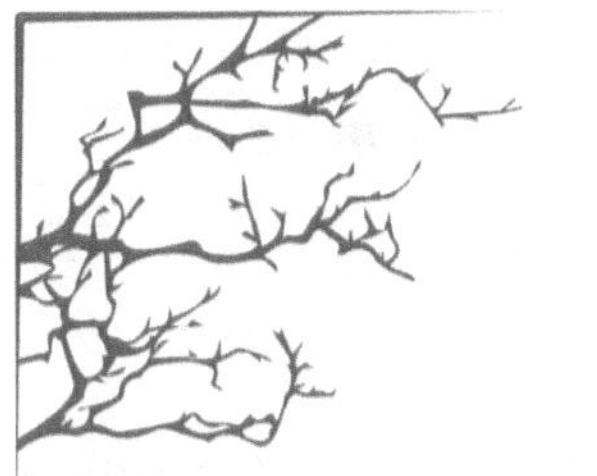

5

Riley

I ran through the icy rain, clutching my side as stabbing pains burned me from my lack of exercise.

The clouds were darker than I had ever seen them, and twenty minutes earlier, the sky opened and rain poured down at me like God's tears.

My stomach was aching because I hadn't eaten since yesterday, and my lungs clamped with the sorrow and fear swarming inside me; my muscles were so tense that I felt they'd break.

God... everything hurt.

When I reached the end of the street, I slowed to a stop, catching my breath.

The streets were empty here; nobody came here, anyway. Especially when it was pouring outside.

I kneeled down onto the concrete and folded my arms over my stomach, attempting to ease the pain coiling inside me.

It never vanished.

But now it hurt—so—much.

Tears sprang in my eyes, and I finally let them out because there was no one to watch me cry, and loud sobs escaped my mouth as I clutched myself tighter.

It was hard to breathe with this much agony... While I was crying, I took loud gasps and tried to calm myself.

But I couldn't stop.

I forgot the reason why I never cried.

It was impossible to stop.

But I clutched my navel through my T-shirt, standing despite my lungs seizing.

And I ran across the street, to the other side where my father rested.

I didn't care how much this hurt, I needed him near me; I needed to feel his presence.

I ran through the millions of graves, knowing where my father was the moment I stumbled through the gates.

I couldn't stop, so I kept running through the damp fields.

The rain was bleeding through my jacket and freezing my skin underneath, but I didn't care.

Seconds later, I dropped onto my knees next to my father's grave, still clutching my stomach when I leaned forward and pressed my forehead to it, the sobs slowing now.

But the pain wouldn't vanquish.

I didn't want to go home; I didn't want to go back to the hospital.

I wanted to stay here—with my father—where I felt safe.

I knew he was gone, but here... I felt secure.

So I lay on the mud in front of his grave, curling up and held myself.

I never wanted to leave.

Never leave me again, dad.

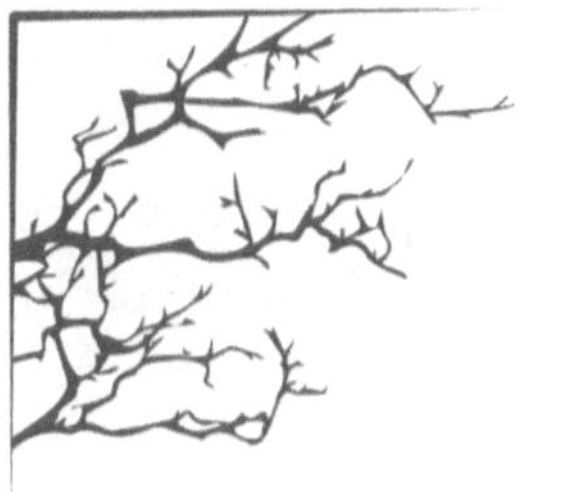

6

Paris

"What the hell are you doing out here?" I questioned as I ran up to Riley.

I put my hands on my knees as she remained curled on the mud, the rain staining her clothes a darker color as she stared off into space lazily.

She wasn't falling asleep; she looked... *numb*.

Quiet, but fragile.

I stared down at her after a moment, blinking rain off my lashes. "Come on," I urged, "I don't want you getting sick."

She never responded.

"Riley," I pressed.

Silence.

I sighed then, staring off into the distance for a moment before gazing around curiously.

My eyes settled on the stone in behind her seconds later. "Why are you here? What's today?"

I searched her for a moment, knowing I'd get no answer—not even a curious glance—so I stared back up at the tombstone, reading it.

Micheal T. Princes.
Beloved Father and Husband.
May He Rest In Peace.

My eyes darkened, and I gazed down at Riley seconds later.

"This is your father's grave, isn't it?" I kneeled down beside her, not earning a response. "Is it the day he died? Or his birthday?"

She was quiet.

I sighed, staring off into the distance for a moment.

And I gazed down at her. "C'mon, Riley. Let's get you home."

She surprisingly didn't resist when I guided her arm around my neck like I did the night before and lifted her in my arms.

She turned further into me as I walked back home; as if she needed my warmth.

Well... she was stuck in the cold for God *knows* how long.

And she was soaked and covered in mud and grime.

Riley let me carry her home with no resistance, clearly too tired to care this time.

Which wasn't entirely normal for her, to be honest.

I walked through the streets for almost twenty minutes when I gazed down at her. "Hey, Rye."

She didn't respond, but I knew she was listening.

"Can you get under my jacket?" I asked her. "Just grab the edges and wrap it around yourself. I can't do it because I'm using both arms to carry you."

She was silent, but eventually listened and caught the edges of my jacket, turning further into me and wrapping the edges around her arms.

I was trying to warm her up with my body heat because I assumed she was freezing.

But when I felt her icy skin press against my chest—*through my shirt*—I knew she was colder than she was supposed to be.

How long had she been lying there for? It took me just an *hour* to find her.

Was she there for an *hour*?

It only took ten more minutes before we stepped onto Riley's driveway, me ringing the doorbell seconds later.

Riley was clearly confused as to why I wasn't afraid of her mother, but she never asked, so I never answered.

The door opened seconds later, and Violet's brows drew together when she saw me.

But they rounded when she noticed Riley was covered in mud, huddled up with me.

"Jesus Christ," she said, stepping out and attempting to assess her daughter, but I didn't let go. "Is she okay?" Violet said. "Did she get hurt, too?"

"No," I responded gently, "she's okay. Just a little numb. Can I take her to her bedroom?"

Violet eyed me for a moment before nodding, letting me in the house willingly.

"Her room's upstairs," Violet stated.

I nodded even though I already knew. "Thanks."

And I carried Riley up the stairs and to the right—where the bathroom was—setting her on the floor gently and testing to see if she could stand before letting go.

She could, so I stepped a little back and smiled.

"Take a shower," I instructed her. "Warm yourself up, okay?"

She nodded numbly.

And I walked out of the bathroom, making my way down the stairs and into the dining room.

"Oh," Violet said, "are you hungry? Do you need anything?"

"No, I'm not hungry," I said. "I wanted to talk to you, though."

"So tea then?" Violet answered.

I nodded, chuckling. "Yeah, that's fine."

Violet and I had been talking for over thirty minutes, and toward the end of the conversation, Violet slouched back in her seat, exhaling a curse.

"I know this was going to happen," she murmured. "I didn't expect it so soon. I was also kind of hoping it wouldn't, either."

I nodded.

"Does she know who you are?" Violet said. "Riley?"

"No."

"Good," Violet said. "Keep it that way for now. She won't understand it yet."

"So, you're okay with this?" I said.

"Yeah," Violet responded. "The way you explained that makes sense, really. I knew my husband was in some bad business with your people, and I know you want redemption. He talked about you all the time, you know. Paris, this, Paris, that. 'Paris is going to change the world' kind of thing."

I just nodded, staring off into the distance for a moment. "Alright, well I guess it's settled then. You need to go in hiding."

Violet nodded.

The moment we heard footsteps receding down the stairs, Violet and I looked up, seeing Riley come down with a straight face, but her brows were relaxed.

Man she looked depressed.

"Hey," Violet said softly, "Paris just said he wanted to take you to the movies tonight. Why don't you two go have fun?"

Riley shook her head after getting a water bottle from the fridge.

She was probably trying to rehydrate after all the crying she did.

"I'm not in the mood," she said in a flat tone.

And she went right back upstairs without another word.

"Wow," Violet said, "usually she's all over things like that. Why is she...?"

"Guilt," I responded. "And also the fact that she knows I'm hiding something and it concerns her."

"You can't tell her, though," Violet said. "She won't understand."

"Yeah," I said, sighing, "that's why this is going to be hard."

Violet scooted out of her chair. "I'll go talk to her, Paris. I'll try to convince her to come down to at least chat."

And she went upstairs, knocking on Riley's door before opening it and stepping in.

I decided to silently follow to hear their conversation, peering through the crack of her bedroom door.

She fucking intrigued me.

Riley was sitting on her window sill, watching the rain pad against her windows.

Wow... text book depression.

That was kind of sad.

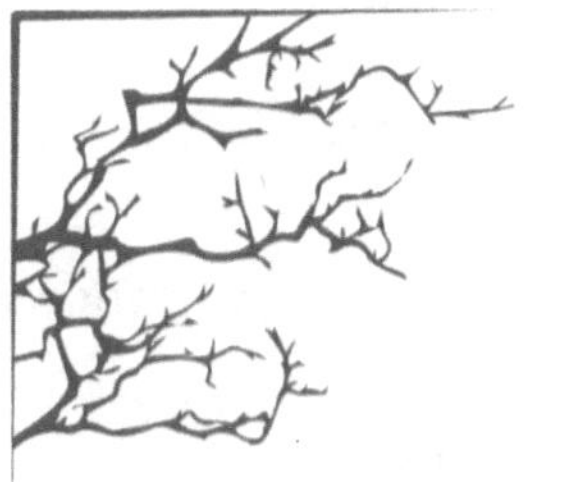

7

Riley

"Why don't you go with Paris?" Violet said gently. "He seems really nice, you know."

I casted her a confused look mixed in with a depressed one. "I don't want to go out."

Violet sighed and cracked the door behind her, stepping over to my bed and sat on the thick mattress.

"Why do you like him so much?" I questioned. "You allow Ryan in my room even though you hate him, and you don't even know Paris and you're acting like he's been a family friend for years." I looked out the window. "You used to hurl when Ryan made kind comments about me, and shoved him out the door at curfew, and now you're allowing a stranger into our house." I sighed, setting my chin on my knees. "I don't think I'll ever understand what's happening to my life. Honestly, it feels like some dream. Some inescapable nightmare."

Violet was silent, clearly not used to this side of me.

Mainly because I prevented myself from breaking all these years, and now the trauma was bleeding out like a sliced heart.

"I'll leave you alone," Violet said then, clearly not knowing what else to do, "okay?"

And she walked out of the room.

I stared off into the distance, feeling uneasy at the sudden silence casting through the room.

I looked up when the rain slammed against the windows and thunder crackled across the sky.

Something wasn't right... Just *something*.

But all the sudden, a sharp pain struck me on the back of my head, and I topped over, blacking out before I could even hit the ground.

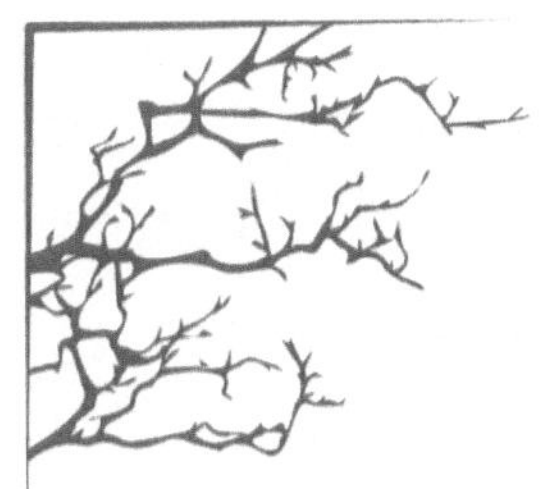

8

Riley

All the sounds came back in a blur, and I felt myself drifting back and forth...

My head was pounding wildly against my skull, and I heard a distant crashing of waves.

I rolled over, groaning in pain.

Why was I drifting in my room...?

But my eyes opened a slit, finding myself outside.

What happened...? Why was I outside?

With the waves and the softness under me, was I on a beach?

How did I get here? Why was my head pounding?

But when I felt odd bumps going through me, I sat up, finding myself lying on an inflatable boat.

But... where was I...?

My heart pounded when I looked up...

The boat was drifting further into the ocean.

What? *What?*

I cried out, using my hands and diving them in the cold sea so I could use them as paddles.

But it was raining, and the waves were getting stronger.

No... no...

How did I get here?

A single wave went under the boat, almost throwing it over but I caught the edges and held it still.

"Help!" I cried, spinning around as the rain poured down on me.

I was getting further and further away.

"Help!" I called. "Someone!"

Did someone knock me out and put me here?

Why?

A second wave came from under me, rocking the boat as it pushed me further back into sea.

I couldn't swim... and I'd been trying to paddle back with my hands, but the waves were too strong.

A third came, making the boat bounce, a forth followed behind it, and a fifth after that.

Thunder crackled across the sky, making me shriek.

I paddled harder, hearing the water crash from behind me.

Oh, God... I was going to die, wasn't I...?

"HELP!" I called, wading further toward the shore but was only pushed back.

And that's when it happened.

I heard water crashing harder behind me, and a sudden shadow loomed over me like my awaiting death.

When I slowly turned, my eyes rounded when I saw it.

The thirty foot wave moving toward me.

Shit.

I started paddling with my hands harder, keeping my eyes on the water.

Right as the thunder cracked across the sky—the rain feeling like needles piercing my skin—the wave came down on me at an instant.

I screamed, the sound drowned out when the cold consumed me like a mother of death folding her arms around my body.

I kicked as hard as I could, piercing through the water as I tried to swim back to shore.

I couldn't swim though, and I slapped the top of the ocean as another wave covered me, and I pierced out again, coughing as the water entered my lungs.

"Help!" I cried, trying to stay above water but my arms were aching. "Hel—"

Another tidal came over me, crashing me through the water.

I came up again, trying desperately to breathe, but the panic as well as the water entering my lungs weren't helping in the slightest.

"Someone!" I cried, the rain piercing down at me. "Help me! Please!"

Another came over, practically drowning me, and I pierced through.

"HELP!" I called. "HELP ME! HELP!"

But another forty foot wall came from behind me, and I stared up at it in horror.

And it came down on me, the impact knocking the breath out from my lungs and I sank further down.

I tried kicking, but the water only hit me harder.

Can't... I can't breathe...

I'm... going to die...

No matter how hard I fought, I only went deeper.

Until the water entered my lungs, and I coughed, only inhaling it further.

My muscles felt so weak...

I can't breathe. It hurts.

And I couldn't fight anymore.

I accepted it. I was going to die.

It was about time. I knew my time was coming eventually.

When my muscles weakened from lack of oxygen, I started finding myself sinking further into the ocean.

It was so dark down here... I wondered how the sea life could see in this darkness.

But a light came down from above me, and I parted my lashes, feeling the water sting my eyes as the light came closer.

And something caught my wrist, and I found myself pulled up by a savior, them holding me body to their body as they kicked up toward the shore.

It was so far... and I couldn't breathe.

I could feel myself fading.

But as their legs kicked harder, the grey sky came through the top of the water.

Was this a lifeguard from the beach...? Did they come to save me?

How did they know I was out here? Did they hear my screaming?

Moments later, they pierced through the water, though the pain in my lungs didn't dissipate.

I started gagging, choking as the water in my lungs came up to my throat and sank back down.

I felt myself fading.

The savior caught me tighter and waded to a speedboat that was slowly drifting into the distance.

I couldn't breathe.

I choked as my lungs seized.

But the figure pulled me on the boat, pushing me up to a sitting position and pressed their hands to my chest, slapping my back and chest at the same time.

What were they doing?

But the moment their their hand collided with my skin, a pound of water exited my mouth, and I started coughing heavily, every bit of ocean exiting my body.

I stared at the figure above me as I started gasping, trying to regain all air back to my lungs.

"*Go!*" the savior called to another person.

And the speedboat rattled as the engine started, and we moved toward the shore.

But... why did his voice sound so familiar?

I gazed up at him, unable to see his shape with all the ocean water burning my eyes.

I started pressing my hands to the boat around me, still trying to get air to my lungs.

"It's okay," the savior promised. "I got you now... I got you... Don't panic... Shhh...."

"Paris...?" I choked, only to start coughing again as my voice rattled my lungs.

I felt his strong arm slip under my back, and he pulled my weak body up and cradled me to him because I was freezing.

It was still raining.

There was too much water... Not enough air.

"It's okay..." he whispered gently, holding me to him tightly. "I got you now. We're almost back to shore."

"I blacked out..." I said, voice raspy. "And woke on a boat...."

"You're safe now," was all he said. "We're going to get you to home where you'll be under protection, okay? And we'll call a doctor to check on you. You'll be okay."

"Paris..." I said, choking still, "I think... someone's trying to kill me."

"I know," he answered. "But I won't let them."

He turned to the man running the boat. "Faster!" Paris said with panic in his tone. "Go *faster*!"

The engine roared and the speedboat launched forward, making its way back to the shore.

"Who is... he?" I questioned.

"My friend," Paris answered. "But it's okay. You'll be okay. As I said, you'll be under protection."

I stared up at the sky as it rained down on me.

I closed my eyes then, letting the darkness consume me.

God, I was so tired.

"Riley!" Paris said, panicked. "Riley, *wake the fuck up*!"

"Check her pulse," the man running the boat said.

I distantly felt him press his finger to my wrist and pull back. "Her heart's beating."

"Then she's fine," the man said. "Let her sleep."

When I felt a pair of warm arms surround me, I let myself fall into my dreams.

"Thank you, Paris..." a voice echoed from the hall. "Thank you so much. Oh, God...."

I stared at the ceiling of my bedroom drowsily while I listened to the conversation.

"It's okay, Mrs. Princes," Paris said. "Please, don't cry. The doctor said she's going to be okay."

"Why her?" Violet cried. "Why are they doing this to her? I don't get it! I hated watching her hurt all these years... but now *this*? They tried to *kill* her! I shouldn't have left the room! I shouldn't have left her alone!"

"It's going to be okay, Mrs. Princes," Paris said, clearly trying to calm Violet down.

"They took my *baby*!" Violet said, almost screaming now. "While I was in the *house*!"

I listened to mom rant, too tired to yell out so I wasn't alone in my bedroom anymore.

But a sudden shadow hovered over me, and my breath caught as my eyes widened.

I couldn't see it clearly, but he had dark skin and bright gold eyes.

Did the killer sneak in my room again?

No, *no*! I couldn't run! I was too tired...

"Paris!" his deep voice called, making my heart stop for a moment. "She's awake!"

He stepped away as the door opened, and Paris came walking in, mom behind him.

Paris sat on the bed, my breaths quickening when his hand inched toward me.

He drew back at this. "Hey," he uttered, leaning a little over so he could see my face, "I saved you, remember? Don't panic."

My eyes darkened when I recalled the memory of me drowning in the ocean.

He was right... he did save me...

But why? And who knocked me out and took me to the water...?

"Riley," Violet said, sitting on the bed beside me, as well, "how are you feeling?"

"Everything hurts..." I said, voice raspy.

"Yeah," Paris responded, "your muscles, huh? Drowning will do that to you."

I gazed at him and back at mom. "What's going on?"

Violet looked at Paris and back at me. "We have to put you in protective custody, Sweetheart."

I tried shifting to my side, but my muscles burned, so I stopped. "Did the police come?"

Violet hesitated. "Not exactly...."

"What does that mean?" I questioned.

"Let's not talk about this right now," Paris stated. "You're going to lose your voice. So just take a break from talking for now, okay?"

"Mom...?" I whispered, knowing she's answer. "What's going on...?"

She sighed. "I don't know."

"It seems like you know," I urged. "I don't want secrets. You always told me to tell the truth, so tell the truth."

She sighed and shook her head. "Riley, there are things going on that are beyond your understanding, Sweetheart. I just can't explain it right now."

"Why does everyone want to hurt me?" I questioned. "Why are they taking everyone I love?"

"Claire is fine," Paris promised. "She's still in the hospital with the two officers. She's going to be alright."

"What about Ryan?" I said.

"He's fine, too," Violet said coldly, "but that doesn't mean you can call him over."

Paris sighed and shook his head. "Everyone's okay. So, just take a breather, alright?"

"I want to see Claire..." I said, trying to sit up, but my muscles burned, so I whimpered and collapsed back on the bed.

"Not right now," Paris stated. "Let yourself heal for a little, okay?"

A knock on my bedroom door came, and I looked to find the same guy standing there that originally called Paris in here.

"Sir..." the man said despite him clearly being ten years older, "we have to go."

"Why?" Paris said, urgency in his tone.

"Code twenty," the man stated.

"Shit," Paris murmured.

"What?" Violet said. "What's wrong?"

"We have to move her," Paris explained. "Violet, you have to get out of here and go into hiding."

"Mom?" I said.

"Remember the meeting place?" Paris stated.

Violet nodded.

"We take the train," he told her, "at five, and then we split. Meet up every week at the café."

"What the hell is going on?" I cried.

No one answered.

"Someone please tell me what's happening!" I cried. "What's happening?"

Violet looked at me numbly. "You and Claire are in good hands, Riley. Remember that." She walked over and kissed my forehead.

"Mom?" I said, tears building in my eyes.

"I love you, Honey," she whispered. "You'll be alright."

"Mom!"

"Paris, *twenty*," the man repeated.

"Violet, you have to go," Paris said again.

She cupped my cheek for a moment before running out the bedroom door.

"*Mom*!" I cried, trying to sit up but everything hurt. "Mom, come back! No! *No*!"

Paris caught my arm and guided it around his neck.

"Stop!" I said, pulling my arm out. "Stop it, Paris! Tell her to come back! *Tell her to come back*! I don't want her to leave me!"

"Riley, we have to leave," he said, pulling my arm up again.

I tried to wiggle out, but he lifted me, running out the door seconds later.

"Mom!" I said, trying to get out. "MOM! Come back to me! *Come back to me, mom!*"

But Paris's guard opened a door to a car, and Paris got in with me cradled up against him, and he quickly closed the door and the man drove off seconds later.

My childhood home started moving further away, and I tried to get out of Paris's grip, but he wouldn't let me go.

"Mom!" I cried.

"You're mom's going to be okay," Paris said. "Look away. Look away now, Riley."

But I didn't, and when I saw a spark of something in my bedroom window.

A loud explosion boomed through the neighborhood, making me scream.

Paris cradled my head to his chest as all the cars parked on the sides of the road echoed their alarms.

When I looked up, my chest caved when all that was left of my house was the foundation and burning wood.

"No..." I whispered, "no...."

I slammed the window then, making Paris yelp.

"No! FUCK! NO! NO!" I tried to get to the door, but he pulled me back down as I sobbed. "No! Stop it! Stop it! That was my dad's house! THAT WAS MY DAD'S HOUSE! NO!"

"Riley, calm down," he tried to reason.

"LET ME GO! LET ME THE FUCK GO!"

"Riley," he warned, "listen."

"LET ME GO!" I screamed. "LET ME THE FUCK GO! NOW!"

Paris cradled me against him when I started screaming, kicking out my legs despite the pain burning inside me.

"NO!" I cried. "Stop this from happening! WHAT'S HAPPENING? STOP THIS FROM HAPPENING!"

"Veo," Paris told the driver.

"Yes?" he said.

"I need the kit," he said. "Now."

The man named Veo tossed him a fabric zip-able box, but I didn't pay much attention, just fought Paris as I watched my childhood home burn down.

Paris unzipped the box and pulled out a syringe filled with some kind of liquid, but I hadn't registered it because I was kicking and scratching and pushing against him.

I knew this was happening but never really acknowledged it.

He quickly ripped off a bag of alcohol wipes and wiped my shoulder, and I tried to fight the wet substance off because it was distracting me, somehow not smelling it.

He then pulled me down against him and pierced the needle into my arm, making me cry out.

"What are you doing?" I cried. "*What are you doing?*"

He held me to him, pressing the fluid into my veins as I exhaled a whimper. "Don't be afraid, alright? It's just going to calm you down. If you want, I can keep you awake. I just can't have you freaking out like this. You're going to kill yourself if you jump out the door, Riley."

I weakened against him. "Please... take it out."

He took the needle out after my plead, but all the fluid was in my muscles anyway, so he just put the syringe back in the kit and threw it to the floor.

I started sobbing silently, and Paris held me tighter.

"I know..." he said. "I know... I'm really sorry. But I needed you to calm down, you're going to be fine, I promise."

I continued to sob.

"Shhh..." he murmured, "what do you want? To look out the window or something?"

"Yes..." I whispered.

"Okay," he said, "I'll move you." And he lifted my limp body in his arms, positioning my head on his shoulder so I could see outside the back-seat window. "You'll be okay," he said again, "I promise."

A single tear slipped down my cheek, and he brushed it away with his thumb.

"Just relax," he said, "we'll be there in a little."

"What did you inject me with...?" I whispered somberly.

"It's just a sedative," he told me gently. "It'll help with your aching muscles, too. But it's not lethal, alright? It's going to help you. You'll be alright."

I was silent.

"If you're afraid to go to sleep because of it," he told me, "then tell me to keep you awake, okay? I'll happily keep you up so you don't feel scared to sleep and never wake up."

Another tear slipped down my cheek.

"Please," he said, brushing it away, "don't cry, okay? You're safe, Riley." He circled his arms around me. "You're safe now. I promise. You, Claire, and your mother are safe."

Why did they never mention Ryan? Did they just hate him or something?

"**R**iley, stay awake for me." Paris lightly patted my cheek when my eyes closed, making my lashes part. "Good, keep those eyes open."

I lazily stared up at him when the car slowed to a stop, and the driver's door closed, Veo stepping over to us seconds later and opening the door.

"Don't worry," Paris told me. "I won't drop you." And he lifted me in his arms, getting out of the car as I remained limp like a rag doll. "Veo," Paris said, "Veo, support her head with something."

The man quickly ran to the car and pulled out a blanket from the trunk, making his way back to us both.

"Here," he said, lightly lifting my neck and stuffing the fabric in between Paris's arm and my head, gently setting my neck back down onto the cushion.

"There..." Paris said as Veo stood back up, "better?"

I only looked at him, silver eyes glistening, and stared back off into the distance.

"I think that was a 'yes,'" Paris said, chuckling. "Thank you, Veo. I appreciate it."

He nodded, waving to the train that was sitting on the tracks

It was like it was waiting for *us*.

Paris walked up to the doors where two men in black suits stood, and they stepped sideways when he entered, and Paris then carried me down a couple cars, passing the dining car that was deserted, the sleeping car that clearly used to be a caboose, getting to the seating car where people just sat and watched the trees pass.

But there was no one there... we were all alone.

Was Paris the president of the US or something?

But he stepped to one of the doors on our right, two men that I now realized were behind us opening the door, and Paris stepped in, sitting down while I remained limp in his arms.

"Is she here yet?" Paris said to the guard. "You put a tail on her, right?"

Who were they talking about...?

"Yes," the guard said, "they said she'd be here in two minutes."

"Good," Paris stated. "The last thing she needs is to lose someone else."

Who were they talking about?

"While we're waiting," Paris told him. "Get a blanket, yeah?"

He nodded. "Yeah." And walked off, the other guard remaining in his position.

"See?" Paris said down to me. "You're going to be fine." And he gazed back up at the guard. "Whereabouts on C.N.?"

"Three minutes back," he responded.

Paris nodded, seeming relieved. "Okay. Take her to the medic car."

"Yes, sir," he stated.

Who was C.N.?

"Paris..." I whispered, still feeling exhausted from the sedative, "Paris...."

"Yes?" he uttered.

"Who..." I said, "even are you?"

He smiled. "Not to be trifled with, so just stay in here with me. I have cruel punishments if you try to escape."

My eyes rounded as something inside me burned.

"Oh, relax," he said, rolling his eyes while still smiling, "I was messing with you. I'm not going to hurt you, Riley. So chill out."

"Are you..." I said, "part of the government?"

He suddenly started laughing, and the guard outside did, too.

"What?" I said sadly. "Why are you laughing at me?"

Paris's chuckles trailed off, and he gazed at me with raised bows. "Honey, we're *far* from the government."

What did that mean?

He shook his head at my confused stare. "If you need *anything*," he stated. "Just let me know, I'll get it. Everyone will be here in about five-ish minutes, and we'll depart in ten. Everything will be okay," he promised. "Everyone you love will be safe now, I promise."

My brows drew together.

What was he talking about? Who *was* he?

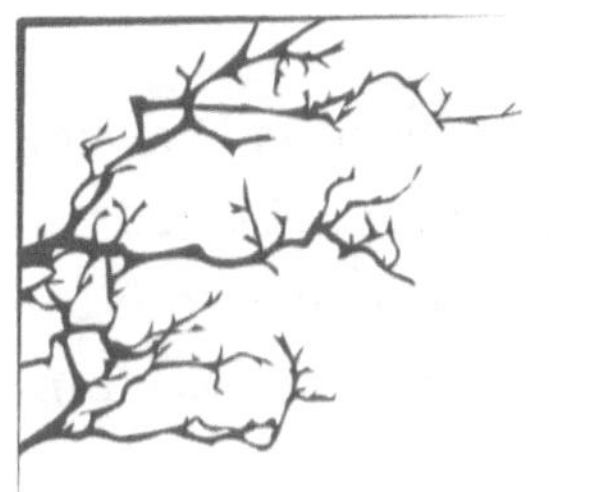

9

Paris

"How long has she been asleep?" Violet questioned me as Riley rested her head on my lap, practically knocked out.

"A *long* time," I responded. "She fell asleep right after we got on here and hasn't been disturbed since."

"Is she okay?" Violet questioned. "Is she hurt? Sick?"

"No," I responded. "Don't worry, she's fine. Just a little loopy. She was freaking out, so I had to give her a sedative."

"The human one," Violet said, "right?"

"Duh," I said as if she were a moron, "why would I give the poor girl *ketamine*? She's not a fucking horse."

"I know she's not really my daughter..." Violet whispered then. "And I know I was supposed to raise her and all after her father passed, but... I still worry about her, you know?"

"You should," I responded. "You kept her safe for the past nineteen years, which was your job. It's only natural that you'd grow an attachment over her."

Violet exhaled a sigh.

"So, Violet," I said, making her look up, "you can stop dying your hair brown and take out the silver contacts now. She'll find out what's going on in about a week, so I need you to go back to your normal look. Is that clear?"

"Yes, Paris," she said.

I gazed down at Riley then. "I know why my father wanted her dead..." I whispered, "but he's gone now... I killed him after he assassinated her father, but... I don't know who's trying to hurt her now. It's concerning. I have my men searching every block, but I can't find anything."

"Why her...?" Violet said. "Why do they want *her* dead?"

I gazed up at Violet. "Riley's real mother had her when she was fifteen. She placed her on the police's doorstep because she was on the run from my father. When Riley was a toddler, her father took her in and cared for her, and he was on the run the entire time, but he somehow managed to hide it from her. My dad was hunting her after her mother died years earlier, but he never found her."

"Why did he want her dead, though?" Violet questioned.

I sighed. "I think he wanted her dead because... my father... *encouraged* Riley's birth."

"What? So you're like siblings...?"

"No," I said quickly, "not brother and sister. He arranged the... sex... because he wanted Riley as a test subject for something he was developing."

"You make that sound like supernatural or something."

"No," I stated, "a disease he mutated to murder people when they inhaled it. Riley's mother was an experiment, and he wanted her pregnant before he gave her the disease to see if it affected the child. It did not. But after Riley's birth and while her mother was infected, she escaped and gave Riley to the police. She wasn't safe, anyway."

"That's screwed up," Violet said, "no offense. That whole getting a teen pregnant thing. And the fact that they were testing on her mother like a rodent." Violet looked up. "Sorry, I interrupted you, sir. What happened to her mother?"

"She killed herself in an alleyway," I exhaled, "so my father would never find out where Riley went."

"That's screwed up on so many levels..." Violet whispered. "I just wanted to say something, is that okay?"

I nodded after checking to see if Riley was still asleep. She was.

"I want you to know, Paris," Violet said, "that after your father passed, we were so relieved to find that you were taking over and all. It was a saint that you wanted to reform. It was amazing. We were all stuck with your father, and the way you're trying to fix things for us is amazing."

I gazed down at Riley. "She was his main target all these years, and since he has a copycat and there's no one else in her life other than her friends, it's our job to make up for it and protect her."

"Thank you, Paris," Violet said. "You're so much better than your father."

"I am," I responded. "My father was a psychotic criminal mastermind. I'm just a criminal mastermind."

Violet chuckled. "Yeah, I guess you are."

Riley groaned in annoyance, shifting in my lap.

I raised my hand so she could move, and then set it back on her head, ruffling her hair slightly when she relaxed back into me.

"Why is she on your lap?" Violet said then. "You could've just spread her along the seat and sat next to me."

"Yeah," I answered, a small smile creeping on my lips, "I could've. But it's easier this way because if she wakes up and runs, I'd be able to catch her faster."

Violet nodded. "Yeah, I guess you're right."

I looked down at Riley then. "I'm sorry I had to tranq you, Riley. But I had to so I could bring you back to my house; it wasn't fun, doing it, I was also worried you'd jump out the car and break your skull."

"Is Riley the *only* one your father went after?" Violet said.

"Riley was the only one who survived," I answered. "Which is pretty incredible because my dad was beyond intelligent."

"I'm actually surprised her father let me in the household knowing I wasn't her mother," Violet said. "I'm *really* surprised that he lied about it, too."

"It was the only way to keep her safe," Paris responded. "He wouldn't leave her side."

"I know, but... who was he? To your father?"

"Her father?" I thought for a moment. "I actually think he was a guard of some sort, and he hated himself after he got her mom pregnant. He left after that."

"Yeah," Violet said, "your dad...."

"Is messed up," I finished. "I know, but I'm in charge now and everything is going to get better."

I gazed down at Riley. "Especially for her."

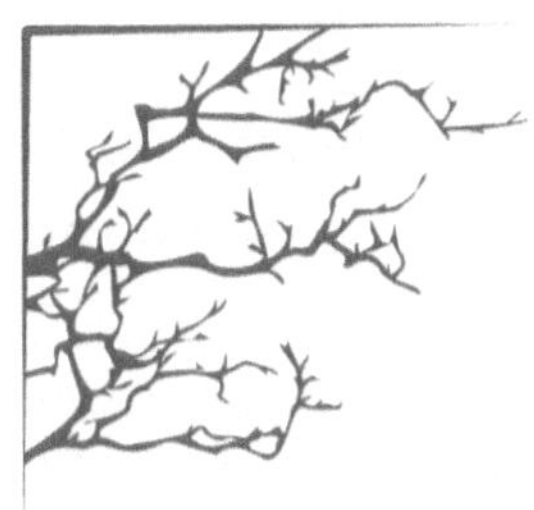

10

Riley

I woke slowly, feeling half-drowsy, half awake.

I honestly didn't know the feeling was possible.

I opened my eyes a slit, looking at the bed I rested on lazily before pushing my hand to the mattress to sit up.

I knew my hair was a mess and that I probably had drool stained on my cheek, but I didn't really care.

I was more curious as to where I *was*.

My brows pinched together when I took in the unfamiliar room.

The walls were white, but bare, and the floors were stone and slightly glossy. I sat fully then, taking in the entire area.

The curtains were drawn, letting sunlight beam onto the bed like I was under a spotlight, and the sheets someone had drawn over me were white and silky.

Where was I ...?

"Ah, finally awake," Paris said from the doorway, almost making me jump. When I looked at him, he smiled. "Good morning, Sleeping Beauty."

My gaze shot around the room before settling back on him. "Where am I?"

He stepped up to me and stopped at the foot of the bed, settling gently on the side as he eyed me curiously. "You're in a safe place now, Riley," he promised, then smiled. "My place."

I gave him a concerned look before wrapping my arms around myself as an attempt to warm my cold body. "Who are you?" I asked him for the hundredth time.

"Paris," he responded, "I'm Paris Lucan."

I gave him a sharp look. "*Who* are you?"

His lashes lowered at my tone. "I just said—"

I shook my head, cutting him off; I knew he was dodging the question, and wasn't in the mood to argue. "I want to go home."

"You can't go home," Paris told me, clearly keeping his distance and I didn't really know why. "It's burned down, Riley."

My heart stopped for a moment, and his expression seemed grim at my reaction.

"No..." I whispered, "no, that isn't possible."

"Riley...."

"It was a dream," I told him. "It was a *dream*."

"Riley," he said, "you *know* it's the truth."

But I ignored his words, immediately snapping into action. "Where's my mom? Where is *Claire*?"

"Riley...."

"Where is CLAIRE?" I yelled.

"Fix the tone," he said, annoyed, "and calm the fuck down, okay? She's in her room, Riley."

"What about Julie?" I said, something hot washing through me at his choice of words. "My niece?"

I was supposed to be watching over the child. Julie practically lived with me and Violet because her parents died.

"Everyone you love," Paris said, "is here, Riley."

My heart pounded in my chest. "Everyone...? Claire? Mom? Julie?"

He nodded. "Yes."

"Take me to them," I said. "Take me. I want to see them."

Three minutes later, Paris and I entered a second bedroom which had similar colors as the one I was in, but this one had a girl in it, and she was seated in a wheelchair, staring out the window blankly.

"Claire...?" I whispered.

She gazed up at my voice, and smiled. "Riley!"

Since she was in a wheelchair, I ran over and tackled her like I did the morning I woke up in the hospital. And Claire hugged me back, burying her face into my hair.

"Riley..." she whispered, "I'm so glad you're okay."

I let go then and stared at her fearfully. "How did they get you passed the security guards? The officers? How?"

"They *were* the officers," Claire said.

"What?"

"The police outside my door worked for Paris."

I shot my gaze behind me to Paris who was leaning against the door casually.

He smiled, the look saying, *I'm everywhere, huh?*

"Why are you doing this?" I questioned him, suspecting a catch.

He sighed, shaking his head. "Because I have some things I have to patch up, and you're in the center of it." His eyes flickered with something that I didn't like.

I looked down to Claire, ignoring his response; I didn't know why, but it was kind of fun to test him. "So... you'll never be able to walk again?"

She shook her head, smiling sadly. "But don't blame yourself, okay? It's not your fault."

I looked taken aback. "I'm fine. I'm not blaming myself."

I wouldn't admit it out loud with Paris standing there; it would show him that I was weak, and that was the last thing I wanted if he was really the bad guy.

"Let's go see Julie," Paris suggested. "You and Claire. Come on."

Claire wheeled out of the room behind me, and me after Paris, memorizing all exits and entrances, and all stairways to the basements if I needed to hide.

How would I escape if Paris had everyone I loved tied into his hands?

About a minute later, we entered the kitchen of Paris's mansion, and Julie sat there, a straw from a chocolate milk bottle pressed to her lips as Veo stood behind the counter, creating shadow puppets on the walls to entertain her.

She giggled at a joke Veo said that I couldn't hear, and I then ran over to her and picked her up without another word, earning a squeal when I stepped away from Veo, watching him with suspicious eyes.

"He's funny, Riley," Julie said, hiccuping when she swallowed the milk too fast.

After everyone kept their distance, I set her down and rolled up her sleeves, checking for bruises or cuts, but found none. "Did they hut you?" I questioned the child. "In any way?"

She shook her head, and smiled happily, the light in her eyes glowing. "Oh! Veo gave me a teddy bear, wanna see?"

She immediately ran over to the counter and set the milk on the granite, grabbing something from a chair and ran back over to me. "Look! Look! See?" She waved it in front of my eyes. "It's exactly like Julie Junior! The one I lost two years ago? I love it!"

When I gazed up at Veo with suspicion, he nodded to Paris. "He told me to."

I gazed at Paris then, questioning him silently.

"Veo's good with kids, too, Riley," he explained, smiling.

I didn't like that smile either. It did something weird to me inside.

I looked down to Julie then; who ran back over to the counter to grab her chocolate milk and sipped it through the straw again.

I wasn't sure what to think of this, honestly.

Was Paris manipulating me or was he really this kind?

"Come here, Julie," I said, the little girl running over to me and I lifted her in my arms. "I want to keep you with me," I told the child. "Don't leave my sight, okay?"

"It's okay, Riley," Claire spoke for the first time. "Paris wanted to take you out. I'll watch over her, okay?"

I glanced at Paris, and then at Claire, then back at Paris again, trying to establish a connection.

"Just you and me," Paris told me. "Traditional. No chauffeurs."

I didn't like the sound of that.

Especially with all these weird feelings he'd been giving me.

"Do I have to?" I said.

Paris tipped his head to the side. "No choice."

I paused when his eyes raked me again, skin burning when they trailed up and down me.

What was so interesting about me that he kept *doing* this?

I looked back down at Julie, hoping if I didn't pay attention to him, the warmth in me would settle.

Well... I trusted Claire with all my heart and knew that Julie would be safe with her, and I wanted answers, anyway.

"Hey, Julie," Claire said in a silly voice, "wanna ride back to my room?"

"Yes! Yes!" Julie said excitedly, making me yelp when she jumped out of my arms, running over to Claire and hopping on her lap.

"Wait!" I said. "I didn't agree yet!"

"Go on," Paris said, and Claire sputtered her lips, imitating an engine.

"Full speed ahead!" Claire yelled, speeding off while Julie's laughter filled the room.

I stared off into the distance, questioning everything that was happening.

Who should I trust? Who should I avoid? Who should I confide in? Was Julie safe here...?

Paris held out his hand, snapping me out of my thoughts. "Well, ready to go?"

I gazed at his hand for a moment before walking past him, showing him I was not in the mood to take it and made my way to the front door, slipping on my shoes that someone left.

I stood by the exit then, waiting.

Paris and Veo exchanged a look before Paris stepped to the door, unlocking the many bolts and holding it open for me.

I stepped out numbly, waiting on the front porch as he stepped out and locked the door behind him.

I couldn't run now.

Not when everyone I loved was in that house.

Paris stepped beside me then, looking at me curiously, though more suspiciously.

I tried to erase every emotion from my expression just like he did.

And I succeeded; because he sighed in annoyance and walked past me, stopping at the bottom the of the steps while waiting for me.

I followed, though silently, and we didn't speak the entire time as he held the passenger door for me and I got in, him getting in the driver's side seconds later.

The drive was also very quiet, and the silence clearly crawled through his skin like bugs.

Good, I liked testing him.

"So," he said, "how are you doing?"

I mumbled something, and he glanced at me.

"Huh?" he said.

"Are you really taking me out to talk or is this a date?" I asked him.

He paused for a moment, and glanced at me with a smile. "Ah, so you knew my intentions. You're very smart, you know that?"

"I can tell because of how you look at me, and are you being sarcastic?" I sounded slightly irritated.

"Partly," he answered. "I just want to go out with you. Is that too much to ask?"

"Yes," I said coldly. "For one: I barely even *know* you. And Two; you are *weirdly* interested in my sex toy drawer. Three? Last time I went on a first date, he suddenly showed his true colors, and I realized I was in denial for so long, so if you're planning on getting in my pants, back off boyo."

He was silent for a moment. "You have trust issues now, don't you?"

"It keeps me safe," I answered coldly. "And something is clearly missing from this situation. I'm starting to wonder if you have an ulterior motive. So what is it, Paris?"

"Who was this guy?" he asked instead.

"Why are you so *interested*?" I said. "And why do you want me alone with you? Are you going to kill me? Go right ahead. I might even give you the satisfaction and stand next to a building so my blood splatters on it, like a painting."

He raised his brows. "That got dark fast."

I looked out the window, silent.

"I'm not going to *kill* you," he said, annoyed. "Fucking god, I'm serious. And I want to know who my competitor is, Riley. Tell me his name."

"He's not a *competitor*," I answered. "I hate him, he's a dick, but I've been stuck with him because he won't leave my fucking friend group. And for the record, I'm not a romantic. So fuck off."

"Wow," he commented, "*someone's* angry. I usually don't let people speak to me that way, so calm down, and there will be no consequences."

"You're egocentric," I said, "good to know."

"Riley," he warned. "Don't test me."

He knew what I was doing? Huh.

I stared off into the distance. "Don't even try with me, Paris. Yeah, you're cute and all, but I know men like you. You're manipulators. One second you want me because you 'love' me, and the next I'm thrown out on the street because you asked the *big* question and I said no."

He was silent.

"You're all the same," I whispered. "All of you."

"Who's the guy?" Paris asked again, making me exhale an annoyed groan.

"It's none of your business."

"I want to know."

"That doesn't mean it's your business."

He glanced at me. "It is."

"No, it's not."

"Tell me, Riley. I want to know who he is."

"No."

"Riley..." he uttered. "Riley. I'll pester until you tell me. Riley—Riley—Riley—Riley—"

"Shut up."

"Riley—Riley—Riiiiiley—Riley—Riley—Riley."

My blood started simmering.

"Riiiiiiiiiiiley—Riiiiiiiiiiiiiiiley—Riiiiiiiiiley."

"Don't push it," I growled.

"Riley—Riley—Riley—Riiiiiley—Riley—Riley—Ri—"

"RYAN!" I yelled angrily. "It was RYAN, OKAY? NOW SHUT IT!"

He glanced at me, smiling in satisfaction despite anger burning in his eyes. "See? Was that so hard?"

"What do you want from me?" I said then. "What do you want?"

"I'm protecting you," he answered, still smiling.

"From who?"

"The person who wants to kill you, Riley," he said. "He won't stop until you're dead."

"Why?" I said. "Why are you doing this? There has to be a catch."

He glanced at me. "What if there isn't?"

"Then I don't believe you," I responded.

He sighed, staring out the windshield. "You're a smart one," he said not for the first time. "But I need you to trust me if you want to live."

"I don't trust anyone," I said, tone sharpening. "Especially when I found that you're the leader of the *California Mafia.*"

Paris froze, swerving to the side and breaking.

He stared at me then, eyes widening. "How did you know that?"

"You didn't think I'd look you up?" I countered. "'*Paris Lucan, son of Jonny Lucan; the mafia boss from 1988 to 2014. Jonny's death was unexplainable, but there were signs of it being a murder.*'" I kept my gaze forward. "I don't know why you murdered your father, Paris. And there's probably a reason, but just know," I glared at him, "I don't trust you. It's going to take a lot more than just giving me puppies and taking me on lovey-dovey dates to earn it. So tell me," my eyes darkened, "what do you want from me?"

Paris sighed, pressing his head to the back of his seat. "Fuck, you're too smart for your own good."

"Mm," I said, "no, I'm pretty smart. But I need it to survive in this world."

We were both silent.

"Riley... there are things going on that you aren't going to understand," he told me. "And I know I'm hiding things, I know you can tell I have a big, bad, terrifying past, but what I want you to understand," he looked to me grimly, "is that I'm trying to reform our culture. My father was a horrible man who hurt your mother deeply."

"She's never told me this," I responded suspiciously.

"She wouldn't," Paris said vaguely. "But the plans my father had were cruel, and had you centered around it."

My lips parted in confusion.

"I killed him because of something dangerous he was developing and he wanted to kill you with it, and now he has a copycat who wants to murder you, as well, but none of us know who it is. I want you to know, Riley," he said, "it's okay if you don't trust me, but I can't let you go with a serial killer out there; one that my father created." His eyes darkened. "The killer is probably one of the people you know very well."

My breathing quickened, and I stared outside, trying to think of who the killer would be.

If it was Claire or mom, then Paris shouldn't have taken them in his own house, and Ryan was too stupid and self-centered to kill someone and risk going to jail and being hated.

Then who was it?

If it was Paris, then why would he tell me these things if it was so confidential?

Ugh, my brain was hurting. Everything hurt.

"So," he said, "we're here. Ready to go inside?"

I looked up, finding us in the same place he parked before.

Oh, wow. I had amazing timing when I shocked him.

"Ready to go ea—" he started.

But I watched him glance in the rearview mirror before his face went white.

And he turned on the car, the engine roaring as he slammed the gearshift into drive.

"Head down!" he called, making confusion swirl inside me when I looked behind me, finding a truck speeding toward us at hundreds of miles per hour. "HEAD DOWN!"

I listened, and Paris slammed on the gas, making me shriek when we launched forward.

I spared a glance at him when the speedometer reached twenty then forty then eighty.

"Paris!" I called in fear. "Paris, what's *happening*?"

He glanced at me. "Clutch the door, *now*."

I caught the handle on the door, and he swerved to the side, making me scream as we entered a field, the bumps rattling my bones.

I heard the truck zoom past us from behind at light speed.

I was gasping, and Paris was too, adrenaline pumping through our veins.

"Jesus Christ," he muttered in panic, pressing his head to the seat as he kept his eyes on the rear-view mirror.

"Paris...?" I whispered.

He clutched the steering wheel suddenly, hands tightening around the leather. "He's coming back. Fuck," he muttered when I found the truck backing up and getting onto the field. "Hold on," Paris said.

And he hit the gas again, lurching the car toward the forest ahead as I screamed in panic, clutching onto the door handle for dear life.

Paris swerved to the right of the trees and sped past us from the side, the truck following behind us.

He then spun the wheel to the right, making me cry out when we entered the road again, zooming down the highway.

"Riley!" Paris yelled.

"What?" I called back.

"I'm about to do something terrifying!" he called, switching lanes on the toll highway until we hit the far right. "But don't worry!" he told me over the engine. "We're going to be okay! This car can handle it! Just press your head to the back of the seat!"

"What are you *talking about*?" I cried.

"Trust me!" he told me.

And we hit a bridge, my eyes widening when he drifted to the right, the truck coming close behind us.

But I was more focused on Paris.

"Paris!" I screamed. "Paris! What the *hell are you doing*?"

"Hold on!" he told me.

"Don't tell me you're going to jump off right now!" I yelled. "That's INSANE!"

"Press your head to the back of the seat!" he said. "Do it NOW!"

I listened, still trying to reason with him. "PARIS, WHAT THE HELL ARE YOU DOING? PARIS!"

And he drove off the edge, making me scream while we flew off, my stomach sinking to my feet when tears left my eyes, and we got farther and farther to the road below us.

"PARIS!" I cried.

"HEAD BACK!" he yelled in response.

I pressed my neck to the back of the seat, and the ground got closer.

Oh, God, I was going to die, wasn't I?

But Paris pressed my head to the seat with his hand; clearly to prevent me from breaking my neck or getting whiplash, but I screamed out as we got inches.

And the tires hit the ground, lurching me forward with inhuman force, but Paris's hand kept my head from falling forward.

And he'd clearly done this many times before, because his head never left the seat.

And right as the impact burst through my body like fireworks, he took his hand away and continued driving, speeding away from the bridge at a hundred miles per hour.

I gasped heavily while my heart pounded against my ribcage, the force from Paris speeding not helping the hollow feeling in my gut.

Twenty minutes later, Paris pulled me through the front door, and slammed it behind us.

"Veo!" he called as I stared at the ground in horror, completely frozen and numb. "VEO! WHERE THE HELL ARE YOU?"

The man came running down the stairs at an instant, standing in front of him and I.

He gave me a concerned look before returning it to Paris. "Yes, sir?"

"Lock down the house," Paris instructed. "Complete lockdown. And I need patrol."

Veo nodded, Paris letting go of my wrist seconds later.

"Riley," he said a little sternly, eyes burning with rage and fear, "go to my room again. The one you woke up in, okay?"

That was *his* room? What was he going to do to me in there?

He wasn't still talking about *consequences,* was he? I heard the hint behind the type of consequences.

It was far from small innocent punishments.

"Paris..." I tried to reason.

His eyes narrowed. "*Now.*"

But I nodded, every part of me still hollow and went upstairs, making my way to the room I woke up in and sat on his bed, contemplating my life choices.

I sat there for a full ten minutes before the panic vanished.

I stood after a moment of regaining my composure, snapping into action, and decided to search through his things to get better insight of who he was.

His room was clean for one—spotless—and I wasn't used to a teenage boy's room being so clear and healthy.

It could've been his staff or '*underlings*' who cleaned it, but I tossed the thought.

Everything was white, not black.

He clearly wasn't goth or emo or whatever, but there was no color either.

He had good taste in bedsheets, I knew as I ran my hands on them.

There were a lot of intriguing things about him, though; like how he was strong and carried me places.

He wore a lot of plain colors like black, grey, or white.

My thoughts started to trail off in the wrong direction...

I found myself wondering how it would feel if his calloused fingers slipped inside—

I slapped myself internally.

No, bad, Riley. Bad.

I gazed up then, eyes locking on his oak dresser.

Usually people hid there dirty secrets in the dresser.

I could raid through his stuff and torment him with *his* sex toys like he did with me.

So I ran over to the wood and opened the top drawer, shuffling through the contents and then went lower.

There was *nothing* in here other than *plain colored* shirts and pants.

Ugh.

But then something caught my eye.

There was an article of blue and pink clothing stuffed inside a bunch of regular clothes.

I pulled it out, curious as to why he had a splash of color in his black and white beauty.

But as I examined it, my breath caught at the sight of the jacket.

It was Bella's jacket; the one she wore the day she died.

Why did *he* have it?

But that meant...

My eyes rounded.

He was the killer.

A sudden knock cascaded on the door, startling me.

"Riley?" Paris called. "You decent?"

I immediately stuffed the jacket in the drawer and half-hazardly closed it, running over to his closet and rolled open the doors, closing them in front of me seconds later.

My heart hammered against my ribcage when he opened the bedroom door and walked in, scanning the area before exhaling, "Shit, she's gone. *Fuck.*"

But I touched the wall, hoping to find some kind of hidden exit.

But that's when something sharp sliced my skin, and I sucked in a breath, gazing down at the source.

It was a mirror... A broken one.

I caught a shard of glass and closed my hand around it, looking back up to find Paris pacing the room impatiently through the crack of the closet door.

"Riley?" he questioned. "Riley, are you in here?"

I backed myself against the wall behind me, hoping to melt into it and become a part of the plaster.

"Riley," he said then, "if you're in here, come out now and your punishment won't *nearly* be as bad."

Well, technically I wasn't *in* the room, I was in the closet, so that was a loophole.

He sighed, shaking his head.

Right as he was about to exit through the bedroom door, his eyes locked on the closet.

Shit.

I clutched the shard tighter when he stepped up to the closet, eyeing the door carefully before catching it.

Slit his throat, a part of me said.

Kill him slowly, said another.

At least wound him, said the third.

He might've fooled Claire and everyone else with his... *kindness*... but he was far from fooling me.

Serial killers were very good manipulators.

The closet door finally rolled open, and I didn't waist a second, I took the shard and slashed him across the cheek, making him yell out.

I didn't wait to see what his reaction would be, I just ran with the shard piercing into my skin, and blood lightly slipped down my wrist as I made my way to the exit.

"RILEY!" Paris screamed in anger.

I'd get the police to come here so they could save Claire and everyone else.

I couldn't do it on my own no matter how much I wanted to, not even if I shot Paris in the balls.

He always had followers lurking everywhere.

I was proven right when Veo suddenly stepped away from the wall and blocked my path to the front door.

I skittered to a stop before he could catch me and backed away.

"Miss Princes..." he whispered.

I then spun around and ran the opposite direction, turning a corner before Veo or Paris could follow me.

I saw a staircase here, anyway.

So I darted to the open door and ran down the stairs two steps at a time, not stopping until I reached the bottom.

It was a basement, but it was cluttered with a lot of weird stuff, so I could hide down here easily.

"Riley, come back here!" Paris called from upstairs, and I only closed my eyes and swallowed down a lump in my throat.

But I ran to a corner hidden by a bunch of boxes, and crouched down in the darkness, holding the shard tighter despite it burning my skin.

I had been in the basement for almost half-an-hour, and during this time, I waited for Paris to stop looking for me.

So since my legs got tired from crouching, I sat on the concrete and pulled my legs to my chest, staring off into the darkness as I still held the shard of glass tightly in my hand.

I even stopped feeling the pain of it eventually.

But then footsteps receded down the stairs, and I stiffened, heart pounding.

And without even a little bit of looking, Paris came around the boxes I hid behind and sighed, shaking his head.

"Wow, you were very lucky. The moment you ran, my guard reset the security systems and it took a while for it to reboot. Otherwise it would've been easier to find you."

He meant they had security cameras? Great.

"Riley," Paris said.

I backed myself against the wall, shaking my head to indicate him to not get closer.

"Riley," he said, stepping further toward me, "don't panic."

I pressed myself further to the wall, rose my hand, and pointed the shard of glass menacingly at him.

He only sighed and kneeled before me, clearly not afraid of the silent threat.

I just noticed the cut I left on his cheek.

It clearly wasn't attended to, and there was blood slipping down his skin like red tears.

"Come out of there," he said then.

I shook my head.

"What happened?" he asked me. "Was it the car ride? I was trying to protect us."

I shook my head again, afraid if I spoke, my voice would waver.

"Then..." he said, tipping his head to the side, "what is it?"

"I found her jacket," I told him, making him blink in surprise.

"Who?"

"What do you mean, WHO?" I yelled at him, though he didn't flinch back. "BELLA'S!"

His eyes darkened as if he realized something and he looked away, sighing. "That's why. I didn't think you would get the wrong idea."

I stared at him worriedly. "But serial killers take keepsakes."

"I'm not the killer," he said, annoyed. "Will you let me explain?"

"*Did you kill her*?" I questioned him.

"No. I was trying to save her."

I drew back in shock.

"I took the jacket to hopefully get DNA from the attacker," he explained. "But I only found his blood-type."

"Show me," I demanded sternly, still keeping the shard at him.

He blinked. "Right now?"

"Yes, right now, you *dumbass*!"

He rolled his eyes at the name and pulled out his phone while sitting—and while I held him at knifepoint.

"Here," he said, flashing the phone's screen to me while I gazed down at it. "The DNA analysis is pretty slow because we got old equipment, and there were some mixups, so this is all I got."

My brows drew together. "A-positive?"

He nodded, and swiped to another analysis.

"B-negative?"

"Yeah," he said, "the B-negative was Bella's blood type, so the killer's must be A-positive."

My heart pounded in my chest when I realized Paris took Bella's blood sample at the crime scene.

But when did he find her...? I was the one who found Bella's body, so how did he get a hold of this stuff?

I didn't even want to *ask* why Paris had a crime lab.

The answer would probably be consequential.

"Do you know anyone with A-positive?" Paris said, pulling the phone away.

I shook my head and gazed up at him with a disgusted look. "I don't go around, asking for blood-types, Paris."

He smiled at my sarcastic response and pushed his phone back into his pocket.

So, he must've been telling the truth, right? Why else would he have done all these analysis and showed them to me?

He could've fabricated them.

But why? How would he know this moment would happen? How would he set all these up in the past and predict this future?

It didn't matter how it was possible in TV... this was real life.

It wasn't possible; my suspicions were irrational.

I started to question if his motives were *actually* to protect. Most of the red flags I had were fabricated because I was afraid of trusting him...

And that he was possessive, but it felt like he became this way because of his father—protective over things he liked.

I became that way, too; I was like a mother figure to Claire and Bella, always preventing them from going places because I didn't want them getting hurt.

But Paris always told me he was going to give me consequences, but he never hit me, never grabbed me tightly enough that my skin burned, and part of me thought the "consequences" was him using a playful method to make me listen.

To not make irrational decisions.

Because everything he did was thought through—calculated—in a matter of seconds.

But... he was mainly showing white flags or whatever you called them.

He really seemed warm-blooded.

No pun intended due to the fiery feeling he was giving me.

"Paris..." I whispered, "who are you *really*? As a person?"

He smiled. "If I tell you," he said softly, "will you come out of there?"

"I'll think about it," I responded, not giving in to his loopholes.

He sighed, setting his knees down and sitting criss-cross in front of me.

I still held him at knife-point, but he didn't really seem bothered by it.

Not even with the *still leaking* wound.

"All of us here are vigilantes," he told me, and I held the knife steady despite my body starting to shake. "Yes," he said, not moving despite the fear weakening my grip on the glass shard, "I know, but we're good people now."

"'*Now?*'" I echoed.

"When we were ruled by my father," he continued, "as you know, we would be considered a mafia."

"What are you now?" I questioned, the shard now shaking.

"Now all we want is to right our wrongs, Riley. To reform." He sighed. "My dad killed a lot of our families, Riley, and threatened us to work for him or others we loved were gone, too."

He pulled up his shirt then, making me suck in a breath when I noticed all the scars lining his stomach.

"He purposely cut me here so no one would know the wounds existed," Paris explained, dropping the fabric back down. "And I hated him for it. I hated him the moment I was born."

I could tell by the fire in his eyes that he was telling the truth. "Why?" I whispered.

"Because he killed my mother," Paris said coldly, making me stiffen.

"Is that why you killed him...?" I said.

He shook his head. "There were other reasons, Riley. Many—many reasons."

My eyes reflected him with concern.

"Yes," he said, "I know this is confusing. Just..." he held out his hand, "just come out of there, and I'll get Violet and I'll explain everything."

"My mom...?" I said. "She's okay, right? Because of the explosion and stuff."

"She's fine," Paris responded softly. "Don't worry, alright? She got out before we did."

I stared down at my bloody hand then.

"Come on," Paris said, holding out his palm. "Come out of there."

"Will you inject me again?" I asked him suspiciously.

He shook his head. "No, I won't."

"Promise?" I stated.

He held out his pinky then, making me look down at it in confusion. "Pinky promise," he told me.

I hesitantly reached out to him, watching him carefully before locking our pinkies together, then shaking hands like goofy adults, me dropping the glass shard when I found no use in it anymore.

He let go then and stood, waiting for me patiently as I got out from the corner and stood with him, Paris pressing his hand to my head. "Oh, watch out. There's a shelf there." And he kept his hand to my head as I ducked and walked out from the space. "There you go," he said, smiling gently, "don't want you to hit your head."

I only stared at him, trying to recognize malice or anger in his expression.

There was none; it was all play and gentleness.

He caught my elbow that was stained with blood from my hand. "Come on, Riley," he said, "let's go upstairs, okay?"

I nodded, letting him hold my arm, and we ran up the steps seconds later.

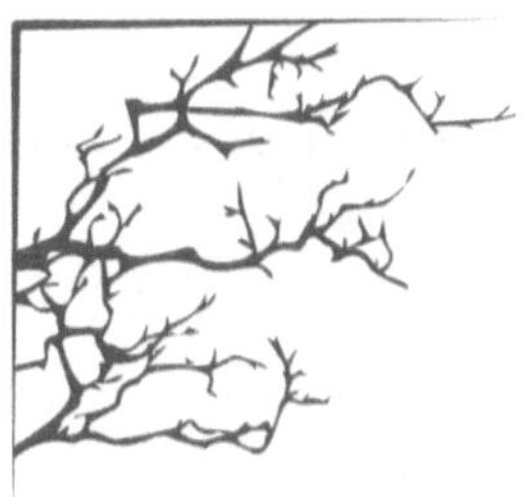

11

Riley

It was an hour after Paris took me upstairs and explained everything to me, and while he spoke, the nurses in his infirmary attended to the glass wounds on both of us.

Every little detail was explained to me.

That Violet wasn't my real mother—that my father had been lying to me all these years—that my real mother killed herself in an alleyway somewhere near the police station I was given to, and that I was an experiment of some infectious disease that Paris's father created; a disease that wasn't really that effective.

But most of all... was that all of my family by blood were dead.

All except for little Julie.

All this time, my birth was a mistake... all this time.

I was currently sitting on the floor of a bathroom upstairs, sobbing into my knees while I pulled my legs to my chest; an attempt to cradle myself.

My life was a lie.

A big, horrible lie.

And now there was a copycat trying to rid of everything in the bloodline.

Because we were all part of the experiment.

And only me and Julie were left, and this killer wouldn't stop until we were all dead.

The thought only made me sob harder into my knees, and my throat constricted.

I couldn't breathe with all the pain consuming me.

Not when my lungs tightened, and not when my throat felt swollen with all the crying I'd done for the past thirty minutes.

Who? Who would do something like this?

Who was the copycat? Who was it?

It was someone I knew, but it wasn't Claire or Paris or Violet, and Ryan was too lazy to commit murder despite his many awards from football.

Then who...? Who would do this?

But without a knock, the bathroom door creaked open, and I heard it close; followed with footsteps padding toward me.

I forgot to lock it.

Shit.

Until Paris kneeled down in front of me, watching me worriedly as I refused to make eye-contact.

I succeeded in stopping the loud sobs, but I knew if I locked eyes with him, I'd start crying again.

And I wasn't sure if I could stop then.

I felt is hand touch my shoulder, though I didn't pull away; just let him do what he was doing.

I trusted him now—somewhat. He was still a little crazy and not a very safe driver, but he'd proven that he wasn't the bad guy.

Because everything added up; everything he said made sense.

It was incredibly hard to lie about something like that and have it so *everything* added up.

I kept my face in my knees, staring at the ground while he started to rub my back soothingly.

I took the back of my hands and wiped my cheeks to get rid of all the tears.

"Hey," he said gently—me loving the tingles running through me while he rubbed my back, "you okay?"

I nodded.

"Can you show me your face?" he said.

I shook my head.

"No?"

I shook my head again.

"C'mon," he urged, "show me your face. I want to see."

I lifted my neck then, staring at him through my blurred vision and seeing his figure smile.

He gently cupped my cheeks and ran his thumbs under my eyes, drying all tears.

"You wanna watch some TV with me?" he asked gently.

I just blinked, confused at the odd question.

"Just, c'mon," he urged, standing now.

I just sat there, staring up at him blankly.

He rose a brow. "Really?"

No response.

A sigh. "Whatever, come on." He lifted me by my armpits and I whined in annoyance, shifting away from him until he finally let go and rolled his eyes. "You do realize you can't sit here all night? Some people have to take a piss, you know."

I didn't respond, once again.

"Silent game?"

I moved my eyes to the wall behind him.

He rubbed a hand down his face. "Do you *not* want to watch TV?"

Yeah, I did. I just needed to recuperate my thoughts, though; mainly because he was confusing the *hell* out of me.

I also was testing him; again.

He clearly saw my slight smile on my blank expression and rolled his eyes, grabbing under my armpits, once more.

I was messing with him, and he knew.

As I tried to squirm away, he only lifted me and chuckled, "No, don't fight. Let's go, now."

And he carried me out the door like I was a child, holding under my hips to keep me up while we went to a new bedroom that was clearly made up for me.

Oh, Jesus... The warmth from his hand was so close to my clit...

I was burning.

At least I didn't have to sleep in his bedroom tonight, right? I could satisfy the burning by myself and I could fantasize him licking my...

No, bad, Riley.

After setting me on the bed, Paris walked over to the dresser while I stared at him curiously, catching the remote in his hand and stepping back to me, settling down next to me seconds later.

He switched on the television, brushing off his pants while I climbed up to the head board and rested my back against it, watching the comedy show on channel twenty-one.

I honestly wanted to watch the news again, but I doubted that Paris would let me.

Everyone was trying to keep me away from it.

And I knew after I almost died that Paris was right; I had to stop looking for the killer.

It would only lead to my demise.

So I watched the show for a moment, seeing the cartoon characters jump around and laugh together; this show was... *American Father*? Or something? It was on that comedy network that showed that other show called... *Friends* that I loved to watch as a kid.

I honestly wished I could feel that way again... Having a family and living happily together.

"You okay?" Paris said, catching my attention.

I parted my lips in response when I gazed up at him, and nodded.

His eyes searched me for a moment before he accepted it and stared back at the TV.

We watched the show for a little while, me feeling his hand move closer to mine almost instinctually, and then he pulled back when he realized it.

I gazed up at him then, curious as to what he was thinking, and I found he was still watching the show, though his eyes had something dark in them.

It was like he was stirring inside because he wanted to ask me something, but was refraining from saying it.

It also looked like it hurt him; not telling.

But I just lifted the sheets from under my feet and managed to pull it out from under him when he was still focusing on the TV.

But I knew he was watching me from the corner of his eye.

I scooted a little closer to him and draped the sheets over us both, looking up to see his expression.

He was still looking at the TV, but his eyes softened a little.

I hesitated when I thought up something, and gazed at him with my face reddening.

He clearly saw it but said nothing.

So I scooted a little toward him.

And rested my head on his shoulder.

He stiffened, and I expected him to say, "*What are you doing?*" or "*Get off me,*" but he didn't.

His response was something entirely different.

He turned a little toward me and wrapped an arm around me, scooting a bit up while I smiled, easing into the mattress more.

I'm glad he didn't push me away.

I knew he wasn't an entirely *good* person; he probably murdered millions of people and such, but...

I honestly didn't care anymore.

It didn't matter how he was an insane driver or ran an entire team of mafia people who were most probably tasked to kill people.

Even though he was practically a crime boss...

He still had a heart.

I turned further into him and snuggled in his grip, feeling his hand gently run up and down my back.

"Here..." he whispered gently, shifting toward me while guiding me closer. "Sit a little on my lap, Riley, and rest your head on my shoulder. It's better for your neck."

My heart warmed at his words when I listened, climbing onto his lap and nestling up with him.

He cared enough to know that this position was a little uncomfortable.

Thank you for not shoving me away, I thought.

I might've been a nervous wreak and had major trust issues, but I needed this right now.

I really did.

Paris gently stroked my hair while he gazed back up at the TV, smiling when he felt me relax into him willingly.

We lay there for a while; so long that it actually was dark outside before a different show switched on; one that wasn't really as interesting.

Paris looked down at me then, and he noticed I was drifting—clearly on the verge of falling asleep.

He snapped into action then. "Here." And lay me gently down onto the bed, pulling the covers over my calm form before staring back up at my face.

I didn't resist one bit.

Something about his warmth... something about it made me feel so relaxed and at ease—and the fact that he smelled so good, too; like leaves and earth—it made me feel safe, in a way.

He smiled down at me, brushing some hair out of my face and my lashes fluttered.

And seconds later he opened the drawer on the bedside, taking out some kind of wet-wipe and gently ran it on my cheeks.

I groaned an annoyance, but he caught my chin gently to wipe my nose.

"You have so many dried tears on your face," he commented while cleaning my chin. "Seriously, it's all salt. Do you even drink *water*?"

I groaned again, trying to shift away but he pulled me back.

"Yeah, yeah," he cleaned my cheeks again, "I know I'm disturbing your calm state, but I promise it'll feel better in the morning when you don't have these white stains all over your face."

He went to wipe my skin with more kindness on my neck and throat, clearly trying not to scare me with the slightest push down.

He was probably afraid I'd think he was choking me or something.

Sometimes, I wondered what this man was thinking; seriously.

But he tossed the wipe in the trash bin and made it, closing the drawer seconds later.

"Paris...?" I whispered groggily before he could get up.

He gazed down at me. "Yes?"

"Can you…" I hesitated, "can you stay…?"

He blinked.

"I just don't want to be alone," I said almost quietly; embarrassed at the question.

"Sure," he said, settling down beside me, "sure. I'd be happy to."

I smiled when he sat, back against the headboard.

When I snuggled up with his lap, though wasn't *on* it, he smiled and stroked my hair softly.

I eased into the mattress more at the gesture and then smiled lazily up at him. "Will you protect me from the monsters under the bed?"

He chuckled at my slurred voice. "Yes, yes, I will."

Moments later while he rubbed my back, I was half-asleep, huddled up with his leg and breathing softly under the covers.

"Good night, Riley…" he whispered, continuously rubbing my back while lying down beside me.

He switched off the light and snuggled close with me, falling asleep next to me seconds later.

I liked this…

It felt nice.

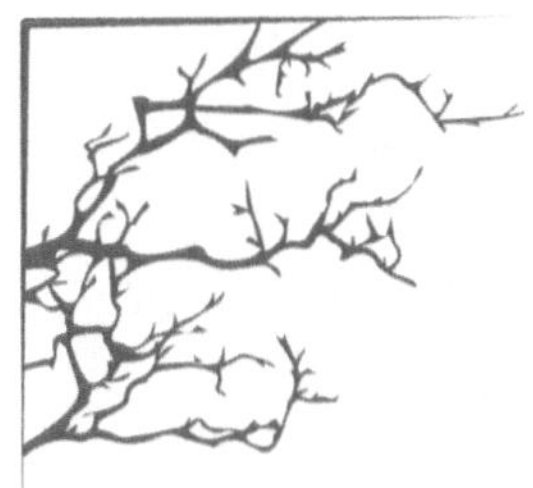

12

Riley

I slid down a wall of ice that thickened the layers of the hills around me, and when I landed on the ground, I looked up to find Paris standing in front of me.

He was smiling down at me with his dark eyes, but there was something unfamiliar about him.

The wings... the wings that sprouted from his back and enclosed itself in black feathers.

He was an angel of the darkness, but an angel, nevertheless.

"Riley," he said softly, "come on, now. Before the storm comes."

I gazed up at him curiously. "There's a storm?"

"A storm of fire and ice," Paris answered. "And I must shield the fiery rain from your skin," he held out his hand, "come on, Riley. You're safe."

I stared at him for a moment, and stepped to him, smiling as I took his hand.

"Paris...?" I asked him. "How can you be so dark? But also so light?"

He gazed down at me. "There's no light without darkness, Riley, and there's no darkness without light. There's a combination."

"What are you?"

"I am the darkness," he told me. "And you are the light. To-gether we make perfection."

"Did you do bad things?" I asked him. "Really bad things?"

His eyes dimmed. "Yes, yes, I have."

"So are you a demon or an angel, Paris?"

"I'm an angel of darkness, searching for my light."

For me? Was he searching for me?

I woke slowly the next morning, staring lazily at Paris's chest as he rubbed my back in tender circles.

How long had he been awake? Seriously, didn't he have to pee or something?

"Good morning," he said to me, though was quiet so he didn't startle my calm state.

He clearly saw my eyes open.

"Good... morning..." I murmured.

He chuckled at my slurred words. "You seem quite tired, Angel."

"Angel?" I liked that name, honestly.

"Sleep well?" he asked, staring down at me softly when I snuggled a little closer.

I nodded in his chest, letting him run his fingers through my hair.

"Seriously," he questioned, "how long has it been since you slept?"

"I sleep," I said with a tired annoyance.

"How long?" he commented.

"Like..." I breathed out a sigh, "four hours? Not counting the multiple nightmares I have at night."

"So less than four hours?" he questioned.

"Yeah, I think so."

He chuckled low under his breath. "That explains it."

"What?"

"The stress, the fears, the horror that you're going through, it's forcing your sleepiness away. Which was why you slept all night last night; you needed a presence, Angel."

"Hmm..." I murmured. "Paris...?"

"Yes?"

I nestled a little into him.

I knew he was probably not the *best* person to snuggle with when he was most probably a drug dealer and a killer, but he was *really* warm.

And I was cold; the window was open, sending a draft into the room, and I just wanted to hug him forever.

"Paris...?" I whispered.

He chuckled. "*Yes?*"

"Have you..." I breathed softly for a moment, "have you been holding me all night?"

He brushed his fingers through my hair, making my lashes flutter as another wave of calm washed over me.

"Yep," he answered. "You squeak like a mouse when you dream. It's so fucking cute."

I shoved my palm gently into his chest as an indication that he annoyed me, but then grumbled something.

"Huh?" he said.

I rose my face above the covers. "Thank you, Paris; for helping me sleep." I glared at him, then. "Although, the mouse comment makes me regret saying it."

He chucked again. "Oh, you're so fun to tease."

I rolled my eyes then, and he slipped off the bed, me staring at him as he stretched out his long arms.

I kind of liked him when he got out of bed; his hair was all tussled and tangled, and his shirt and jeans were wrinkly and ruffled.

It showed his imperfection, and I liked it.

"Well," he said, yawning as if he woke minutes before I did, "I'm going to shower."

"Wait..." I said before he could walk out of the room.

He paused and looked back at me as I slipped off the bed. "What's up?" he said.

I stepped over to him. "Can I... try something?"

He eyed me suspiciously. "Uh, sure, but you better not stab me."

I stared at him for a moment. "Please, don't judge me."

"I'm starting to worry that you're going to stab me," he stated.

But I caught his shirt and reeled him down to me as I raised myself on my tip-toes, clasping our lips together seconds later.

Paris gave in for only a second before he pushed me away, his eyes looking slightly glassy.

I took a couple steps back, pressing my hands to my chest.

Oh... he didn't want me to do that... Maybe all his kindness was based off of a friendship not a relationship.

My eyes burned with tears.

God, I was an idiot.

I stared at the floor as Paris eyed me sharply, his gaze slicing my skin.

I breathed out shakily. "I—I'm sorry. I wasn't really thinking. I—I'll go now."

I stepped past him and almost exited through the door.

"Wait," Paris said, making me pause.

I wasn't in the mood for him to scold me right now.

I heard the bed ruffle as he sat on it.

"Come here, Riley," he told me.

"You don't have to make me feel better," I said to him. "I'm serious. I accepted the mistake, it was my bad—"

"Riley," he warned not for the first time. "How many times have I told you not to fucking test me?"

"I'll just go," I said, facing the door and took one step.

"Riley, one foot out that door and I'll force you to eat ten tubs of ice cream."

I still faced away from him. *"What?"*

"It sounds neat until you get brain freeze, so if you don't want the punishment, come here right now; before I lose my patience."

Wow... he was being pretty serious right now. I wasn't really used to it.

So I turned and stepped further into the room, keeping my eyes on his collarbone when I stood in front of him.

He caught my waist then, making me yelp when I collapsed onto his lap.

I had no where to put my hands, so I really just collapsed on him like a fainting elephant.

I looked up in shock when the act made me straddle him, and my cheeks burned at his cold stare so I moved my eyes to his chest when I pushed him away.

He only caught my hands and pulled them forward, and I yelped when I collided with his chest and he guided my arms around him.

"I said I was sorry," I stated angrily but with a hint of fear.

"You sure did," he answered, flipping me over until my back met the bed.

I stared up at him when he climbed slightly on top of me. "What are you doing?"

He paused and looked up at me. "I was going to kiss you again," he told me. "I thought that was what you wanted, is it not?"

I was silent.

"I can stop if you want me to," he said to me, making my brows draw together at his kindness.

Wow, a mafia boss that didn't want to one-night-stand every pretty girl he saw?

That was new.

It was nothing like those weird novels I read.

"Okay," I said before I could think it through.

"Good girl," he praised, lowering himself so our lips clasped together, and I drew up against him as he lowered to my level, twining his fingers in my hair as I wrapped my arms around him.

He tasted so good... It was so minty and sweet at the same time...

I loved it.

Paris pulled away slightly and got the tangled covers, draping them over both of us as he gazed down to assure me, "You're cold. You've got goosebumps. I can't kiss a girl if she's not comfortable, right?"

I honestly didn't feel it; all I could focus on was him, every hint of cologne, every speck of gold in his blue eyes.

He was gorgeous.

I nodded in response, letting him lower himself back down as he lightly kissed the corners of my mouth and lowered his lips back on mine.

I used my arms to pull him closer, letting him know that he wouldn't crush me.

He listened, and set his elbows on both sides of my head as he leaned down further and kissed me harder.

He was so warm.

Closer... I needed him *closer*.

But he caught my arms and pinned them above my head, making me stiffen as he smiled against me.

But he separated our lips, me staring up at him with lust-filled eyes as he smiled menacingly.

"You like kisses?" he said. "I can kiss you anywhere. That acceptation was very vague."

Before I could respond, he dipped his head down and caught my nipple through my shirt, making me whimper when he let it slide through his teeth and caught it again, doing the same after.

Oh, fuck. What the hell was happening?

Heat swarmed inside my belly, and I moaned softly when he started licking the sensitive bud through my shirt and trailed kisses up my chest and gently started devouring my neck.

He let go of my hands so I could twine them in his hair.

"Paris..." I moaned. "Paris... Oh, god."

And his hand trailed down my leg—to my thigh—and lightly started stroking up toward my heat and back again, making my back arch as I started burning worse down there.

"Have you never done this before?" he whispered with a smoky tone, leaning up and kissing my lips gently before continuing the strokes on my inner thigh. "You've never been kissed before?"

"Kissed, yeah, *that*, no..." I moaned, trying to shift. "Fuck, please stop doing that to me."

"Doing what?"

"It burns," I breathed. "It hurts."

"Does it?"

"Paris!"

"I said I'd punish you," he stated. "Is this not a punishment?"

"Paris, please," I begged, sliding my hands to touch myself but he only caught my wrists, pinning them both above my head.

"Ah—ah," he said, "I can't let you do that."

I wiggled painfully from under him. "Please, just fucking *touch* me already!"

"Mmm..." he said, "nah. But I can give you more kisses, would you like that?"

"Touch me," I writhed from under him, "please, stop that."

He only started teasing my nipples with his mouth again.

"Paris! Fucking God! Stop being so cruel!"

He only pressed his mouth to mine, silencing my cries.

Right as he lowered himself further, a knock cascaded on the bedroom door, making us part in shock.

I panted from under him, eyes shaded over with lust, and he smiled.

"I'm mean," he told me. "This is what happens when you use that tone with me. Did you learn your lesson?"

I nodded, breathing harshly from under him.

The knock came again, making his smile replace with an annoyed look.

"Fuck. Such horrible timing."

Another knock.

"One *second*!" he called to them, looking down at me as I shivered from under him.

Thinking I was cold, he lifted himself up and got off me, covering me in the layers of blankets as I stared up at him.

I'd never felt this way before.

He chuckled. "It sucks, doesn't it? But I'll be one second."

I nodded.

He then got off the bed and made his way to the door, prying it open to reveal Veo standing there.

"I was in the middle of something," Paris said. "What is it?"

"I—sorry, sir, but…." He whispered something in Paris's ear.

Veo gazed over at me and then back at Paris again.

Paris rubbed a hand down his face, exhaling a curse. "Yeah," he said, "thanks. Get it ready for us, okay? I'm not leaving her, you should know."

He nodded and walked off.

Paris looked to me as I sat up on the bed, wrapping the blankets over myself.

I eyed him curiously as he stepped over to me.

"What's wrong?" I said.

"We need to move rooms," was all Paris explained.

"Why…?"

"Just come with me without fighting or you know what happens," he said, lifting me up until he could carry me outside the room.

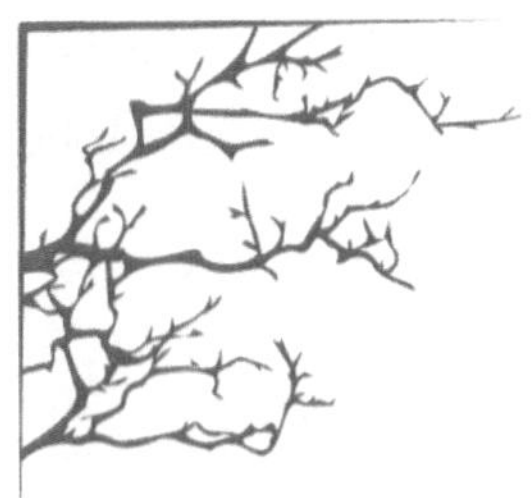

13

Riley

"Where are we?" I questioned as Paris closed the door behind me.

It was some kind of house... it was like an apartment—it had two bedrooms and a bathroom in each chamber, a large living space with a giant L-shaped sofa, and a kitchen that rested on our right—but it was really fancy and... *big.*

"Where are we?" I repeated again as I turned to him.

He was smiling, leaning lazily against the door while he continued eye-fucking me. "We're on Earth."

"Duh," I responded harshly. "But what is this *place?*"

"It's new to you, huh?" he commented. "I've lived here for many years. It's a loft, Riley."

I gazed at him. "You're seventeen, how can you have a *loft* all to yourself?"

He pushed himself off the wall and stepped over to the kitchen. "A lot of my guards are adults," he explained, snatching a water bottle from the fridge and looking up to me with a smile. "And I'm twenty, Sweetheart. You don't assume someone's age, you know. I can pay for anything because I'm an adult, and I'm a billionaire."

"But I thought you went to my high school," I said.

He chuckled. "You know how easy it is to make fake backgrounds? I told them I was turning eighteen on Tuesday, I look that age too."

"But you're... *twenty*?"

He nodded.

"So... you're an adult? That means you can give...."

He raised his brows.

I shook my head. "Never mind."

"No—no—no," he smiled, "what were you going to say?"

"Don't push me," I growled.

His lashes lowered. "What did I say about that tone?"

I stared at the floor. "Sorry."

"I don't like apologies either, stop that."

"Then what do you *want* me to say?" I countered.

"I want you to watch your tone," he stated. "Or I will punish you again, hear me?"

I nodded numbly.

"Good," he stated. "You're a good listener, aren't you?"

I nodded again.

"Good," he said again, smiling.

"Paris...?" I whispered.

"Yes?"

"Are you a good person?"

"Yes."

"Are you sure?" I whispered.

He nodded.

"Paris... who are you? What are you thinking? I can't read you... ever. It bothers me. I want to know what you're thinking."

He shook his head in amusement and gazed back up at me. "Your curiosity is entertaining, you know that?" And he downed half the bottle of water in one go, setting it on the counter seconds later.

"Paris," I urged, "who do you think the killer is? You told me before you have a suspicion."

He looked at the floor for a moment. "That's just it, it's a suspicion. I don't know if I'm right, therefore I will not tell you."

I sighed in defeat. "How did you get ahold of things at Bella's crime scene? How did you know I was drowning in the ocean?"

He didn't hesitate responding, "I got ahold of Bella's jacket because I have a friend in the police department. And I knew you were in danger because I sensed it, and when I went up to your bedroom, you were gone. But when I looked out the window, you were over some guy's shoulder."

"Whose?"

He shrugged. "He wore black clothes, but I do know he has some kind of build. I'm really glad I was able to get to you in time, though." He leaned on the counter. "I was almost too late."

The slight shade to his eyes told me he was being honest, and I wondered how often he'd been saving me without me knowing.

It seemed like he was beating himself up inside.

He smiled then. "Are you *blushing*?"

I shook my head, covering my cheeks. "No."

"Liars have to be taught lessons, too, you know."

My cheeks reddened more.

"Go on," Paris urged, nodding to a bedroom on the far right of the wall, "make yourself at home."

I nodded numbly, stepping up to the bedroom and flipping on the lights.

I gasped.

It was so pretty; the white walls and the bleached white carpet, and the bed sheets were a silky black, the throw pillows also covered in black and white swirls and designs, and the nightstand—as well as the dressers and doors—were painted a coal black.

It felt like I was in one of those luxury hotels.

I would have no problem settling into *this*. This was so beautiful; I felt the urge to vacuum and make the sheets every chance I could; just to make it stay pretty.

So I walked in the room, dropping my backpack on the ground and collapsed on the bed, belly down.

Maybe I would take a nap before me and Paris went out for dinner.

After taking an hour nap, I lazily walked out of my bedroom and to the kitchen to find Paris at work at the cutting board.

There was a pot steaming, and a grill set on the stove that was sizzling with the meat on it, and Paris was skillfully slicing a tomato.

I rubbed my eyes, yawning, and looked up to him. "What are you doing?"

The corner of his mouth tilted, and he glanced up at me while still cutting the tomato. "Making burgers for dinner."

"Burgers?" I echoed tiredly.

"Yeah," he said, "you know, lettuce, cheese, tomato—"

"I know what a fucking *burger* is!" I responded harshly.

He chuckled, shrugging while focusing back onto what he was doing.

We were silent for a moment, and I stared down at what he was doing.

The way he cut the fruits was so graceful. I'd never seen something like this before.

It was like he was a Bollywood dancer, waving his hands everywhere and such.

I didn't even notice how close I was to him; how I was practically breathing down his neck while he diced the first tomato and opened the steaming pot, gathering all the fruit and dumping them into it.

It was clearly a side dish of some sort, and I kind of wondered what it was.

He seemed like an expert chef or something.

He got another tomato from a plastic bag, and set it neatly on the cutting board, turning to me while I glanced up at him in surprise.

He smiled. "You look bored. Come here. I'll teach you how to make burgers."

I yelped when he caught my arm and reeled me in front of him, so we switched places.

"Let me see what you do," he uttered, setting a knife on one side of me as he leaned on the wall, clearly watching.

I breathed shallowly when I picked up the knife, sloppily sliding the point into the middle of the tomato until the blade slipped and I yelled out, dropping it before it cut me.

Paris laughed then. "Angel, it's a knife, not a rattlesnake."

He walked over to me then, pressing himself to my back as I stared down at the cutting board, breathing shallowly still. "Let me show you," he whispered, breath warming my neck.

He slipped his hands around me, catching my wrists as I closed them back around the knife.

"You hold it like this," he told me, adjusting my fingers as my cheeks reddened. "And then you do this." He guided my free hand to one side of the tomato and held it there, and then he neatly pressed my wrist so I could slice the tomato. "See?" he whispered, making sweat stick my hair to my temples. "There you go, now let's do it again."

He guided me as I sliced the tomato neatly this time.

"Do you have to stand this close?" I whispered.

"Would you rather slice your hand off?"

"Never mind."

He chuckled. "Here, I'll guide you through the whole tomato."

And I stood there, face reddening as he stayed overwhelmingly close and did as he said.

Guided me through the whole tomato.

But about halfway through the piece of fruit, his lips brushed the side of my neck as he spoke in whispers, but I couldn't focus on what he was saying because of the shocks of heat that went through me.

I was overwhelmed with the warmth of his body, and the stove wasn't really helping.

But one thing that I noticed... I wasn't uncomfortable.

I was actually liking how close he was.

Though, I didn't really know why, honestly.

I never felt this way with Ryan.

Was that bad?

But while I started getting close to the end, Paris kept a hold of my hands as I sliced the tomato, but then lightly started kissing the skin on my neck, making the shockwaves get stronger.

"Paris..." I murmured.

But he never responded, holding my wrists as he kissed me slightly harder, making me moan as he gently suckled on the skin.

He moved to my ear, and I dropped the knife when he flicked the lobe with his nose and moved to trailing his tongue along the side of my neck.

He continued teasing the skin until he tasted my sweat, and drew back, kissing behind my ear softly before whispering in it, "And that was for talking back to me when we came in here."

"It's burning..." I whispered to him, clutching the counter.

"I know," he responded. "And you're not easing it tonight, Sweetheart. I know what you're planning, and I'm going to make sure you don't touch yourself tonight by coming in at random times in the night. This is a lesson, hear me?"

I nodded, the space between my legs throbbing.

Almost twenty minutes later, Paris and I sat at the mini dining table beside the living room and ate our burgers happily.

Paris smiled when I let out a silent, "Mmm...." And the fact that my cheeks were lighting at how good it tasted.

My clit was still throbbing, but I was able to ignore it.

"You like?" he said.

"Yeah," I told him, "I feel like you were a professional chef before."

He shrugged. "I cook for myself a lot."

I kept eating, making him smile.

I never really finished my food before, and now I was almost three-quarters of the way through the burger.

"Well," he knocked the table, stretching out his arms when I looked up at him curiously, "I have some work to attend to, so I'll be out for the night."

"Outside?" I said.

"No," he told me, "I meant I have something to do on my computer, and *yes*, I'm still making sure you're not disobeying my orders."

"Oh."

"Yeah, I'm mean, huh?" He stood and ruffled my hair. "Holler if you need me."

And he walked off to his bedroom.

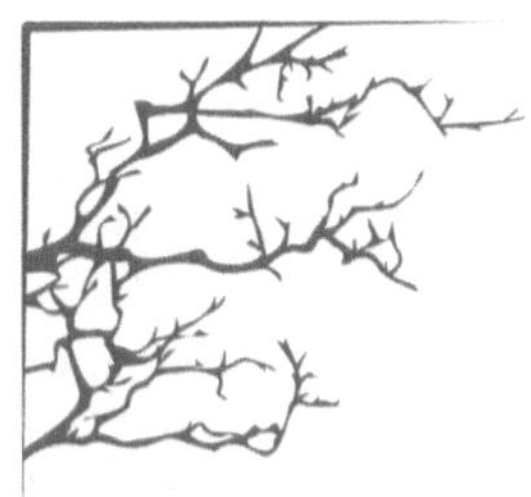

14

Riley

It was around twelve in the morning when I walked into Paris's bedroom, wearing one of my T-shirts but refrained from the shorts because the shirt covered to my mid-thigh, anyway.

I knocked on his door first to let him know I was there, but he never responded.

His door was open, though, and I clearly saw that he was at work on his computer, typing like a maniac.

He was probably busy, but maybe he didn't see me or something.

So I knocked again.

He never responded.

Was he ignoring me or was he hyper focused on whatever he was doing?

I then decided to walk in, glancing around the room to find the tables covered in papers.

Even from my distance, I could tell they were wanted posters and documents from the police department.

I saw the manilla folder with "Bella Swans" on it with papers from it pouring all over the dresser.

Was he trying to find the killer or was he trying to find a motive?

My eyes ran along the room before they settled on him.

He looked slightly restless; hair tussled, eyes almost blood shot.

If I didn't know he was stressed, I probably would've thought he was on drugs or something.

But I understood, I couldn't sleep either.

That was why I came in here.

"Paris?" I whispered quietly, slightly embarrassed at the next question. "Can I have a good night kiss?"

I had been staring at the mirror in my bathroom for the last thirty minutes, repeating the question over and over until I stopped blushing.

"I'm busy," he said a little harshly.

My stomach sank at this sudden anger. "I know, but... It'll help me sleep better."

He looked up at me then, eyes burning in anger as he slammed the computer shut. "I said, I'm *BUSY*."

I drew back in surprise, seeing the anger in his expression.

Then something cold washed over me, followed by a similar heat.

I knew what it was; guilt and anger.

"Oh..." I uttered, looking down at the floor in shock. "Sorry, I guess. I was just asking for help. I... I'll leave you alone then."

And I walked out the door.

"Riley," Paris said before I could leave. "Don't leave this room."

"Good night," I said, walking across the hall and slamming the door shut behind me with a sudden anger.

I headed straight for my bed, eyes burning with tears as sobs edged up my throat.

He had a right to say no, but it still hurt.

His whole reaction hurt.

I climbed into bed and let some of my tears slip into the pillowcase, staining it with my guilt and sorrow as I pulled my knees to my chest and held myself.

He didn't have to get so angry. I just wanted help sleeping.

The more I thought about it, the pain in my lungs expanded, and it got so unbearable that I started crying silently.

I just wanted someone to lean on, someone to trust.

Was that too much to ask? Was it?

Almost a minute later, my door cracked open, and I heard Paris enter silently.

But I didn't want him to see me cry.

"I told you to stay," Paris stated angrily, "but did you listen? Do you need to be taught another lesson?"

I didn't respond, just tried to hold myself.

"Are you ignoring me now?" he stated angrily. "Seriously? Do I need to start keeping a tally chart?"

I let out a slight sob, and covered my mouth.

His silence told me he heard it.

"Hey," he uttered, sitting on the bed beside me.

"Leave me alone," I said, voice shaking.

"Riley," he uttered, "I'm sorry, I was busy."

It wasn't what I wanted to hear. He was busy, fine, but it didn't change the fact that he treated me like I was a burden to him.

"Riley," he said at my silence.

"LEAVE ME ALONE!" I screamed, making him gasp.

I really didn't want him to see me cry right now.

Paris didn't listen then, clearly knowing I needed someone to calm me down. "Don't push me away."

"I'm pushing," I said.

He touched my shoulder, but I flinched away making him draw back slightly and set his hand on the bed. "Riley."

I let out another sob escape and cursed internally. "Please, just go... You're busy, I get it."

He was silent. "I'm being patient right now, so tell me what's going on."

"I don't want to."

"You're going to tell me," he stated.

"I *don't have* to."

"Riley, my patience is depleting."

"I don't fucking CARE!"

He drew back in surprise and I shot up from the bed.

"I told you to leave," I stated, slipping off the mattress. "You didn't listen to me and now I hurt you. You see what happens when you get too close? Apparently, I don't ever learn my lesson of how I act around people when I'm like this. I'm sorry. You should've really just let me get murdered. I'm sure—whoever they are—they have reasons."

And I walked off to my bathroom, shutting the door behind me.

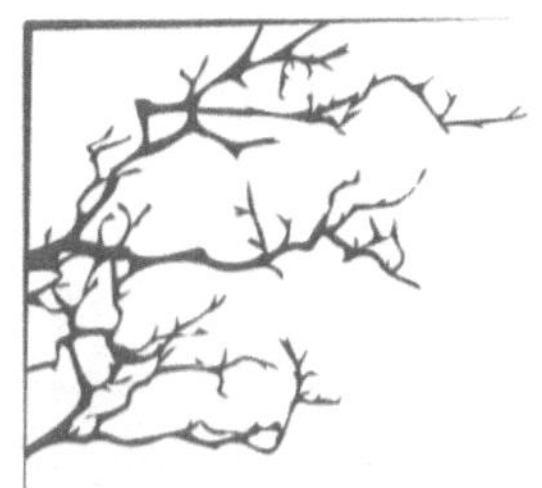

15

Paris

"**R**iley," I said, standing up while walking to the bathroom door, "are you planning on lying on the floor in there and crying all night?"

"What does it matter to you?" she questioned.

That was a "yes."

I rattled the handle. "Let me in."

"No."

"Are you going to hurt yourself?"

"I'm *not* SUICIDAL!"

"That's what a suicidal person would say," I commented.

I heard her groan in annoyance and slide down the wall, clearly sitting on the floor.

"Riley," I stated, "come out of there. *Now.*"

"No."

"If you don't—"

"Then you'll punish me? Yeah, I know. But it's better to be punished later than to possibly scream at you because I'm so stressed out right now."

"Then scream," I stated.

"I'm going to say things I don't mean," she told me. "And you'll be hurt. So it's better for you to walk away now and go do something else."

"Riley."

"*Don't* try to reason with me, okay?"

"I guarantee I've been hurt worse," I stated.

"Probably, but you hated him."

My father.

I sighed, leaning against the wall. "Riley, come out of there."

"I will if you leave."

"I'm not leaving."

"Then I'm not coming out."

I dragged a hand down my face. "Can you *not* test me right now? My patience is wearing thin."

"And it should," was all she said.

I stared at the door then, blinking in annoyance. "I will pester you again until you unlock the door."

"And I'm turning on the fan," she stated. "See? Hear it?"

The fan suddenly came on after a click of a switch.

Fuck, now she couldn't hear me.

But... I kind of expected that.

I unlocked the door with a thumbnail, stepping in the bathroom seconds later.

Riley—once again—had her face in her knees, and there were headphones covering her ears as she kept the position.

I kneeled down beside her, lightly flicking her forehead.

Her face shot up, cheeks red with tears when her eyes rounded, and she took the headphones off. "How did you get in here?"

"Rule one," I said, "when you lock yourself in a room in hopes to isolate yourself from me, make sure the lock can't be opened with a penny. Rule two," I eyed her, "I don't give up, now come out."

"Can you stop this? Can you *please* stop?"

"No."

She sighed, setting her chin on her knees. "I hate you."

"Is this you trying to get me angry and leave?" I questioned. "Yeah, Honey. I do it, too. So I know what you're doing, sweets. Now get up and walk out of here willingly, or I'll drag you out and teach you *another* lesson." I paused. "For the what.. *third* time today?"

She was silent.

I sighed. "Second option it is."

She yelled out when I caught her wrist and dragged her out of the room like her arm was a leash.

"Paris!" she exclaimed. "Let go of my fucking arm!"

"I don't really feel like it," I answered, smiling down at her before gazing back up to her room. "My room's kind of a mess..." I said, a wicked smile spreading along my lips, "I don't honestly feel like sleeping in there tonight."

Her eyes locked on me, clearly getting the hint. "Another lesson?"

"You can't learn without consequences," I stated.

"All night...?" she said then.

I gazed down at her, dick throbbing in my jeans, but I was able to ignore it for now. "You'll have to see, won't you?"

She looked away when I dragged her against the bed, letting go of her arm seconds later.

"I can't handle that all night," she stated.

I picked her up, earning a gasp when I set her on the bed and leveled my eyes with hers. "Then maybe you should learn you lesson, no?"

She was silent.

"Ask me," I told her, kneeling down to her level.

"Ask you what?" she said, looking at me now.

Her eyes were glimmering like a fucking excited child.

Oh, fuck me. My dick was pulsing harder.

"Ask me again. What you wanted to help you sleep. Ask."

She shook her head. "But you said you were busy, and then got mad at me. I don't feel like asking, Paris."

Could she *not* do this right now?

I sat down beside her, attempting comfort while brushing some hair off her neck and left a gentle kiss there, lightly running my thumb on all the marks I left from the kitchen. "I'm not anymore. Go on, ask me, Riley."

She sniffled, hugging her arms around herself. "Can I...?" but her voice trailed off.

"Can you what?" I prompted. "Finish your sentence."

"Can I have," she looked down to the floor, holding herself tighter, "a good night kiss?"

I smiled, slightly satisfied. "Of course, you can," I uttered. "See? Was that so hard?"

"Yes, because you're forcing yourself now."

I wanted to slap her with how passive she was being right now, but I wasn't that kind of guy.

"Riley," I lightly tugged her shoulder, "come on. Face me."

She shifted so she faced me, eyes glimmering with unshed tears. "Can I have a good night kiss?" she asked again.

"I said, yes." I smiled.

She closed her eyes, leaning into me and waiting for our lips to touch.

But when nothing happened, she opened her eyes to find me staring down at her in amusement.

"What?" she said.

I chuckled, choosing to tease her. "Aren't you going to kiss me?"

"I was trying to," she commented.

I smirked. "Try again."

She stared at me for a moment, then scooted further toward me and clasped our lips together.

That's when my playful self vanished, because the moment our lips collided, I gave in with no hint of reluctance.

I caught the back of her head and brought her closer, cradling her so she would hopefully stay in place.

But I then shoved her away—not parting our lips—and held her under me on the bed.

It was too much... it was all too much.

I trailed my kisses down her neck again, feeling her hand catch onto my shirt and twine the threads into her fingertips.

She let out soft moans as I continued down to her shoulder, and she started whining again when my fingers lightly grazed on the hem of her panties.

I drew back then, surprised, continuing to run my finger on the hem, and she groaned on annoyance, turning her face away at the worsening burn.

"You're not wearing shorts," I commented, gazing up at her. "Naughty girl. You were planning on this, huh?"

She shook her head. "No, I swear. I just thought the shirt was long enough to cover it."

"Liar," I slipped them under the fabric, making her cry out as my hand slowly moved down. "Tell me the truth."

"It is the truth!" she told me, wincing as my fingers hovered a millimeter over her clit.

"Liar."

"No!" she said. "I'm not lying. Please, just touch me!" She wiggled from under me. "Stop teasing, please!"

"But you wanted a good night kiss," I said, enjoying her begging. "And now you want more?"

"Yes," she said, "yes, please."

"Well, I'll give you want you wanted, but I'll decide myself if you deserve more."

"Paris..." she sobbed.

My dick was throbbing... it was aching.

I lowered my mouth to hers, kissing her gently.

But when she drew up against me to get me closer, I pulled back.

"No," I said, "I'm the lead. Repeat it."

"You're the lead," she said.

"Good girl," I praised. "Keep yourself still, got it?"

She nodded.

And I kissed her again, cradling her head to me as she whimpered softly.

The kiss lasted for what felt like hours.

Until, almost instinctually, I lightly moved my knee to hers, and slightly parted her legs as she tried to kiss me back.

She clearly felt my hand slowly trail down her stomach, and she whimpered.

"I know," I whispered on her lips before lightly pecking it, "hot, isn't it? Does it hurt? Does this hurt?"

She nodded, hands twining onto the covers as I ran two of my fingers on both sides of her labia, still not touching her clit, and she arched her back, not used to this sensation I was giving her.

It clearly burned.

"Touch me..." she begged. "Please... just a little. Touch me... Touch. Touch."

"Why?" I said. "You wanna give me a reason?"

"I need it..." she whispered, "please."

"But I thought you hated me," I stated.

She shook her head. "No."

"Then why did you say it?" I questioned, continuing to stroke her.

"I was scared..." she told me desperately. "Please, touch me... Just a little, please."

"Why were you scared?" I asked her, continuing the burning act.

"It's throbbing!" she told me, aching her back in hopes to rub her clit on my hand, but I shoved her back down, making her whimper in annoyance.

"Why?" I said. "Answer, now, Riley."

"Why are you making me speak?" she questioned. "While doing this to me?"

"It's part of your punishment," I stated. "Now answer the question."

She turned her head to the side. "I'm afraid of getting close..." she told me. "Please, just—"

"Why are you scared of getting close?" I said.

She sobbed at the throbbing pain between her legs. "Paris, please!"

I started playing with her nipple through her shirt, leaning down while whispering, "Answer my questions, and I'll think of letting you come."

She looked up to me, glassy-eyed. "I don't want to hurt you... and I don't want you to hurt me...."

"Explain," I said.

She caught the covers tighter, sweat sliding down her temples. "I don't want to fall in love with someone..." she exhaled, trying to keep her composure, "only to figure out they were using me... only to find how cold it is an night when I have no one to hold me...."

"Ryan did that?" I said.

She nodded, breaths quickening. "I got used to it, so please just... touch me. Goddamn it."

"Why are you afraid of hurting me?" I asked then.

"Because someone is killing everyone I love... everyone I care about... and I can't handle another person, Paris, *please*."

"Hold on," I said, making her groan in annoyance. "Why were you so restless?"

"Because," she answered.

"Because why? Something was bothering you, I can tell, Honey."

She threw her head back. "Paris, it hurts. I need to touch it."

"You're going to keep your hands right where they are," I instructed, "got it?"

She sobbed due to my denial, clearly knowing I'd just pin them above her head if she disobeyed. "How are you not plunging inside me right now?" she asked me.

"Oh, I want to," I stated honestly, "my dick is throbbing like fucking crazy, but I know it would satisfy you, and I can't have that. This is a punishment, isn't it?"

"Paris..." she cried softly. "Please."

"You're very sensitive," I said. "Most girls can handle a light brush on their nipple, but you?" I ran my thumb along it, earning a gasp. "Mm... you are very sensitive. I kind of wonder how it would feel for you if I touched your clit right now... but I can't do that, can I?"

"Paris..." she whispered. "Paris, please, stop teasing me."

"What do you want me to do then?" I said.

"What do you want me to say...?" she whispered. "What do you want me to say to make you..." she arched her back when I ran my thumb on her nipple again, "to make you satisfy me...?"

"Do you like this?" I said. "This attention I'm giving you? Do you like the punishments, Riley?"

She nodded.

"Say it aloud," I ordered.

"Yes, I love it."

"Love what?"

"When you punish me... I love it. I really do. I never feel this way with anyone... It makes me wanna...."

"Wanna what?"

"I want to do *so* many things," she responded, "please, just touch me. I need to satisfy it... It hurts *so* much."

"Beg," I said.

She gazed up at me. "What?"

"Beg," I stated. "Beg me to touch you. Beg."

She closed her eyes, turning her head away as she whispered, "Please, touch me."

"What?" I said. "Louder."

"Please, touch me," she said.

"Again."

"Touch me... I need it, please. Please, just a light brush. Just a light one. I don't have to come. I don't have to."

I blinked, confused. "Since when does a girl as desperate as you *not* want to come?"

She shook her head.

"Answer the question, Riley."

"I've never."

"Never what?"

"Never come before... I don't know how to."

I paused, staring up at her.

"I can't handle holding the vibes to my clit," she said. "I can't handle thrusting the dildos inside me. It's too much and I can never get to the 'climax' or whatever."

"You," I said, not believing a word, "have never come before?"

She shook her head.

"When Ryan asked you to have sex with him," I stated, "did you?"

"A little..." she responded.

"He went inside you?"

"With a condom," she made sure to clarify.

"He came?" I said.

She nodded.

"*You* didn't?"

She shook her head.

I leaned back, running my fingers lightly over her panties until they passed over her clit, making her gasp.

"Did he know you didn't come?" I asked her, doing it again.

She shook her head. "No... I faked it."

I stopped then, making her exhale a groan as I sat up on the bed.

"What?" she said.

"Riley," I said, "get out."

Her eyes widened. "What?"

"Get out of this room. *Now.*"

Her heart pounded ice in her veins. "Why?"

I shot a glare down at her. "Does it look like I'm in the mood to reason? Get OUT."

She froze for a moment.

But she nodded then, and got out of bed, making her way over to the door as tears filled her eyes.

God, she drove me fucking crazy. She pissed me the fuck off.

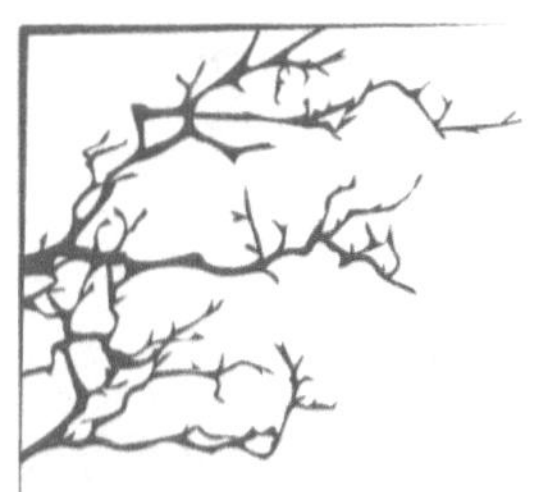

16

Riley

What did I do?

When I got to the front door, I shuffled on my jacket and shoes, covering myself as I started to slowly cry.

What did I do to make him so angry? He wanted answers... did I share too much? Did he hate me now?

When I reached for the doorknob, I heard an irate, "Where are you going?"

I looked up at him, trying to blink away tears when I saw his burning blue eyes. "You told me to leave...."

"I told you to leave the *room*, not my house. Go sit at the dining table."

I felt my heart shattering.

"I don't understand..." I whispered to him.

"DINING TABLE."

My eyes stung with tears as I padded over to the table, sitting down seconds later.

"Do you know why I'm angry?" he asked me.

I shook my head, sobs edging up my throat.

He sat on the table in front of me. "It's because you lied to me."

I closed my eyes as a cold pain consumed me.

"You've never climaxed, yes, I get that," Paris continued. "But did you really fake the climax with Ryan? Or did he never give you one?"

I was silent.

"Answer me."

"He... never gave me one," I whispered, "and I did fake it, but... he knew."

"How did he know?" Paris said.

I blinked away tears. "Because... I'm... apparently guys can tell."

"We can," Paris responded, "even if you don't scream when you do it, we can feel you tighten everywhere. So why did you lie?"

"I didn't... really..." I told him. "I just... didn't tell you the whole truth."

Paris eyed me over. "Do you need to go over my knee?"

I shook my head. "I can't come, Paris. I just can't... I was faltering because I have performance anxiety."

He gazed up at me then, eyes softening.

I shook my head. "I know how to please a guy... They don't know how to please me, and when I told Ryan that... that I wasn't satisfied, he just took me again and told me that he'd continue until I was. But I never came... I just...."

"Just what?" Paris said. "Finish your sentences."

"I told him to stop because I knew he was only pleasing himself, and... he just left."

"Was that the night you broke up?" Paris said.

I nodded. "He's continuously trying to hook me in again... I think it's because girls get tired when they come and since I never do... He could take me for as long as he wants."

Paris eyed me. "You're not lying now, are you?"

I shook my head.

"I can tell," he responded. "Well," he stood and gazed down at me, "I can tell you're very aware right now, so I'll wait until your least expecting me to sneak in, and I'll fuck you in my own little way." He pushed my back when I gave him a confused look. "Off to bed now. Go on."

I numbly walked back to my bedroom, not looking behind me to see if he was following.

"Sneak in" my ass. He was stalling.

I somehow turned him off...

By being myself.

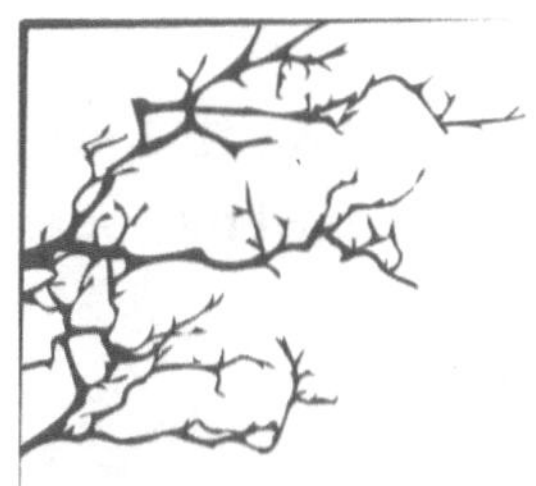

17

Paris

I was shuffling through my nightstand, smiling wickedly as I pulled out some ropes and some vibrators.

Riley went back to her room all sad, thinking I was messing with her or something.

I wasn't.

I pulled out the clit brush that I found in her nightstand, and I pulled out a big ass dildo that was somewhat grainy so it would rub against her and feel *so* much better than a normal one.

Ah... I was so mean.

She hadn't come before? Fine. It's normal.

She was just one of those girls who needed extra time with the vibes and the fucks.

She'd come eventually.

I wanted to push her to her limit.

Right as I closed the nightstand drawer, a flash of light beamed through the sky, followed by a crackling thunder.

Oh, that was right. There was a storm tonight, wasn't there?

But there was a large thud in the room next to me, followed by a painful scream.

My heart stopped when I dropped all the toys.

Oh, shit.

And I darted out of my room, busting through Riley's door until it slammed against the wall as I scanned the room.

Shit, shit, shit.

She was gone.

Fuck.

Another flash of light burst through the window, and the thunder boomed through the city.

But right as my panic settled in, I heard another scream that trailed off into a sob.

What?

But I followed the sound, circling around the bed and hearing faint sobs as I got closer to the source.

Another flash of light, another booming thunder.

The glass tables in this room rattled with it.

"No!" a girl cried. "Stop it! Stop it!"

Was someone hurting her?

I finally stopped at the end of the bed, finding Riley under the desk at the left side of the bed, curled up with herself as she covered her ears.

Who was she scared of?

"Riley," I said, scanning the room for threats as I made my way to her, "what's going on?"

She never responded, just held herself under the table and pressed herself to the wall as if she was attempting to melt into it.

"Riley..." I murmured, "is there someone in here?"

She shook her head, tears staining her cheeks. "Make it stop... Make it stop, please... I don't like it."

What was she talking about?

I stepped over to her and kneeled down next to her. "Do you need my hand, Honey?" I held it out to her.

She stared down at it, her entire body shaking.

Jesus... it made something inside me shatter.

She was terrified... I'd never seen someone this scared before.

Was it something I said? Was she upset with me?

"Give me your hand," I whispered to her, wiggling my fingers. "Don't be afraid. I won't hurt you. Come out of there."

She reached slowly to me, fingers lightly brushing my palm as I kept my place, hoping not to startle her more.

"It's okay," I whispered. "Don't be scared of me. Give me your hand, Honey."

She started to settle her palm on mine.

But another light beamed through the room, and the thunder came after, bursting my eardrums.

Woah. That one was close.

Riley drew back immediately and covered her ears, crying out as she turned further into the wall.

I stared down at her in concern.

Another flash burst through the room, followed by thunder rattling the house.

Riley cried out again, rolling over more and covering her ears.

I just eyed her carefully.

This was why she needed help sleeping, wasn't it? This was what was bothering her all night.

Riley had a phobia of thunderstorms, and there was a severe weather warning.

But I didn't really understand why she was afraid.

"It's okay," I breathed softly, running a hand down her arm as she exhaled whimpers. "Don't be scared. It can't hurt you."

Another boom shook the house, making her scream until she started crying again.

"Here," I said, picking up a blanket from her bedside. "Come here."

"No!" she cried when I pulled her out from under the desk and lifted her onto my lap. "No! No, stop it! *Stop it*!"

I cradled her against me, rocking her slightly like she was a child in need of protection, and wrapped the blanket around her, trying to sooth her with the softness of it.

"Hold onto me," I told her and she curled up. "No, no, not yourself. Me. Wrap your arms around me."

Another bolt crackled across the sky, followed by a loud rumble and I could hear the cups in the kitchen start rattling.

Riley screamed in fear and hid her face into my neck, hands latching onto my shirt.

"There you go," I breathed. "There you go."

She kept sobbing into my shirt.

"How do you go through this yourself? Jesus."

"I..." she sobbed, "I have headphones and I hide in my closet, but the closet here won't fit me."

"Do you have headphones?" I asked.

She shook her head. "I left them in the bathroom and I can't get to them...."

"Yeah, that's a problem," I commented. "Will earmuffs work, Honey?"

She nodded.

I breathed out a sigh and shuffled through the contents in the nightstand.

And I pulled out some grey earmuffs, lowering it over her ears gently before going back to holding her tightly.

She probably could still hear me, but I still gently pushed her head against my chest so she could avert her eyes from the lightning.

She listened, turning her face into my neck.

"There you go…" I soothed, running a gentle hand along her arm through the blanket. "Shhh…."

Another flash burst through the window, followed by an echoing thunder.

She only murmured in annoyance this time, but shifted further into me, giving into my comfort.

She clearly felt the house shake, but it didn't bother her as much.

Good, she couldn't hear it anymore.

Earmuffs didn't really block sound, I also was covering her ears.

"Shhh…" I breathed, rocking her still. "There you go… There you go. See? This is how much of a good girl you are. You can be a good girl if you try."

She started easing in my grip, shifting closer until she could feel my entire body heat.

"Ease up," I murmured into her hair. "Just breathe, okay?"

Despite the constant flashes of light and the loud, booming thunder, she let go of the back of my shirt and folded her arms between our chests, huddling close with me.

"You can fall asleep," I told her. "I won't leave, I promise." I rubbed her arm gently again with my free hand, still closing her exposed ear with my other. "I'm sorry for being an ass. You can hold onto me, though. For however long you want, Angel. However long you need."

She exhaled some kind of whimper and snuggled up with me, nestling into my grasp.

She could stay like this.

I smiled as I brushed some hair away from her eyes.

Punishments could wait until later.

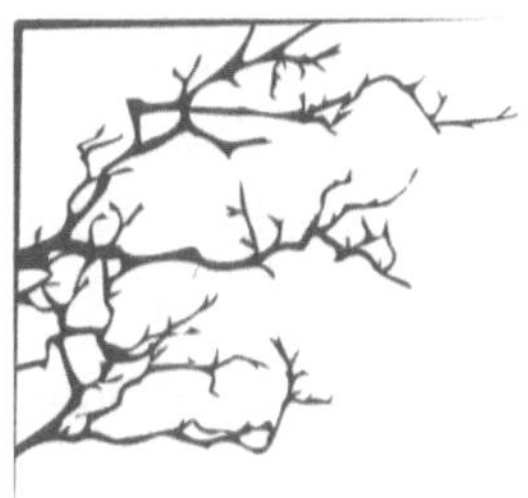

18

Riley

"Yaaaaaaaaay!" a child said, running into the room. "I found you!"

I smiled as Julie hopped up on the bed and tackled me, giggling uncontrollably.

She snuggled into my grip, me holding her tightly as I nuzzled my face into her hair.

"Oh, you're so adorable," Paris said, rubbing the top of Julie's head.

"I like Veo," Julie said, wrapping her arms around me. "He's nice to me."

"Boss," someone from the doorway said, and all three of us looked up to find Veo standing there, something dark in his expression. "I need to talk to you," he said to Paris.

Paris stood and stepped out of the room, my brows drawing together as he vanished outside.

Hold on... This didn't feel right.

Why was everything... distant?

I could feel Julie in my arms, but I... *couldn't*.

Paris's suddenly came into the room, and before I could comprehend what was happening, I was shoved down onto the bed as he lowered his mouth harshly on mine, and as Julie exhaled a squeak, he let go. Paris then pressed his forehead to mine and wrapped his arms around me, eyes looking darker than I had ever seen them.

Why did it feel like there was a sudden chill in the room? Why did it sound like I was in an abandoned mall?

So quiet and... distant.

"Everything will be okay, Sweetheart," Paris whispered to me.

Something cold twinged inside me. "What's going on...?"

"I won't leave you until this blows over," he whispered in response.

"Paris..." I argued.

His grip tightened on me. "Don't move."

"What?"

Veo got down on the bed beside us, enclosing Julie in his arms.

"No..." I said, "no... what's happening? *What's happening?*"

"You'll be okay," Paris said.

The room was getting colder.

But before I could respond, the window in the bedroom shattered inward, making me scream at the deafening noise, and I burrowed my head into my savior's shoulder.

"Paris!" I cried.

"Shhh..." he soothed.

When I looked up a final time, my eyes rounded when there were black feathers drifting down from above me.

What...?

"Paris...?" I whispered. "What's happening?"

"Death has come for us all..." he told me, wings sprouting from his back as my heart beat rapidly against my chest. "But I will not let it take you."

"*What*?" I cried.

This was unreal. What was happening?

But before I could look up, a loud screech came through the room; like a demonic cry for war.

And I screamed, closing my eyes as tears slipped from my cheeks.

I shot up from the bed, sweat sliding down my temples.

I gasped for air, looking down at my hands to find them trembling from lack of oxygen.

But a sudden pair of arms surrounded me, and I nearly screeched again before I was pulled into Paris's embrace.

"Stop screaming," he said sleepily. "It's fucking annoying."

I turned into him, letting his warmth sooth my panic sweats.

"Where's Julie?" I questioned. "Where's *Claire*?"

"*Again* with the questions?" He sighed, clearly letting his mean side go. "They're safe. It was just a nightmare. Whatever you saw isn't real, okay?"

I clutched onto his shirt, heart pounding as I continued to gasp for air.

My chest hurt... It hurt so much...

"Hey—hey," Paris said, shifting a little so I was leaning against the headboard and he could kneel in front of me, "breathe.... *Breathe.*"

I was crying because I couldn't get enough oxygen to my lungs, and my chest hurt so much—the sharpest pain stabbing my lungs—and I couldn't breathe for the life of me.

His hand suddenly roamed up to my chest, fingers spreading gently along my collarbone, but he wasn't touching any... *girl parts*...

None *yet,* anyway.

But even though I started crying, he rubbed my chest in small, up-and-down motions, whispering, "Breathe. Breathe for me. Breathe."

I started calming when soothing chills ran through me, and I gazed up at him, finding him staring softly down at me with one arm wrapped around my back, the other still rubbing my chest.

"There you go..." he murmured as I calmed. "There you go... Shhh...."

I eventually grew quiet, closing my eyes as he continued to rub, and then opened them when I was calm and he pulled away.

"What do you need from me right now?" he said.

I leaned forward and hugged him tightly, making him gasp slightly at the gesture, but I didn't let go. "Don't let me go..." I whispered. "Please, don't."

After a moment of surprise, he hugged me back, burying his face in my hair.

I was awfully clingy tonight, but he didn't seem to mind it.

He felt like he needed someone to hold, anyway.

We were both silent for a moment, and I started softly whimpering, making him glance down at me in curiosity.

"What's wrong?"

"Paris...?"

"Yeah?"

"Am I going to die?" I asked him, heart pounding again.

"No," he said way to confidently, "no, I promise you won't."

I was silent then, staring softly into space.

"You're shaking," he commented. "Are you cold?"

I nodded slightly as if embarrassed.

And he draped a blanket over me. "There, better?"

I nodded again.

"Good girl. See? Is it really *that* hard to give into me?"

I shuffled further into him, watching the darkness swarm outside.

It was still night.

"I don't want to sleep again," I told him.

"Then don't," Paris stated. "Just stay here, alright?"

And he started gently rubbing my arm, making me relax into him.

"Do you promise?" I said after a while.

"Promise what?" he said.

"Do you promise that I'm not going to die...?"

He circled his arms around me at the comment. "I swear it."

I stared off into the distance then.

"What?" Paris questioned.

"I like this..." I told him, "do you mind if we do it more often...?"

"I don't mind at all," Paris told me. "In fact, I have plans for you before the sun comes up."

I looked up. "More punishments?"

His smile made me burn. "You're smart, aren't you?"

I stared off for a moment. "I'll never learn my lesson. It's not how I work."

"Then I'll tease you until you start sobbing," he answered, "is that what you want?"

I was silent.

"I know you a little better than I did before," Paris told me, "I'm not a sadist and you're not a masochist. But one thing you love?" He smiled. "Bondage."

I looked up, shocked. "How did you know that?"

"While you were sleeping," he told me, "I shuffled through your desk. Found some pretty explicit short stories in a notebook, Hon. One about an anime character, one about you fantasizing being with someone, and one of a book character fucking his girlfriend."

"You're not supposed to raid through my stuff," I stated, annoyed.

Paris only flipped me over until my back met the bed, and I stared up at him in surprise.

"I'm going to show you," he promised, "how it feels to come. And then I'll torture you until you start learning your lesson, hear me?"

"But..." I looked slightly afraid, "I thought you said you weren't a sadist."

"I'm not," he explained. "There's a thing that I've learned about you girls. When you come through clit stimulation, it's *very* sensitive after." I winced when he started walking his fingers slowly up my stomach. "And I'd like to play a game," he told me.

"You always say that..." I told him as the throbbing returned. "Games this, games that. Is everything a game to you?"

"It is," he leaned down over me and lightly kissed my neck, "and I'm determined to win."

"What game...?" I dared to say.

He smiled wickedly up to me. "I'll give you ten minutes to come," he told me. "And if you come before, I'm holding the vibe to your clit and torturing you for the amount of time left, and if you come after, the same thing happens, but for however much time is left after the ten minute mark."

My brows drew together. "Hold on, so... *if* I come, I'll only win the game if it's right at *ten minutes*?"

He nodded. "Such a smart girl."

"But..." I argued, "I can't come...."

"For the record," he stated, "you can barely hold the brush to your clit for a *second*. And secondly, you've never come before, so you don't know your limits, do you?"

I was silent.

"*Do* you?" he repeated.

I shook my head.

"So..." he told me, "I'm setting a timer for every part of the game. The first is one minute for you to get ready to be fucked, the second is after I tie you down to the bed: you're going to be teased for three minutes, then the third is me drinking you for a full five minutes, and then for ten minutes or *more*, I'm going to simulate you, and fourth, you get the clit torture which I already explained, and lastly," he leaned down to whisper, "I'm going to fuck you."

I closed my eyes, sweat sliding down my temples at his hot breath.

"And don't worry," he promised seductively, "when I'm done with you, you're going to pass out. I don't think you'll wake until ten-ish tomorrow."

I looked up at him. "What if I don't come?"

"Oh, you will," Paris told me. "Quickly."

"I've never...."

"It doesn't matter," he said. "And stop arguing or I'll gag you."

I shut my mouth then.

"One minute," he told me, "keep these clothes on. Wait one minute before coming in my room. Not a second more, not a second less. Got it?"

I nodded.

"Good," he said, slipping off the bed, "you might want to set a timer on your phone."

And he walked off and disappeared into his bedroom.

I immediately set a timer on my phone, questioning what the hell I was doing.

I wasn't really uncomfortable with it, honestly. I had sex before, and it didn't really hurt as much as other girls said.

It was odd, though. The first time you have sex, it's like nerve-racking and you feel like God's watching you with his disapproval.

But it didn't really sound as bad when you finally did it once.

That didn't mean I wasn't nervous as fucking hell right now.

I'd never done it...

This way.

And Paris was well aware of the fact that I was a submissive.

I'd never told anyone that before.

And he just knew from the stories I wrote on my desk.

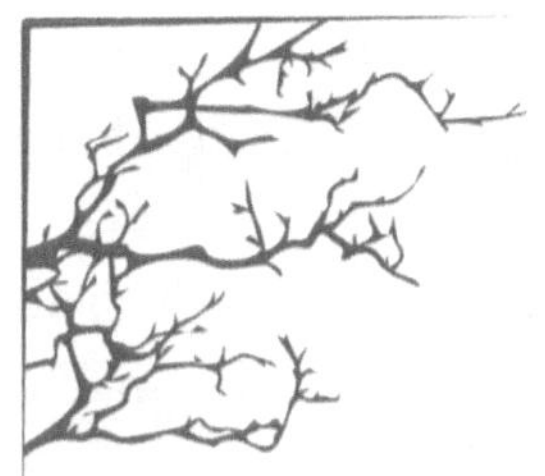

19

Riley

"**P**aris...?" I whispered as I entered the dark room, heart pounding at the menacing silence. "Paris? Are you in here?"

All my ears met were silence, and I was about to exit—to look somewhere else...

But I was shoved against the wall suddenly, crying out, though it was muffled by a hand.

"Shhh..." Paris murmured, voice low, "don't scream."

What was he doing? And why was it so dark in here?

But it only took a moment before I felt his hand slip in between my thighs, and I clenched.

Fuck... he was going to tease me in the *beginning*?

Goddamn it.

Why was I comfortable with this...?

"I'm going to take you tonight," he whispered in my ear, still covering my mouth as warmth pooled in my belly. "I'm going to take you and make you mine, will you let me?"

I nodded numbly, heart pounding.

"Good," he responded. "Now I'm going to take my hand away, and you're going to be a good girl and be quiet."

I nodded.

And he took his hand away from my mouth, me keeping my head to the wall as little whimpers escaped my lips from his delicate stroking.

He leaned forward, me closing my eyes while I waited for the kiss, but he only whispered, "Let the games begin. Do you want to see who will win this game?"

I nodded despite knowing *he* would win.

He clearly formed it that way; the role of a dominant.

"Say it aloud like a good girl."

I winced as he kept stroking ever-so-gently. "Yes, please."

And I was pulled away from the wall suddenly, and yelped when I landed on his bed, Paris climbing on top of the sheets while I stared up at him.

"Does it have to be dark?" I asked him.

"You're not allowed to see what I'm doing," he answered, pulling some ropes up from the sides of his bed, "so yes."

I stared up at the ceiling while he fumbled with the bindings.

And I gasped when he harshly caught my arm and wrapped the rope tightly around my wrist, shining his flashlight on my hand while pressing his finger to the skin, clearly making sure the bindings weren't cutting off my circulation.

I wouldn't be able to fight him with my arms tied above me.

When he was in the clear, he moved to my other arm.

"Paris...?" I whispered.

"Yes?"

"I'm nervous," I admitted.

"I can tell," he responded, wrapping the bindings around my other wrist, "you're sweating."

"Is it gross?" I asked him. "Do I smell bad?"

He stopped and looked at me, raising his brows. "You have performance anxiety, I know. But I assure you that you'll do fine."

I stared at his shirt. "Are you not going to... take off my clothes...?"

"There's a thing called a knife," he responded, making me stiffen. "No," he assured me, "I'm not going to threaten or cut you with it, just the clothes."

I watched him carefully as he started tying my right leg down. "I'm nervous," I said again.

"Then pick a safe word," he responded. "Something other than 'no' or 'stop' that will let me know when I'm going too far. What is it?"

I gazed at him while he checked my circulation on my right and moved to my left.

"*Necromancer*," I responded then.

He gazed up at me. "You'll remember it?"

I nodded. "Yes."

"Good." And he finished with that leg, gazing up at me seconds later. "What's next now?"

I stared up at him. "Uh, making me come?"

He chuckled. "No, nice try, though. What is it really?"

I sighed in annoyance. "Tied and teased."

"For how long?"

"Three minutes."

"Good girl," he responded, turning a knob on one of those old-fashioned hand-held timers. "Three minutes."

And he set the timer on the nightstand, me watching him as he climbed in bed beside me and lay down.

I winced when he trailed his fingers up my stomach, then walked them back down, and then went back up again.

No, no, not the burning again...

Fuck.

"It must be throbbing *hard* now, huh?" Paris said, moving the hand to gently stroke up to my heat and back again. "Pulsing?"

I turned my head into the bed, making him smile when I tried to pull on the bindings.

"Yeah, the ropes make it hotter, don't they? It's arousing when you're restrained."

"Stop talking..." I moaned, making him smirk.

"Why?"

"Just stop it."

"Is it making it worse?"

"Yes, now stop."

"But I like to talk," he responded. "I love it, honestly. Stroking, hearing your moans...."

"Paris..." I warned.

"How bad is it?" he said then. "How bad are you pulsing?"

I wiggled from under him, the pain getting worse. "You're such an ass...."

"I know," he responded. "You love it, though."

Why the *hell* was I okay with this?

"You have one minute left," he told me.

I groaned in annoyance, arching my back before settling it on the bed.

It was too long... Too long... Goddamn it.

"Thirty seconds," he told me.

I moaned in irritation, arching my back again.

"Keep doing that and I'll tie down your stomach, too," he threatened.

I settled back down, pulling at my bindings.

"I know," he said, smiling, "hurts, right?"

"Paris!"

But the timer went off, and I breathed out a sigh, stomach raising and falling with the leftover burn from his teasing.

He smiled then. "Part two of the game, what is it?"

"Drink..." I murmured, voice husky. "But I don't know... what that means...."

"You'll see," he responded. "How many minutes?"

"I think, five...?"

He smirked. "Good memory, Riley." And he turned the dial, making me suck in a breath while he stepped to the foot of the bed, where my panties covered my heat, and kneeled down, lightly running his thumb along the hem before taking his pocket knife out of his pocket and slicing the fabric, tearing the panties off seconds later.

"Paris...?" I whispered. "What are you doing?"

"Drinking," he responded, leaning further into me. "And I'm *parched*."

"Paris...?" I whispered. "I can't see you. What are you doing?"

He lightly blew on my clit, making me stiffen.

"No..." I said, "no, you don't mean you're going to suck me, right? It's gross down there. It always smells."

"It smells good," he responded.

"No, no, not there," I told him.

He smiled. "Especially there."

"Not there," I said again. "I don't want you getting sick, and…."

"Riley," he said.

I was silent for a moment. "Yes…?"

"Do you trust me?" he asked me.

"Yes, yes, I do."

"Then will you let me do this? And if you don't like it, what do you say?"

"Necromancer," I responded.

"Yes, good girl."

And he blew on me gently again, making me gasp at the tingles running through me.

"Jesus…" he responded, chuckling low, "you're soaked down here."

I felt a shiver run through me at his dirty words.

He didn't waste another second, he dipped his head down.

And he drank.

I let out a whimper of surprise, feeling his lips curve into a smile against my soft pink skin as he lightly suckled my clit into his mouth.

I cried out, legs pulling against the bindings as he licked me with his tongue.

When he put his full mouth on me and sucked in the pink flesh, I let out a cry of pleasure, pulling on the bindings as warmth continued to pool in my belly.

I let out a sob when he let go, lightly stroking my clit with his tongue.

"I can't…" I whimpered, "I can't…."

But I didn't say the safe word yet.

"It's okay," he responded, fingers gently stroking my entrance. "You're doing good."

"I don't like how I moan..." I whispered.

"I personally think it sounds beautiful," he responded, then lowered his mouth to me, drinking me while lightly pushing his index finger to my entrance, invading me slightly.

I let out a choked cry, hands and feet pulling at the ropes.

He let go. "You have approximately twenty seconds left. And that whole time I'm going to be harsher, okay?"

"Okay..." I said in a small voice.

He did the same thing before and lowered his mouth on me, but he sucked me in harder, making me cry out.

But it didn't stop there.

He started licking through the suction, earning a loud moan.

And his finger started pumping in and out of me, and I pulled against the bindings because it felt so good.

The timer went off, and he let go, making me gasp for air.

"I can't come!" I cried to him, feeling like a complete idiot. "I can't, I'm so sorry!"

Paris stood up then, giving me silence while turning the timer, and then raised two stick-like things in his hand.

But he only climbed onto my stomach, straddling me as he slowly slid a rocky dildo into my entrance, making me moan softly.

And then he spread open my lips, letting the sensitive button of my clit poke out from the skin.

"Paris..." I said, "Paris, I'm sorry."

"Don't be," he answered low. "I wasn't expecting you to come, anyway. I had my reasons for doing that."

He kept me open with two fingers, starting a vibrator with a click.

I heard it. "What is that...?"

"You'll see," he responded, and since my clit was too sensitive to have the brush placed on it directly, he kept it on the lowest setting and set it on the skin right above the button, making me gasp and freeze.

I breathed quickly. "Wait... don't move it. I... I like that."

He smiled. "You never tried the skin above?"

"I didn't think it would feel like this..." I answered, then arched my back slightly, letting out a high-pitched moan. "Please, don't stop...."

He glanced at the clock. "It's been five minutes. How close are you?"

"Close...?" I echoed. "What does that mean?"

He rolled his eyes. "How close are you to coming, Riley?"

I wanted to feel innocent... I really did.

He made it hard, though.

I froze for a moment. "I... I can't tell."

"You'll realize it eventually. Six minutes," he said then.

"Wait..." I said at the warmth overwhelmingly pooling in my belly, "wait... I feel something."

He gazed down at me. "There it is, your clit's spasming, I can tell you're close."

I froze. "I feel something, Paris. I feel it. Keep... keep the brush there. That exact spot, please. I want to feel it..." I started shivering, "oh... god... Jesus... fuck...."

"You're *so* fucking close now, Riley," he said as I shook from under him.

And he pressed the brush harder to the skin.

That was the edge.

I came.

Paris kept the vibe there so the whole thing passed, while I let out a soft cry, body shivering from under him.

It lasted a full minute.

A full minute of me screaming and crying and shivering from under him.

It felt so good... it felt so good. I'd never felt something this good before, and I loved it.

"There you go," he said when the orgasm eased, taking both toys away. "See? Good, isn't it?"

I stared up at him lazily, and he smiled in amusement.

"Yeah..." he said, climbing off until he could face me, then brushed my hair away from my face, "good, huh?"

I nodded, eyelids hooded with exhaustion.

"Don't worry," he whispered at my calm state. "Those other two parts of the game were threats."

"But..." I gazed down at his length that looked as if it poked uncomfortably through his pants, "you didn't come."

He sighed, gazing up at me. "Are you asking me to fuck you?"

"I can try to..." I wiggled against my bindings. "I know how to please men... *somewhat*. Can you free me so I can try to give you a release?"

Paris eyed me for a moment before accepting my offer, untying all my bindings and sitting up while I scooted away from the headboard. "You might want to lean against something," I told him.

Paris sat against the headboard as I climbed around him and gazed down at his dick that was hardened under his jeans.

And I lightly ran my hand on it, making him exhale a growl.

"Good?" I asked him.

"Don't you stop now," he muttered.

So I didn't, then deciding to lightly tease him through his pants for a couple minutes.

"Riley," he growled, "if you don't stop teasing me right now, it's going in your mouth."

Little did he know the threat wasn't far off.

I smiled then, lightly unzipping his jeans.

And his dick sprang free, making me giggle slightly as I wrapped my hand around it.

Before I could go further, he put a hand on mine, telling me to stop.

I sat up then. "Am I bad?"

"No," he responded, "no, you're *so* good. But can you take your shirt off for me?"

I stared for a moment before listening, sliding my shirt off my form as my breasts lightly bounced at the gesture.

Paris eyed me with shock for a moment, and I didn't waste my time, I lowered my mouth on him, making him grunt as he threaded his fingers through my brown locks.

"Fuck, Riley..." he growled. "Jesus. Not so fast."

I didn't listen, just gently moved up and down, tongue roaming around his skin while I sucked, my free hand stroking the base of his cock gently.

"Riley," he groaned, holding me in place. "*Fuck.*"

I kept my pace even though he started coming, drinking every bit of him while he slouched back into the bed, gasping.

I pulled away then, looking up at him, still exhausted. "Good?"

"*Very* good," he responded, lying on the bed. "Now snuggle up with me. You look tired as hell."

I listened to him, lying down beside him as he pulled me into his embrace, draping the blankets gently over us both as he stroked up and down my bare spine.

He clearly did all this to me to make tonight all about me... To show me how it was like to come, and he knew if my fear was heightened just a *little*, I would've came faster, hence the *clit torture* threat.

But I threw it back in his face, knowing he was hurting himself in the process.

He was satisfied... for *now*...

Later, I knew, that his desire to fill me would be unbearable.

But I was glad I satisfied it.

He ruffled my hair as I pretended to lay asleep huddled up with him.

"Such a good girl," he whispered to me. "Such a fucking good girl. Jesus fucking Christ I don't know how I got you."

I smiled in his chest, hoping he wouldn't see it.

I liked being praised, it made me feel good.

"Riley," he said to me, though I still pretended to sleep, "I'm going to ruin you."

I didn't know why, but I liked the sound of that.

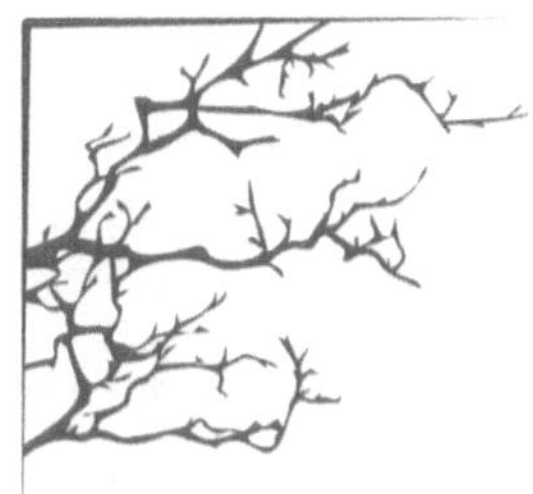

20

Paris

"Riley," I whispered, shaking her as she slept on my lap. "Riiiiiiley."

She groaned in annoyance, shifting further into me.

So cute.

"Riley," I pressed. "Wake up. Come on."

"Leave me alone," she grumbled, turning her face into my neck. "I was having a nice dream."

I chuckled at her slurred voice. "Come on," I coaxed. "Wake up."

She opened one eye a slit and gazed up at me, her beautiful silver gaze glowing with exhaustion. "What?" she asked tiredly.

"I can't sleep," I told her, brushing some brown hair away from her cheeks.

Her lashes lowered in annoyance. "So you wake *me* up?"

I smiled innocently down at her despite my dominant side screaming to put her in her place.

She needed to stop using that fucking tone with me or I was going to throw her down on the bed and thrust my dick inside her until she started screaming.

Part of me knew she wanted that, though, but I was going to force myself to be patient and give her time to build up that desire that was in her eyes.

She *wanted* me to fill her.

She *wanted* me to ruin her, and I wanted to see how long it took before she would start pleading for me to take her.

But my dick was throbbing in my jeans, and I needed a release *desperately*. All the teasing and the licking I did to her last night—and the fact that I made her come for the first time—gave me the most hot and sexy dream ever, and now I needed her to give me a release.

I was so glad I didn't come in my sleep.

"Do it again," I told her.

She gazed up at me, eyes glistening with confusion. "Do *what* again?"

"Fix that tone," I said, dick throbbing harder as her eyes slightly shaded over with a fire, "and what you did last night."

She set her cheek on my chest. "Paris, *really*? You woke me up for *this*?"

"I'm desperate," I told her.

"Clearly," she responded.

I was, though. The way she made me feel last night was unexplainable. I'd never felt that way before when a girl went down on me.

She was special.

"Do it," I told her.

She gazed up at me, and I could tell by the look in her eyes that she was testing me. "Is it *that* hard to say *please*?"

My dick thrashed harder, and *painfully* pushed against my jeans.

I was going to put her in her place.

"Do you want to be punished again?" I asked her.

She rolled her eyes, still testing me. "No."

"Then maybe learn your lesson," I said to her, "and fix your fucking tone or I'll will force you to do things you've never thought of doing."

She gazed up at me with the anger in my voice, and I looked down at her feet that were barely poking out of the sheets.

Her toes curled.

Oh. She liked being scared, didn't she?

I looked back up to her.

"Alright..." she said, sitting up now, "what do you want?"

I smirked when she gave in.

"Do what you did last night," I told her. "But again."

She sighed, getting down on her elbows in between my legs.

Jesus, I could already feel her breath through the fabric.

It hurt.

"I can't believe you woke me up for this," she told me.

"I *will* spank you," I said to her.

Her toes curled again at the threat.

I smiled, leaning back against the headboard. "Do you like being scared?" I asked her.

She looked up at me, and I nearly pushed her back down so I could feel her breath again.

But I refrained, and it was fucking hard.

"What?" she asked me.

"You," I said, "do you like being scared?"

She looked slightly taken aback, and shook her head. "No."

"So if I yelled at you right now," I asked her, "and threatened to do something horrible, would you be wet?"

Her irises beat in her eyes, and she hesitated. "N—no."

I cocked an eyebrow. "Are you lying?"

"N—no."

"You hesitated," I answered, moving my hand silently to the back of her thigh, but made sure she didn't feel it.

She looked back down at my dick and shook her head, clearly not feeling my hand move further down. "I'm going to do it again," she told me, "and you let me sleep, okay? And if you threaten me, no, I do not get wet. I'm not aroused by fear. I know myself better than you know me."

And she started teasing me again through my jeans, making me throw my head back, but I still didn't touch her skin.

She palmed me, for *minutes*, and then I could tell she was exploring me with curiosity.

"Riley," I warned, "stop fucking teasing me."

"No," she answered.

"No?" I echoed, hand moving closer to her ass. "Did you just tell me no?"

"Yes," she answered, "you tease me, I tease you."

"Riley," I warned, stomach rising and falling with the pain flowing through me.

"Yes?" she answered.

"Stop testing me," I said.

"Stop being an ass," she responded.

"*What* did you just call me?" I questioned.

"You heard me," she said.

"If you don't stop talking down on me," I told her, "I'm going to throw you down on the bed and thrust something huge in your pussy."

She winced at my words, and shook her head. "No, I don't think your dick's that big, Paris. I've had bigger."

Oh. Oh, no. She was asking for it.

"What about a lampshade?" I asked her, making her stiffen. "A boot? A shoe? Oh, what about a cup? Or a ten inch dildo all the way up in that pussy of yours?"

"You're scaring me," she said.

"Am I?" I responded.

She never said her safe word.

But I slipped two of my fingers into her pulsing heat, making her cry out and nearly collapse onto me when I thrusted slowly in and out.

"Why are you so wet then?" I asked her. "Surely, if you weren't aroused, you'd be *very* dry."

"Paris..." she tried to reason, unable to get up with I thrusted, "it's too much."

"Too much for your safe word?" I said.

She was silent.

"That's what I thought," I responded. "You're a liar, aren't you?"

"I'm sensitive," she reminded me.

I inserted a third finger, making her clench around me. "I know."

"Paris..." she tried to reason.

"I'm going to do this until you give me a release," I told her. "Take my dick out of my pants right now, and give me a nice and slow blow, and when I come, I'll take my fingers out of you, deal?"

She nodded, hands shaking from the good thrusts as she unzipped my jeans and took my dick out, making me thrust my fingers a little faster when her hand brushed the head.

She cried out, nearly collapsing back onto me.

"You know what to do," I told her.

Her hands were slick with sweat as she lightly stroked the base with her hand, and lowered her mouth on me.

Oh, god... it was so warm and wet.

And her tongue started roaming around me, and the strokes from her hand weren't really helping my arousal either.

I smiled evilly when she started going a little faster, stroking and licking and sucking.

And I pounded my fingers in and out of her, making her cry out on my cock at the pleasure I was giving her.

"Continue," I told her, keeping the pace.

She started licking and sucking harder.

"Yeah, I know you like this," I said, "you're getting wetter and wetter."

She started sucking faster, lowering her mouth on me and going back up, and then she tried something new, she took her mouth off me and lightly kissed the side of my dick, dragging her tongue up and down the length before lowering herself back onto me.

She was enjoying this, naughty girl.

"Keep going," I told her, feeling the release build up. "Faster."

She sucked harder, making me groan, and then she used her tongue and lowered and rose her mouth twice a second, stroking the base with her hand.

And I came, thrusting my fingers harder in and out of her while my other hand twined within her brown locks, keeping her mouth in place while I instructed breathlessly, "Drink it."

She listened, surprisingly, drinking me while shivering as my fingers pumped in and out of her at the other end.

And when I finished, she let go with a little *pop*! and the beautiful girl set her forehead on my thigh as I took my fingers out of her, deciding that I didn't want to give her a release just yet.

"There..." she said, panting, "better?"

I only threw her down on the other side of the bed, making her squeal when I kissed the corners of her mouth and then trailed them down her neck.

I earned a gorgeous moan.

I hated how she demeaned herself, telling me she didn't like how she moaned, it was ridiculous.

Her sounds were beautiful.

"Moan louder," I told her.

She shook her head.

"That's an order," I responded. "Moan louder or I'll make you."

Her eyes glittered when she looked up at me. "Paris...."

"Don't argue with me," I said. "Moan louder, *now*."

She shook her head.

Oh, I'll break her. I'll break her right *now*.

I thrusted two of my fingers inside her, earning a gasp.

That wasn't what I wanted, though.

I pumped them in and out.

Just a couple gasps.

Oh, this fucking girl.

So then I took it to another level, I thrusted in and out while using my thumb to harshly rub her clit, and I lowered my mouth to her bare nipples.

She let out a soft cry, then another louder one, and then she let out a cry mixed with a moan.

I wanted a full moan, though. None of this *cry* bullshit.

So I pumped faster, rubbed harsher, and sucked harder.

And then came the moan; a loud one, too.

I wanted to hear it again.

So I kept the pace.

She twined her fingers in my hair, and let out strangled moans, writhing from under me, as her fingers tangled in my blonde locks.

There it is, good girl.

"Paris..." she tried to argue, "Pari—Oh, God...."

I felt her start shaking.

I let go of her nipple but kept the pace on both spots on her pussy. "Are you already coming?" I asked her.

She turned her head away, and nodded.

"I'll let you come," I told her, "only if you keep moaning. And when you come, I want you to let out the scream, okay? Don't hold it in like you did last night."

She had no room to argue because I lowered my mouth back on her sensitive bud and let go of her clit, using my free hand to grab the clit brush I used last night that was on the bed, and I turned it on, thrusting my fingers back inside her and lowered the brush on her little clit.

That was the edge.

She cried out, writhing from under me while she came, and I could feel her shivering and screaming rattle through my body.

I smiled and kept the pace, thrusting and vibing her and licking her buds.

Until the orgasm settled, and I let go of her bud, taking everything away until I saw her face.

Her face that was covered in sweat and her flushed cheeks.

And a clear sign of exhaustion.

"Wow," I said then, "you came *hard*, huh?"

She looked up at me, her eyes glistening with unshed tears.

"You did good," I told her, knowing what she needed to hear, and set the clit brush on the nightstand, "sit up, okay? Sit on my lap, Hon."

When I got off her, I rested my back on the headboard as she pushed her tired body up and climbed over to me, settling on my lap seconds later.

She rested her head on my shoulder, and I couldn't help but run my fingers through her brown locks, holding her tired body up as I soothed her.

"You did good," I told her gently, "so very, very, *very* good. My good girl."

She rested her cheek on my shoulder, and I smiled.

Yeah, she came hard.

"Go back to sleep," I responded then, feeling her ease up into me. "Back to sleep, my good girl. I'll let you sleep now, Honey."

Seconds later, she passed out.

Ah, I was going to ruin her.

I already started.

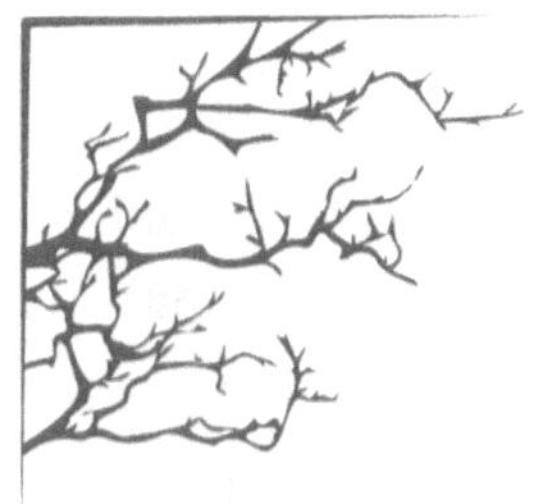

21

Paris

THREE MONTHS AGO

"Where is she?" I questioned, anger rising in my throat as the man tied to the chair sat in front of me.

His hair was matted with sweat, and there were black bruises ringing around both his eyes and his cheekbones.

He glared at me as he responded in his Russian accent, "I don't know what you're talking about, boy."

I struck him across the face and caught the back of his head, pulling his hair as I forced him to face me.

There was blood tricking down the corner of his mouth.

"THE FUCKING GIRL!" I growled. "WHERE THE FUCK IS SHE?"

He smiled menacingly up at me, the blood on his teeth only adding to the horror in his expression. "'Fucking girl?'" he echoed. "That would be a horrible name for a child, no?"

I struck him across the face again, earning a grunt, so I did it once, then twice.

Until his whole face was purple.

"Where is she?" I repeated, pulling his hair so he looked at me. "Where is the girl, you *bitch*?"

He looked back up at me, and spat blood at my feet.

I only pulled him up higher, making him grunt as I leveled my face with his. "I could give you surgery with no anesthetic," I told him, "have my men take your organs out *one by one* until there is nothing left inside you. And you'd die slowly and slowly with no liver—no heart—would you like that?"

"You are a sick boy," he said.

"Do you think I was joking?" I asked him, and I stood, waving one of my men over.

"Yes, sir?" he said.

"Get Doctor Gin over," I told him. "Now."

He went on his earpiece and called someone on it.

"You're bluffing," the restrained man said.

I turned to look at him. "I never bluff." And I nodded to my men.

One of them walked over and untied his bindings while the other two caught his wrists and ankles, pulling him up kicking and screaming.

He wasn't strong enough to fight them with all the blows to the head I gave him, I wouldn't be surprised if he had permanent brain damage.

They threw him down onto a metal cart in the middle of the room; a bed we stole form a hospital room a ways away, and they restrained him with those cuffs as he writhed against the bindings.

I loved the sight of him suffering.

I walked over to him. "Do you really think I was bluffing?"

Almost a second later, a man walked in the room, rolling a cart of medical supplies in with him.

He stopped next to me, and I nodded to the man tied into the chair. "Take his liver out first."

The Russian man looked up to me, startled as he pulled against the bindings.

Was I bluffing? No. Was he going to give me answers? Yes. I wouldn't let him die, I needed answers from him.

When the doctor pulled up a rusty scalpel...

That's when it clicked.

"Okay! Okay!" he said, making me stop as I turned to him. "She's lives in California!"

I nodded to the doctor, making him stop. "Where in California?"

"23465 West thirty-third street!" the man said. "In Sanediego!"

I looked to one of my men, and he gazed back up at me after looking at his phone. "He's right, Violet's there."

"Why did she lose contact with me?" I asked my victim.

"I don't know," he said, "please...."

With a quick nod from me, the doctor sliced the skin of his chest open, making him scream.

"Answer," I told him, "or he's going to slowly slice your heart open."

"We tapped her phone line..." he sobbed, chest rising and falling faster, "so she'd lose contact. We killed her husband so we could leave the girl vulnerable without her father. We hired an assassin to kill her in the most horrible way possible."

"*What* way?" I said.

He looked up at me. "Emotional torment. Kill everyone close to her first and make her the final target."

My eyes darkened. "Did my father order you to do this?"

He hesitated, and the doctor pierced the scalpel into the already open wound, making him scream. "No! No! It is a copycat who runs our company... A billionaire...."

"Who?" I said.

"Mister Raymond," he responded. "That's what we call him."

I looked at his panicked gaze for signs of him lying.

He wasn't.

"Kill him," I said, starting out of the room.

He started writhing in the bed as the doctor started a rusty saw.

"No! NO!" he said. "Please! Please! No! I beg you!"

I turned to him, eyes darkening. "No one hurts Riley. I won't allow it."

And I kept walking, hearing the saw cut against his ribs when I closed the door behind me, and his pained screaming.

P RESENT
     I brushed my fingers through Riley's hair as she slept in my chest, the gesture keeping her asleep as I stared down at her relaxed expression.

She was completely naked and huddled up with me, and I decided an hour ago to take off my shirt so I could give her some of my body heat along with the blankets over us.

I wanted her comfortable and warm.

She turned further into me and murmured something soft in her sleep, and she buried her head in my chest.

I smiled at how comfortable she was with me.

She kept murmuring sounds and her hands folded in between us as she lightly snuggled closer.

"Shhh..." I cooed, holding her tighter, "you're safe now. It's alright, Sweetheart. It's alright."

She seemed to relax at my voice.

"I got you..." I told her, "and I will kill anyone who attempts to hurt you."

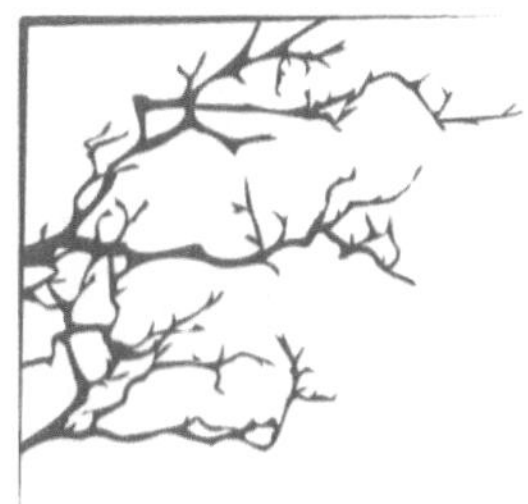

22

Riley

I woke slowly to a light feeling, and to little bumps going through me as if I were wading into the ocean.

My eyes opened then, and I looked up to see Paris above me, and he was walking to someplace in his *"loft"* while holding me up with him.

Why didn't he wake me up first?

"Paris...?" I whispered, making him look down at me. "Where are you taking me?"

He smiled at the sight of my confused stare and looked back up. "To the porch," he answered, "I thought you might like it there."

I looked down at myself, finding my shoulders and ankles bare despite the blanket wrapped around me, and I gazed up at him. "But I'm still naked."

He raised his brows then. "Is that a problem?"

"I don't want your neighbors seeing my tits, Paris."

He tipped his head back and laughed, fucking *laughed*, and he looked back down at me softly. "Ah, you're so cute."

"How is that *cute*?"

"How you're self-conscious about your body."

My brows drew together. "I never said that."

He opened a door to his porch. "Don't worry, I'm not taking the blanket off, but in exchange, you're not allowed out of my arms, got it?"

I narrowed my eyes, suspecting a catch but nodded.

"No matter what I do to you," he continued, "you're not out of my arms, okay?"

Okay, now I suspected a catch.

He walked outside, holding me as he stared off into the distance, then deciding to sit on the bench as he rocked forward and back, still holding me.

I looked up at him, watching his eyes for any malice or playfulness.

It was blank.

Until something sparked in it, and he smiled.

Oh, fuck.

Before I could comprehend what he was planning, he slipped two of his fingers inside me, making me yelp.

He smiled down at me when he started pumping them in and out. "Quiet if you don't want everyone to hear you, got it?"

I nodded, letting out soft whimpers.

He pumped faster. "I said, *quiet.*"

I rested my head on his shoulder, letting out fast, silent breaths as he kept torturing me.

"Oh, hey, Paris!" clearly one of his neighbors said, leaning over a banister to see us, and Paris smiled, still torturing me under the blanket as I tried not to shiver against him.

"Hey, miss Daniels!" he responded. "How's your little kitty?"

How could he speak while *doing this to me*?

"She's good," the neighbor said. "Who's this lovely lady?"

Paris looked down at me, eyes glowing with menace. "Tell her your name."

I shook my head, knowing if I opened my mouth, I would let out something less innocent then a moan.

He started pounding his fingers harder, making me suck in a breath. "Don't be shy," he said, "tell her your name."

"R—Riley," I said, keeping my eyes on his chest.

"Aw," the neighbor said, "you got yourself a shy girl, don't you, Paris?"

Oh, I fucking hated him.

"Very shy," he responded as I broke a sweat, "right, Riley?"

I nodded, trying to hold back a moan.

"Yeah," he said, looking up at his neighbor, "she's a shy one. It's very cute, really. She gets all worked up around me."

Shut up, please, for the love of god, stop.

I heard him chuckle as he continued the torturous act.

"Well," the neighbor said, "I gotta go feed my little kitties." And she walked off.

Paris looked down at me. "Wow, you're fucking *wet*. Did you like that?"

I shook my head, trying not to give in to him.

"No?" he said. "When I first entered you, you were slightly wet, but when she started talking to me and I was doing this to you, it started coming like a waterfall, no?"

"Paris..." I murmured.

"Be honest, you like it when you're scared, don't you? It makes you hot."

I shook my head.

He pumped harder, making me suck in a breath. "Don't lie to me."

"Paris..." I whispered.

"Tell the truth," he said, "and I'll stop."

But I didn't *want* him to stop.

"Paris..." I moaned.

"Tell the fucking truth, Riley," he said.

"No," I responded.

"No?"

"No."

He pumped faster, making me suck in a breath. "No?"

"No."

He stopped then, me gasping as he took his fingers out. "Liar, you were only saying that so I wouldn't stop, didn't you?"

I decided to test something out, acting all passive and shy as I responded, "Yes, sir."

He looked down at me. "Did you just call me *sir*?"

"Yes, sir."

I don't know why, but I liked calling him that.

He smiled. "You know, since you let that come out of your mouth, you can't stop calling me that, do you hear me?"

"Yes, sir."

"Good girl," he responded, "let's go back inside."

"Don't stop," I told him. "Please continue."

He raised his brows.

"Sir..." I added. "Please."

"Mmm..." he thought for a moment, "no." And he picked me up, carrying me inside.

I started whining and wiggling in his arms, hoping to get him to let go so I could run to the bathroom and satisfy the burning myself.

He held me tighter to him when he stopped in the dining room. "Stop moving."

"I want down!" I whined like a child. "I want *down*!"

He looked down at me with a bored gaze. "Keep acting like a child and I'll *treat* you like a child."

I stuck my lip out in a pout.

"You are *asking* to get spanked."

"Why are you so mean to me...?" I asked him. "I've done *nothing* to you."

He looked down at me and took a deep breath while closing his eyes, then he opened them again, the blue now as dark as the ocean. "You're testing my patience."

I tipped my head to the side, and he continued the cold stare. "I like testing you," I stated. "It's fun."

"Riley."

"*Sir*," I added with a touch of sarcasm.

He dropped me then, and I stared up at him as I landed on my feet.

He eyed me almost angrily. "Knees."

"Huh?" I said.

He pointed to the floor. "Get on your knees."

I only stared up at him.

"*Get on your knees*," he repeated.

"Make me," I said.

The anger rising in his eyes made a cold euphoria wash through me.

Ooh, scary.

He caught the front of my throat, not choking me, but brought my face to his.

I felt another cold shiver run through me.

I could smell his minty breath.

"You are going to listen," he told me, eyes piercing into mine. "Or I will do something drastic."

"How drastic?" I whispered.

He shoved me down then, making me yelp when I landed on my knees and the blanket fell off me, and I looked up at him, trying to grab for the blanket that shielded my body from the window, but he kicked it out of the way.

I tried crawling over to it, but he caught the back of my head and brought me back.

"I want the blanket," I told him, trying to get out of his hold but he only held my head tighter. "Give me the blanket."

"Why should I?" he countered. "You're being awfully rude to me, you know."

"Paris," I said, "everyone can see me."

"I don't care," he responded. "Let them. At least it would put you in your place."

I felt another cold shiver run through me at his words.

"Who are you?" he said.

"I—I'm Riley Princes."

"Who do you belong to?" he questioned.

"Me."

His eyes narrowed, and he shoved my head back, making me yelp when he growled in my ear, "*Who* do you belong to?"

"Me," I said.

"Riley," he warned. "If you continue testing me, I'm going to fucking kill you."

"Then do it," I said. "I dare you."

His eyes darkened. "Riley, you do *not* want to do this."

I smiled, loving the anger rising in his eyes.

"One more time," he said, leaning down so our faces were mere inches from the other, "who do you belong to?"

I was asking to get murdered by my next words, "I only belong to Ryan."

Something inside him snapped, and he glared at me.

Uh—oh, he's *maaaaad*.

He shoved me until my stomach met the cold floor. "That's *it*," he hissed in my ear, "you need to be taught a lesson, and clearly what I've been doing hasn't been enough. Now stay here while I get my tools, got it?"

I nodded, stomach freezing at the cold tile.

"Good," he responded, "if you get up, I won't be too happy, understand? Stay here."

And he got up and left me.

I stayed in this uncomfortable position for a couple minutes despite my urge to test him more.

And that's when I heard his footsteps tapping toward me, although I couldn't see him with my face turned toward the wall away from him.

I felt him kneel down beside me, and a cold shiver ran through my naked body as he ran his hand down my back.

"Who do you belong to?" he repeated. "Answer wisely."

I opened my eyes, smiling as I repeated, "I belong to Ryan."

Though, this time, it didn't seem to faze him.

Awww...

"Why do you belong to Ryan?" he responded, gently running his hand along my thigh.

Oh... that felt kind of good.

But the burning was coming back.

He brought his hand down on my ass when I didn't respond, making me squeak.

"Answer the question," Paris said.

"Be... because."

"Because why?" he said.

"Be... because."

I heard a click and a firm vibration.

Oh, shit.

Paris's hand lay on my back, clearly to keep me from getting up. "Who do you belong to?"

"Where are you putting that?" I questioned him.

"Answer the question," he responded.

"No," I said.

He let out a *tsk* noise.

And the large vibrator pressed directly onto my clit, making me buck my hips and cry out.

He only climbed slightly on top of me and pressed me down with his weight, making me squirm as he pressed the toy harder to it.

I squirmed from under him, screaming and crying and pleading for him to let the weight of the vibrator off just a bit.

He never responded, instead just massaged it gently on my sensitive skin, and I kicked out my legs to try to close them, but he held one open and shoved it harder to me.

"Paris!" I cried. "Paris! It's too much!"

"Too much for your safe word?" he said.

I never answered.

"Hmm…" he responded, massaging it a little faster as I screamed and writhed from under him, "sensitive, huh?"

I nodded, reaching out for something to hold but there was nothing to clutch on, so I just grabbed the floors as he kept torturing me.

I felt his weight get harder on my lower back, though I couldn't see what he was doing.

It was too much. I was too sensitive right there, and he found a way to teach me to listen.

"I can spread you open," he told me, still massaging the vibrator on my aching core. "And put this directly on it, Riley. Would you like that?"

I shook my head.

"No?" he responded. "No, you wouldn't? Is it really that sensitive here?"

I nodded, sobbing into the ground.

Paris looked down to my clit. "You have no idea what clit torture is, do you?"

I shook my head.

"No? After you come, Riley. It's ten times more sensitive than this. Can you imagine that?"

I shook my head.

"You *can't* imagine it or you don't *want* to?" he responded.

"It's too much!" I cried. "Please, Paris!"

"Then answer my question *honestly*," he told me. "Who—do—you—belong—to?"

"Me..." I responded, shaking from under him, "I belong to me and you, sir. Me and you."

He took the vibe off and stood, gazing down at me as I shook and trembled from under him, tears staining my cheeks and the floor. "That's right," he said. "Let's get that implanted in your head."

Before I could respond, he caught my arm and carried me back to his bedroom, me shaking as he opened his closet door to reveal a secret room.

Oh, Jesus, have mercy on me.

It was a dark room with chains on the walls and there also were swings painted with a not-so-innocent rubber, and there was also a wall with vibrators and ropes and ties.

Oh, wow.

Paris carried me over to a bed in the corner and lay me down on it, and I stared up at him as he pulled some ropes, the vibrator, and a hang-thing with a long pole and some wires.

"Hold still for me," he responded.

For him? Okay, I'd do that.

He hung the pole on the ceiling and it dangled above my waist, and he caught my arms and tied my wrists together faster than I could handle.

Seconds later, he pulled my wrists above my head and used a wire to tie them to the railed bed frame.

I watched as he got more ropes and picked up my feet, tying my ankles to the pole that he hung on the ceiling, and he then took a blindfold he grabbed from the nightstand next to me, and he pulled it over my eyes and then tied it behind my head.

Oh, god... I couldn't see what he was doing.

I heard him ruffle with more ropes, and I heard more metal squealing.

Until I felt him lower something onto my clit, and he then used some kind of soft rope to tie the cold thing to my waist to keep it there.

Oh, fuck. I couldn't move away from it—whatever it was.

Seconds later, I felt him open the lips of my pussy until my clit was directly pressed onto the cold thing.

I tried moving to get out of it, but it didn't really work.

It felt good, though—rubbing against it.

"Trust me, Honey," Paris said, pulling at my nipples as I exhaled a groan, continuing to ride the cold object. "You don't need to do that," he told me.

"Why?" I whispered to him, trying to face the sound of his voice, but I was completely blind.

"You'll see," he responded, and I heard him lean away from me.

And something clicked.

All the sudden, vibrations rattled through my most sensitive spot.

And I started screaming, writhing against the ropes as the vibrator stayed in place.

I couldn't move out of it! Fuck!

"I know, I know," Paris cooed. "It sucks when you don't listen to me, doesn't it?"

I started crying, bucking my hips and pulling my ankles and my wrists, but the bindings wouldn't budge.

"Paris!" I cried. "Paris! Paris!"

"Yes, Hon?" he said cooly.

"It's too much!" I said, trying to move out of it, but only ended up rubbing my clit harder to the vibrator.

"Is it?" he responded. "I'll give you two more seconds, then it's going on high for another ten minutes—even when you come, it's not going to be taken away."

I tipped my head back, the fact that I couldn't see adding to the pleasure building up in me.

"Alright," he said, picking up something from the night-stand next to me and turned a device.

A timer.

"Ten minutes," he said, walking over to me and flipped a switch.

I screamed.

I screamed, and I cried, and I screeched, trying to get out, but it never worked.

And he only ran his hands all over me as I bucked my hips and pulled on my wrist and ankles.

I was stuck.

I was stuck in this thing for another nine minutes.

But as the next couple seconds passed by, I felt something pool in my belly.

No, no, no. Not now. No.

Paris plucked at my nipples as my back arched, and he chuckled as he looked down to me. "Already?"

"Turn it down!" I said to him. "Turn it down! I'm gonna—I'm gonna—!"

"Why should I turn it down?" he said to me. "You never listen to me, so why should I listen to you?"

I writhed on the bindings. "Pariiiiis!"

"Sir," he responded, "that's what you call me now, got it?"

"Yes, sir," I said shakily. "Please, sir... take it off."

"No," Paris said as the pooling got worse. "Because if I did, then you'd find a way around your punishments, and I can't have that, can I?" His hand ran down my stomach as I clenched and unclenched my abs. "In three," he said, "two, one."

I came.

I came hard.

I screamed on the top of my lungs and I swear I squirted across the room.

And when it settled.

That's when it came.

The torture he was talking about.

I writhed against the bindings, kicking and screaming, but he didn't seem to care.

Oh, Jesus... It felt like someone was putting an entire massage chair on my pussy.

I heard Paris's chuckles as he continued to rub his hand along my stomach.

"You have five minutes," he told me, "endure this for a little longer, and I'll reward you."

I started sobbing through the blindfold even though this felt good.

It didn't feel *good*... it felt *too* good. I wasn't supposed to like this.

But I did.

I liked being punished, and I knew no matter what he did to me, there would be one thing I would most probably avoid.

Orgasm denial.

Hopefully he didn't know that existed, though.

I looked it up last night, and with how the arousal burned me, I didn't want to see how much denial burned.

I had to listen to him, and he wasn't being an abusive ass.

I liked being dominated.

It felt good.

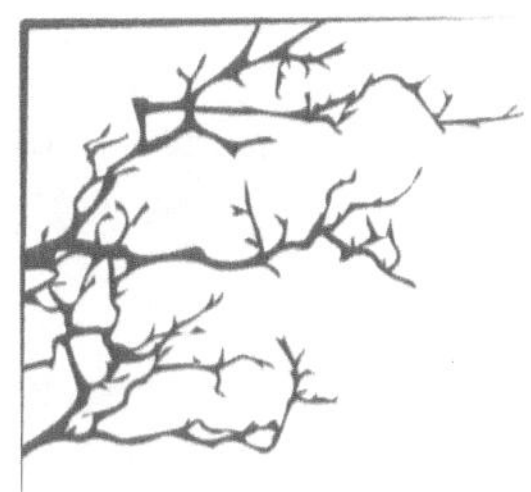

23

Paris

When I walked out of my bedroom to check on Riley, I found her sound asleep on the couch in my living room, her chest rising and falling slowly to her delicate breaths.

I stepped over to her and gently kneeled down by her side, smiling at how peaceful she looked.

So cute.

I felt bad for ruining it, but she needed me to care for her so she wouldn't be scared of me.

Aftercare was an urgent need in our types of relationships.

I gently shook her. "Riley..." I whispered gently, making her breath suck in as she woke. "Come on, get up."

Her eyes opened a slit, and she looked hazily up to me. "Is something wrong?"

"The shower's ready," I told her as she turned over and yawned. "Come on," I held out my hand, "let me treat you nice for the rest of the night."

She gazed up at me. "Why? Did I do something?"

I shook my head and gazed softly up at her. "Let me give you a nice shower. Come on."

She hesitantly took my arm as she stood.

Right as she put her full weight on her feet, her knees buckled.

I caught her before she hit the floor.

"It's okay," I whispered, draping one of my soft robes over her shoulders. "I got you. Come on."

I wrapped an arm around her waist to keep her from falling as she lazily stepped to my bedroom with me, stumbling every second.

We eventually met my white, marble bathroom, and I looked down at her to see if she was alright.

"Sit on the toilet," I told her as I guided her down. "There you go." And I peeled off my shirt, jeans, and underwear and stepped up to her while lightly pulling the robe off her shoulders.

She shivered at the cold and nearly fell to the side, but I caught her again, helping her stand as I guided her into the shower.

With all the writhing and fighting and screaming she did, I would suspect her muscles were hurting—possibly her throat, too.

I also thought that a nice warm shower where I could hold her and wash her off would be a good first experience of aftercare for her.

When we made it under the hot water, she almost collapsed again at how good it felt, but I—once again—caught her.

I lowered us both on the ground and ran my fingers through her hair, letting the warm water pad on her skin and make her more comfortable.

After a couple minutes of soothing her, I grabbed one of my loofas and poured some of my body wash on it, lathering it under the water while Riley rested her head on my shoulder.

And I gently ran the loofa all over her body, lathering her up in my soap as she eased more into me at the gesture.

Yes, I'd done this before. Yes, it was with some strippers.

No, it did not feel anything like this; this emotional attraction I felt toward Riley was indescribable. The way she fascinated me was enraging.

I wanted her body, yes, but I also wanted her to trust me, I wanted her to know that I would take care of her—protect her.

She'd never done anything like this? Yeah, I get it. It's normal for people like her to not be used to their desires. She was pretty young, too. I was, also. But I was pretty rebellious as a kid.

I honestly felt myself getting angry at the thought that Ryan took her first. That I was her second... It bothered the hell out of me.

I wanted to be her first. *I* wanted her to be mine when she was first learning her desires. She probably never had an orgasm with Ryan because she wasn't into it and never really understood what she wanted.

So she wrote it in her notebooks—the ones I read.

I just knew from the beginning.

I just knew she wasn't the innocent girl she put on display.

I smiled down at her while she lazily stared off into space, and raised my hand that was covered in soap suds, poking her nose. "Boop."

Her nose was covered in soap suds then, and she stared off into space before inhaling.

"*Achoo*!" she squeaked, lurching forward while I chuckled and caught her.

The soap suds made her sneeze.

So cute.

She rested back into me. "Ow."

"Sneezing hurt?" I said, brushing some hair out of her face.

She nodded. "Everything hurts. I think I'm gon' die." And she went limp in my arms, making me smile when she stuck her tongue out. "Blegh."

She was so fucking cute when she was tired.

I kept rubbing her arms with the loofa as she rested back into me, absently stroking my chest as I continued to clean her.

"I like your scars..." she whispered, running a finger along one of them. "They're pretty...."

I smiled down at her, heart warming.

No one had ever told me that... No hookers, no strippers.

It also felt good coming out of her mouth.

She was special.

I washed her body off with the warm water.

And she was fucking adorable.

"Ready for bed?" I asked her.

She looked up at me, sad. "But I want to stay awake with you."

I ran my fingers through her hair. "Honey, you're half-dead right now. Let yourself sleep."

She sighed and nodded, staring back down at my chest as I turned off the water.

Wow... she looked so depressed.

"Ready?" I said suddenly, making her look up to me. "Three—two—one, *Whee*!"

I lifted her up in my arms, making her giggle when I set her back down on her feet, draping a towel over her shoulders as I kept an arm around her, taking her to bed.

I didn't care about clothing either of us, just let her dry off before getting in the sheets with me.

I let go for a moment to pull the sheets back.

But I heard a *thud*!

I turned around, panic settling over me when I found Riley on the ground stomach-first.

Oh, shit. Did she pass out?

I ran over to her and kneeled by her side, moving some of her hair away to see her face.

Her eyes were open, and I exhaled a sigh, staring up at her seconds later. "You okay, Sweetheart?"

"I hurt..." she murmured.

"Where?" I said.

"Everywhere."

"Your muscles?" I whispered to her.

She nodded.

"Here," I said, "let me help you to bed and I can make us some tea, and then I'll give you some pain meds, okay?"

She nodded again.

I lifted her up by her arm and held her up as she tried to stand, and despite her already standing, I decided to scoop her up and lay her in bed.

She let out a squeak but didn't fight.

I started the kettle machine in my room, the heater rattling it as I grabbed two mugs from my nightstand and put some powdered tea in them, pouring some hot water in her mug before mine, stirring after.

When both out teas were ready, I grabbed some med bottles from my nightstand before pulling out a muscle relaxant that I got sent in from Canada.

I sat beside her in bed then, handed her the tea, and held my hands out in case I needed to catch it.

I was worried that she wasn't able to hold anything.

But she held it, and I then shook out two pills and placed them in her hand. "Take them both," I instructed gently.

She did, plopping them on her tongue and took two chugs of the tea before swallowing it down.

I brushed my fingers through her hair as she held the cup to her lips, continuing to drink the tea.

"Tastes good, huh?" I said.

She nodded. "I like it."

We were both silent for a moment.

"Paris...?" she whispered silently, but I couldn't tell by her tone if she was exhausted or depressed.

"Yeah?" I asked.

"I..." she hesitated, "I'm scared."

I turned to her, finding her staring down at the sheets while rubbing her fingers together on them.

At first I thought she was scared because I went too far, but I found myself wondering why she didn't use her safe word then.

I didn't gag her mouth shut for a reason.

"Why are you scared?" I asked instead.

She wrapped her arms around herself, the top half of her body exposed, but she didn't seem to care.

That also gave off something *other* than me going too far.

"I'm scared..." she repeated, "that you're going to go."

I eyed her for a moment. "I'm not one-night-standing you, Riley."

"No..." she responded, tears blooming in her eyes, "I... I'm scared you're going to... to...."

My lashes lowered when I realized what she was talking about.

She was worried that I was going to die.

I took her mug and placed it on the nightstand, pulling her in for a hug when she started crying softly, covering her face in her hands.

"It's alright," I promised her. "Shhh... Don't cry. Don't cry."

"Don't leave me..." she sobbed, hugging me back. "Don't let him get to you, please."

"I won't," I promised. "I won't. So don't cry."

She buried her face into my shoulder, hot tears sliding down my skin as I rubbed her bare back gently.

She calmed after a moment, but I could still hear the sorrow in her voice when she whispered, "I'm scared. I don't want to die either. I'm scared."

"You don't need to be," I told her. "I'll protect you. I'll save you. It's alright. Shhh...."

She calmed after a minute, and I stared down at her expression to find her back in that numb state.

The one where she looked so tired and agonized.

"Oh," I said, grabbing a bottle of lotion, "I almost forgot. Turn to me, Honey."

She twisted her body until she faced me, and I pumped out a glob of lotion onto my finger. "Let me see your wrists," I urged.

Without hesitation, she pulled her wrists out from under the covers and stared up at me as I rubbed the lotion into the marks left from her bindings earlier.

"Ankles, too," I said, holding her up with one arm as she pulled them out from under the sheets.

I rubbed lotion in them, too.

"And your stomach," I said.

She listened, pulling the sheets down to expose her waist, and I delicately spread some lotion on her still-reddened skin.

"There," I told her, smiling as she glanced up at me. "Beautiful as always, huh?"

"Thank you..." she told me, resting her cheek on my shoulder as I caught her still-warm mug and gave it to her. "No one's done this for me after sex... It makes me feel...."

"Loved?" I said.

She nodded shyly.

"You are loved," I responded.

She glanced up at me, a question in her eyes, but moved her gaze away.

"You are loved," I repeated, knowing what the question was, "and yes, I love you, Riley. I love you."

"Don't say that," she whispered, sorrow in her voice.

"I am saying it," I responded. "Now, you don't have to say it back yet, okay? Think on it over night, Riley, and respond in the morning."

She nodded.

"Drink your tea," I instructed. "And lights out after."

She smiled, a soft one. "Yes, sir."

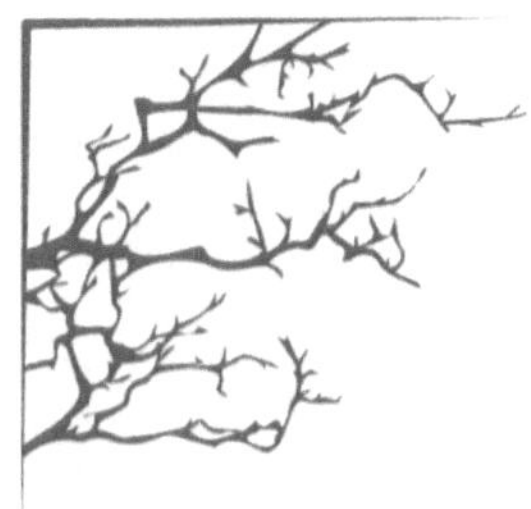

24

Riley

I woke up early the next morning, and when I stared down at Paris, I found him sound asleep next to me.

And since I didn't want to wake him just yet, I got up off the bed and took a small shower, deciding to dampen my hair so I could brush it out.

I still smelled like his body wash from last night, so I didn't really care to add more.

After I got out, I pulled on some of my old clothes, a pair of jean shorts, some black leggings, and an anime T-shirt that had a hole in the side because I wore it everyday in middle school.

And I padded out of the bathroom, still barefoot, and decided to go do something useful.

They had this romantic thing in the novels I read where the man gave the woman breakfast in bed to show how much he cared about her.

What if it was flipped? Woman giving a man breakfast in bed?

I didn't really care, I just threw the pot on the stove and cracked some eggs, placing two slices of cheese in top and a pinch of salt, and I continuously folded the food over until it solidified.

I smiled.

Perfect.

After pouring him a glass of orange juice, I walked over to his pantry and pulled out a tray, carrying it over to the counter as I put the plate of eggs, the cup of orange juice, and a fork as well as a knife placed on a napkin.

I carried it into the bedroom.

After placing it on the nightstand, I hovered over him as he lay asleep.

And I shook him, making him exhale a groan.

"Paris," I whispered, shaking him, "wake up. Waaake uu-uup."

His lashes parted and I smiled. "What?"

"I made you some breakfast." I gestured to the plate of food on the nightstand.

He rolled over and glanced at it, and then back at me before sitting up. "I thought you can't cook."

I placed the tray carefully on his lap before crawling into bed beside him.

"I only know how to cook eggs," I responded honestly.

"Only?" he echoed, sparing me a glance before picking some up and taking a bite.

"Yeah," I said, "only. My dad taught me how to make them."

His eyes lit up when he swallowed. "OH, JESUS FUCK, THIS IS GOOD!"

I smiled when he started eating the entire plate in a matter of seconds.

I watched as he finished, and he first set his tray back on the nightstand, then smiled down at me before catching my chin and lowering his mouth to mine.

I gave in then, raising myself up until our foreheads touched and heat flashed through me like waves.

And he let go of my lips, staring down at me with a smile. "Good morning."

I gazed up at him, feeling a calmness wash through me due to the soft kiss he gave me.

I studied his blue gaze, getting lost in his beautiful ocean. "Good morning."

He patted his lap, and I crawled over to him, sitting in it sideways as I rested my head on his shoulder.

He ran his fingers through my hair, and I nearly purred like a cat, but refrained because that would've been creepy.

It only took a moment to hear his breath catch, and I felt him tug my hair out of the pony tail.

I opened my eyes when I felt the thickness fall down to my shoulders.

Oh, shit. I forgot I couldn't straighten it... He wasn't used to it yet.

After I showered the first time last night, the water got rid of the waves because I used a straightening iron every morning before school. It didn't fully curl until it dried.

And my hair was naturally curly and had ringlets and coils, but I hated it because it always frizzed no matter what hair products I used.

Paris ran his fingers through my curls, and I spared a glance up at him to see if he was repulsed or disgusted.

But his eyes were sparkling.

He looked... *amazed.*

"I've never seen ringlets like this," he said, though I couldn't tell if it was directed toward me or not. "Jesus... they're like springs. So beautiful." He looked down at me then, taking a curl that spiraled down my cheek and ran his fingers through it. "Is this natural or did you do this with an iron?"

I blinked, cheeks dusting slightly. "Uhm... natural."

He gazed up at me. "Why do you straighten it?"

"Because..." I responded, "it's an American thing."

"I don't care if it's a fucking American thing," he told me, still playing with the curls. "It's beautiful. Do you mind..." he gazed up at me, "keeping it this way? I love it."

My heart pounded harder in my chest, and I nodded. "Yes, sir. I would love to."

His eyes locked with mine, and they softened as he whispered, "You have a right to say no, Riley. I'm not trying to control you."

"No," I responded, "no... It... It's hard to straighten it every morning anyway... And I like it when you play with it... It... feels good."

He smiled softly. "Thanks, Riley." He pulled on another spiral, running it through his fingers and watched in awe as it popped back in place. "So cool. I've never seen curls like this."

I smiled. "Thank you, sir."

He ran another one through his fingers and looked down at me. "I'll give you the satisfaction."

I gazed up at him, confused. "Huh?"

"Ride me through my jeans," he instructed, but his tone was soft now compared to his original stern, dominant one, "through your leggings and shorts. I'll let you control the pace, and I'll let you come. Only if you keep your clothes on, okay?"

"May I ask why...?" I said.

"Because the orgasm would come slower with our clothes on," he smiled, "and I want to see if your wetness bleeds through your shorts."

"No, sir," I said, then gazed up again, "I meant why are you letting me be in control?"

"I'm rewarding you," he told me.

My heart jolted. "For... what?"

"For being kind to me this morning and giving me breakfast."

I was silent then.

"Ride me," he said, "and the only rules I have are one, keep clothes on, and two, keep your eyes on mine, okay?"

I nodded.

"I don't do this often," he told me. "So be a good girl."

I nodded again.

"Go ahead and start," he said.

I got slightly off his lap and climbed back on, straddling him as I lowered my covered pussy onto his hardness, and I gazed down at him as he smiled up at me.

"Eyes on me," he instructed, "go on now. Don't be shy."

I started slowly moving my hips forward, lashes flutter-ing at how good this felt, and I kept going, focusing my gaze on his as I dry fucked him.

"Good girl," he praised, settling his back on the head-board as I rode him a little faster. "Keep going."

I felt wetness pouring out of me as I went faster—my clit firmly rubbing on his cock—lashes fluttering closed as I started moaning at how good this felt.

"Eyes on me," he said, and I immediately opened them, wanting to listen this time.

His blue gaze was soft now, but with a hint of fire, and he smiled up at me as my eyes locked on his.

Like I was stuck in a trance.

The hue in his gaze was so warm but so cold... It looked nice in there.

He tipped his head back exhaling a groan, but kept his eyes on mine as I ground him faster.

I could tell by the slight hint of pain in his eyes that he came.

I could feel it, too, I could feel his jeans dampening un-der me.

It made the arousal burn worse inside me.

"Keep going until you come," he told me. "Ride me how-ever long you want."

I listened, and we went on like this for almost an hour, and I made him come almost two more times before I ground him a little faster, catching his shoulders.

He knew I was close—I could tell because he put his hands on my hips to guide my hips better as the orgasm crested inside me.

"Oh, God…" I whispered, going faster. "Oh, God. It's coming. It's coming."

"Let it out," he told me. "Don't hold in your scream."

"I'm coming," I told him, my body screaming at me to stop but his hands stayed at my hips, forcing me to continue. "I'm coming."

And I did, crying out as I shook in his hold, though even as I came, he kept me going until I rode out the orgasm.

I stopped then, pressing my forehead to his chest as I caught my breath.

He laughed softly, gently rubbing my back to help my breathing steady. "You made me come *three* times. Jesus."

"Are you satisfied?" I asked him, still breathless.

He nodded into my hair.

But he only threw me down on the bed, making me squeal as he kneeled down and spread my legs wide, staring down at my damp shorts seconds later.

"Wow," he commented, "soaked. Fucking hell, you have a fucking *waterfall* in here, don't you?"

Before I could respond, he lightly teased me through my shorts, rubbing my clit in little circles as I moaned softly.

"More's coming," he said, his other hand running along my vulva through the fabric. "Wow, Honey."

"Paris…" I whispered, "Paris…."

He gazed up at me. "Yes?"

"Can you please rub there a little more?" I asked him. "Please, sir?"

"You came, didn't you?"

I nodded, but stared up at him. "It feels ten times better when you tease me for a little. Through the jeans and stuff…."

He smiled. "Sit up."

I listened, and when he patted his lap, I crawled over and sat on him like he was a sofa, facing forward.

"Rest your head on my shoulder," he said to me, guiding it down so we didn't smash faces, "good girl. Open your legs." He praised me again when I listened. "Teasing doesn't take much focus for you or me," he explained. "It feels good to you, yeah, but you're able to talk while I do this." He started rubbing my clit gently through my jeans, and I leaned back into him, moaning softly.

"So let's talk," he said to me, gently kissing my forehead as he continued the torture. "You've been looking upset," he said, "what's wrong?"

"Nothing..." I lied.

I didn't really need to dump all my trauma on him right now. He was right, I could focus while he did this to me, but I still didn't want to talk about anything.

"Don't lie to me," he urged, pulling me up a little more as he teased me a bit slower so I could focus. "Tell me what's going on."

I sighed, shaking my head in disapproval but still responded, "I'm growing a strong attraction to you, and I'm not used to it."

He looked down at me quizzically. "You didn't with Ryan?"

"No," I said, "I did, but... this is different." I sighed. "Ryan was an infatuation. This one never goes away and I don't want to ever leave your side. It's not the sexual part, but it is. I'm growing a physical and emotional attraction to you that I can't even comprehend, and it scares the hell out of me.

With Ryan, I broke it off and it hurt, yes. But with *you*? I'm scared you're going to die and it drives me crazy. The things you do to me make me feel like I'm going insane, and I don't know how to stop myself from getting closer, because every time you push me away... I just wander closer. Every time *I* push you away, I just wander closer. I have no control over myself and it drives me *crazy*."

I took a gasp after my rant and tried to calm my breathing. He was still teasing me, and I could feel the arousal coming, but barely acknowledged it.

"I feel the same," he said finally, and I gazed up at him as he smiled down at me. "I've tried to push you away, too. I told myself that I was just protecting you from that killer and such, but... I felt myself growing an attachment—like you said—one I couldn't get over. I've hurt people in the past, had sex with them, too, yes, but you? You just... *feel* so much better than all the strippers. I know, yes, I had strippers over, what a shock, but never again." He looked me over. "Not with you. It will never feel the same."

My eyes glittered with tears.

"And the emotional attraction," he let out a breath, "never have I *ever* felt that in my life. The need to be near you, the need to protect you, the desire to show you all the beautiful places I've been to in this world. Before... I never really understood why I was so... *intrigued* by you. I honestly didn't know anyone with your personality. You test me a *shit ton*, yes, but you also so kind and loving, and I don't ever want to leave your side. I just—"

I got off his lap and straddled him instead, silencing him by pressing our mouths together, and I parted my lips to let his tongue roam in my mouth as he explored every inch of it, and I pulled back, kissing his forehead seconds later as he stared up at me.

His eyes were so dark, so mesmerizing. I loved it so much.

"Paris..." I whispered, brushing my fingers on his cheeks, "I—I love you, too. You know, what you said last night. I love you, too."

He smiled and leaned in for another kiss, and I let him, lowering into him as I felt him harden slightly under me.

I pulled away and giggled. "Already?"

He only scooped me up, making me squeal as he carried me over to the kitchen.

He set me on the counter then, placing his hand on my navel as I gazed up at him curiously.

"How's your tummy?" he asked me.

I nearly laughed at the childish word he used. "It's fine."

"Good," he responded. "Sometimes during sex, it can start hurting here because of built up air pressure."

I nodded. "It's fine."

"Good," he responded then leaned in for a small kiss before drawing back, pulling some hair out of my eyes. "So... what do you want to do today, Hun?"

I pondered for a moment, staring off into space and recalling all the stupid things couples did.

But I came up with something that many would consider boring, but I would love to experience it. "Can you read to me?"

He smiled. "You want me to read to you?"

"Yes, please, sir."

He chuckled at the name I called him and sat up fully, and lifted me by my armpits as he carried me to the couch in his living room.

He sat with me—once again—in his lap, and pulled open a drawer in his coffee table, pulling out one of Shakespeare's plays, *Macbeth*, and draped an arm around me as he started reading:

"'*This is a dagger which I see before me. The handle toward my hand? Come, let me clutch on thee. I have thee not, and yet I see thee still. Art thou not, fatal vision, sensible To feeling as to sight? or art thou but a dagger of the mind, a false creation, proceeding from the heat-oppressed brain?*'"

I started drifting halfway into the Act, only hearing bits and pieces of the book as he continued to read to me, absently stroking my arm.

I loved hearing his voice... so calm. I loved feeling his and brush up and down my arm in a soothing manner. And I loved the smell of him... so minty and fresh, and I also loved that I smelled like him, too. Because I used his body wash.

I didn't want to ever buy my own again.

But I was rudely woken when his phone came to life.

Paris sighed, muttering, "*Mother fuckers. My day off and you...*" he sighed and picked up his phone, pressing it to his ear while saying, "What?"

There was inaudible rambling on the other line.

"Yes," he said, still annoyed, "thanks, bye."

He sighed, turning to me while brushing some hair away from my eyes. "Sorry about that, you were so peaceful and they have horrible timing." He smiled sadly. "Sorry to ruin this moment, but... we have a lead and I don't want to leave you alone so," he held out his hand, "c'mon, beautiful. I'll take you anywhere while we're out to make up for it."

I happily took his hand and he smiled.

"Yes, sir," I said, eyes glistening with his reflection as he smiled. "Thank you, sir. I love you, sir."

"I love you, too, Rye." And he guided me out the front door seconds later.

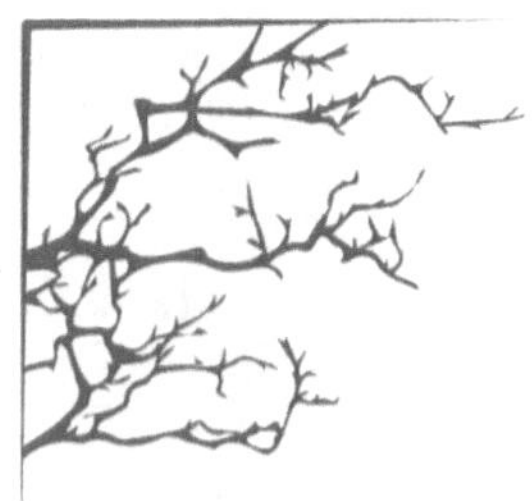

25

Riley

Paris dragged me into some kind of club that was for eighteen-and-older, and since we were both over that age, we were let in with no question.

I was currently sitting in a booth because he had to go talk to some "people that I shouldn't trifle with." So he left me alone at a booth and told me to stay unless I wanted to get murdered, I just nodded and let him go off.

I was currently staring into the crowd, kicking out my legs at the booming music as everyone danced in front of me.

This music was good, too. It was my favorite type, electronic-pop, and I seriously wanted to stand up and dance, but I decided it was better to listen to Paris, anyway.

He'd been gone for about thirty minutes, and I found myself wondering if he was okay.

But I still didn't move, I knew what would happen if I didn't listen.

But seconds later, a shadow hovered over me, and I looked up to greet Paris.

It wasn't Paris, though.

It was two men. One looked in his twenties with black, combed hair, though his eyes were shielded with sunglasses.

The other looked about thirty, with long, red hair that felt to his shoulders, and another pair of sunglasses.

And they both wore casual wear.

"Hey, baby," the younger one said, making me internally cringe. "What're you doin' by here all by you-self?"

"I'm waiting for someone," I told them.

"And yet, here we are," the older man said.

"Can you just back off?" I asked them cynically. "Seriously, it's not that hard to back off."

"But, my babe's lonely. Gotta show her a good time, no?"

"Leave me alone," I told both of them.

But the black-haired one sat beside me, running his fingers through my hair. "You ain't gotta talk to us like that, babe. Just gotta let us fuck you and we'll leave ya be."

I stood then, deciding being punished by Paris was better than getting flirted on, so I went to the girls bathroom downstairs, slamming the door behind me and locking it, splashing cold water on my face and patting it dry seconds later.

When I turned, my heart froze when I saw both men in the doorway.

I looked to the lock.

How the hell...?

"Ooh," the younger one said, pulling a gun out of his pocket when he said in a colder tone, "cornered you, girlie."

I stepped back. "Leave me alone."

The second man pulled another gun out, aiming it at me while my breathing shortened. "Don't worry," he said, chuckling lowly, "we won't rape you. We're assassins, and you're our target. Riley, right? Riley Princes?"

My heart beat rapidly when I realized something.

They made me nervous on purpose so they could corner me in a quiet environment.

Shit.

"You know you're not supposed to be alive, Riley," the twenty-year-old one said. "You're supposed to be dead by now. But things keep getting in the way of our leader. He told us that we should tell you, Riley," he leaned forward, "if we could kill your father, Johnathan Princes, we could kill *you*, Riley. Very, very, *slowly*."

I breathed shallowly. "I thought my dad was murdered by the original mafia boss."

"Nah," the older one shrugged, "he *ordered* him to be killed, but he didn't kill him."

"Then *who did*?" I said.

"You'll never find out." The younger one smiled, clicking off his safety. "Any last words?"

I breathed shallowly, heart thudding against my chest.

Another gun clicked behind them. "Yeah," a young man said, "put your guns down, fuckers."

I gazed up to find a familiar man standing there with golden hair glistening in the lighting, and there were two men behind him, guns trained on both of the attacker's heads.

Paris.

And she guessed the other two men were his underlings.

Paris held two revolvers in his hands, one aimed to each of the men's heads as the other two men next to him had their gun on each, as well.

The assassins were defiantly outnumbered.

"Alright..." the younger one said, raising his hands as the other one did, too. "Alright."

He turned around then, aiming his gun to Paris, and I screamed his name before—

Boom!

Boom!

Boom!

I felt liquid splatter on my face, and my heart stopped when I heard two bodies thud to the ground.

My vision was red with their blood, and I felt tears warming my eyes when I couldn't see.

I can't see.

Was one of them Paris?

I dropped to my knees, sinking down onto the wall as the cold overwhelmed me inside.

I didn't know what was happening... I couldn't *see.*

It felt like I was on another planet.

Everything was so red... It was so... *red.* It felt like my vision was tainted one color.

No.

No.

No.

No.

"Riley," someone familiar said, trying to get my attention as I stared down at the two bodies on the ground. "Riley, come on. We have to go. Riley. *Riley!*"

No.

No.

Stop.

Stop it.

No.

I heard a sigh, and I felt the man raise my arm and wrap it around his shoulder, helping me up until he scooped my body in his arms and ran out of the club.

Too much blood.

I can't see.

Help.

Help me.

I can't.

I can't do this.

Stop.

Stop it.

The man shoved me into a car and drove off seconds later, and I heard screaming and sirens from a distance.

No.

Stop.

"What the fuck is wrong with her?" a male voice said, though I heard it before.

"Riley," someone whispered, turning my head until I could look into his blue eyes, "Riley, can you hear me? Are you hurt?"

Stop this. I can't.

"Riley," he urged me, but I barely acknowledged it.

"Is she dead?" the man driving the car said.

"No," the one trying to talk to me responded, "she's looking at me. But I don't know if she's paying attention. She looks lost."

No.

Please, stop.

I can't.

I can't.

"I'll get a doctor," the man driving said. "We're at your place in a minute."

I can't do this. Stop it. Stop it. Stop.

No.

Not again.

Too much.

Stop it.

"We're here," the driver said, "Paris, carry her out."

I can't do this anymore.

Enough.

I felt another arm cover me as he lifted me up, carrying me inside the building seconds later, I could feel the bumps go through me like he was running.

Stop.

Stop it.

I can't feel. I can't think.

I felt myself engulfed in comfort seconds later, and I heard a snap, but it didn't take me out of my trance state.

I felt like I was flying. I felt like I was *flying*.

"Riley," someone urged, "Riley, look at me."

I couldn't. I was frozen.

I can't breathe.

"Riley," he said, moving my chin, "Riley, are you hurt?"

I'm hurting. I'm hurting.

"Riley," he said again. "*Riley.*"

A knock cascaded on the front door, and I heard it open. I then heard whispering.

I can't focus... I can't breathe. I'm hurting. I'm hurting.

A man kneeled by me—someone I didn't recognize—and I saw something bright flash in my eyes, but I didn't wince away like usual.

Help me. I can't see.

"Get me a towel," the man said, and I heard someone run over to the kitchen and shuffle through drawers. "And dampen it."

I heard the sink run.

I can't breathe. I'm hurting.

"Riley," the man said, grabbing the blob from the man in the kitchen, "Riley, can you speak to me?"

Save me.

"She's not responding," another voice said. "What's happening to her?" I distantly felt something cold touch my arms, and the fabric rubbed everything away, even on my face.

But I still saw red.

"There's blood in her eyes," the doctor man said. "Get me my medical bag."

I heard more shuffling.

"Is it her blood?" a guy said.

"I don't know," the doctor man said. "Riley," he spoke to me, "Riley, I'm going to use some saline and wash out your eyes, okay?"

I never responded.

I can't... think.

I'm hurting.

"Is she hurt?" the same man asked.

"Not on her body," the doctor responded. "The blood on her arms and face look like its from someone else."

Stop me from hurting. I'm hurting. Stop me from hurting. It hurts.

"Riley," the doctor said, "I'm washing out your eyes now. Don't worry, it won't hurt, okay? I'm just using saline, and the plastic bottle I'm using is sterile."

I felt something press to my eye.

It hurts.

It hurts.

But something squirted into my eye, and I felt myself distantly blink at the intrusion.

But the red slowly washed away.

Make it stop. I'm hurting. I'm hurting.

He did the same to my other eye, washing out the red tint in it until I could see clearly again.

"There's no wounds in her eyes," the doctor said after a moment, flashing the bright light in my vision again. "No hemorrhaging. It looks like that was from someone else, too."

Stop this. I'm hurting. I'm hurting.

"What's wrong with her then?" a guy said.

The doctor pulled away. "She's alright. *Physically.*"

"What?" the man said again.

"Emotionally," the doctor said. "She's scarred. She's in shock. Just let her rest a little, and she should heal. I have to go back to my project, but keep an eye on her. I'm not sure if there's long-lasting effects emotionally. With what she's been through, she might have some scars from this."

I heard footsteps pad away.

"Paris," the driver man said. "Paris, do you want me to go?"

"Yes," Paris said again, "yes, just... just... I need guards out there."

"Yes, sir," the driver man said, and he walked outside.

"Riley," the Paris man said, sitting on the couch beside me, "Riley, close your eyes. Go to sleep. Let this pass, okay? You're okay now. You're safe. Close your eyes."

I didn't want to... but I was so... tired.

I closed my eyes and let myself fall asleep.

It was around ten in the evening when my "shock" phase settled, and I found myself following Paris as he guided me to his master bathroom.

I eventually learned that the people who died were the people wanting to kill me, and the man who drove us back here was, Veo. Paris wasn't hurt, but the other one of his underlings had a slight injury because one of the bad guy's bullets skimmed his shoulder.

I still felt a little uneasy and loopy, but I was able to function now that I took a nice nap.

Paris guided me to sit on the toilet before kneeling down in front of me, running his fingers through one of my tight coils as he smiled up at me.

"You still look a little lost," he said softly. "You okay?"

My automatic response was to nod, and I did without thinking.

"You don't have to lie to me," he said, tucking the coil behind my ear. "You can be honest with me, Riley. Don't be scared, okay? I won't hurt you."

I knew he wouldn't... I knew. It was just that earlier... the blood and the gore... it triggered a memory that I didn't like to think about, and I reacted badly.

I knew it wasn't Paris's fault. In fact, I knew it was most probably my fault because I left the seat and got myself cornered in the first place.

Paris eyed me worriedly before patting me gently on the thigh, and he got up and started the shower.

I watched as he walked back over to me and kneeled down. "I'm gonna help you take your clothes off, okay?"

I nodded.

He slipped his hands under the hem of my T-shirt and shuffled it up, pulled it over my head, guiding me to stand seconds later so he could pull down my bloody shorts and leggings, and my underwear, and he guided me back down to sit while he unclipped my bra and lowered it over my shoulders.

I watched him take off his clothes seconds later.

"There," he said, looking back up to me, "c'mon."

I took his hand as he gently wrapped his arm around my back so he could guide me into the shower.

When the warm water padded against my skin, I suddenly felt a wash of relief, and I turned further into Paris as he ran his fingers through me hair.

"Sit down for me again, Sweetheart," he said, and I listened, sitting on the floor as he followed suit, pulling a bottle of shampoo out from a shelf on the wall, as well as his body wash.

Seconds later, I eased into him as he ran shampoo through my brown locks and massaged my head seconds later.

That felt good...

I rested my head on his shoulder as he continued to massage, smiling softly as he grabbed his body wash and his loofa, rubbing the soapy loofa on my back seconds later.

I murmured a soft sound as he continued the act, warm tingles washing through me as he continued to my arms, my legs, and skillfully my stomach while I remained in my position.

He caught my chin then and tipped it up, and with more gentleness, he washed my face.

"There," he said, pulling me into the water and running his hands on my clean skin, "no more blood."

I smiled against his skin while he continued to soothe me, though I knew he couldn't see it.

But when I recalled the memory of earlier... the blood, the guns, the death, I felt myself start shaking as my loopy state slowly came back.

I felt so... numb. But I was... hurting.

"It's okay," Paris whispered, clearly feeling me shake against him. "I won't hurt you."

I shook my head, sobs edging up my throat as I shook harder. "N.. no. I know you won't... they... they found me."

He only set his cheek on top of my head and rubbed my back as I started sobbing silently. "Shhh..." he murmured.

I didn't like crying in front of him, but all the emotions swarming me inside felt so overwhelming and horrible. I knew I needed to let it out eventually, but not in front of him.

But I couldn't stop.

I couldn't.

"Do you need me to show you I'm not bad?" Paris asked me.

I honestly didn't know how he would do that, but I shook my head. "No, I—I trust you."

I felt his lips curl into my skin, and he pressed a kiss to my forehead before drawing back and turning off the water. "Let's get you to bed," he said.

And he lifted me seconds later, wrapping a towel around me and carrying me out of the bathroom.

After he sat me on the bed and dried me off, he got one of his soft throw blankets and wrapped it around me, smiling as he pushed me down on the bed, draping the covers over me, and slipping in moments later.

I relaxed into him as he stroked my hair softly, running a wet coil in his fingers again.

He must've been really fascinated by them. Seriously.

I relaxed into his form while he ran his warm hands down my body and finally lightly cupped my breast, kneading it gently until my nipple started hardening under his hand.

He brushed his finger on it, making me gasp softly at how gentle he was, and he smiled, gazing up at me seconds later.

"Do you want me to make you feel good?" he asked me gently. "Will that make you feel better?"

I gave him a small nod.

He leaned away from me to get something out of his nightstand and turned back toward me, whispering, "Open your legs."

I listened, rolling over onto my back and parted my legs as he came on top of me.

I winced when he slid something rubbery inside me, and something else pressed to my exposed clit as he lowered himself onto me.

"Hold still," he said.

He pressed a button and I nearly screamed, feeling the rubber inside me vibrate as well as the thing on my clit... but the one on my clit...

Oh Jesus... it started sucking me into it.

I writhed from under him while he pinned my hands above my head with one arm, the other holding the vibrator in place so when I clenched I wouldn't push it out.

"Good?" he asked me, dipping his head down to catch my nipple in between his teeth and pull out and I exhaled a moan. "How is that?"

"It's—strong," I said, shaking from under him. "It's *strong.*"

"It's only on low," he commented.

"Parriiiis..." I whispered, shaking harder. "Paaariissss!"

"Already?" he said, chuckling.

I cried out when I came, shaking under him like a live wire while the vibrator only made the pleasure roll harder through me.

"Shhh..." Paris cooed when I settled back into myself. "There you go. Want a little clit torture?"

I shook my head, and he chuckled. "No? Maybe just a little?"

It was still on low—handleable right now—and he smiled evilly while clicking the button once, making me tense.

I started trembling, whimpers coming out of my lips.

"Medium," he told me, "clearly not high enough."

He clicked it again, and I started screaming, writhing from under him while he held me down, chuckling.

"Alright, alright," he turned it off, making me pant heavily as he took the toy out from inside me.

He examined it for a moment. "Wow... that must've felt good, huh? This thing is soaked."

I just gazed up at him, eyes watering as he set the toy back on his nightstand and looked back down at me.

"You don't look satisfied," he commented as I blinked away tears.

I stared up at him, finding him looking at me curiously.

Without thinking, I rose myself up and pressed my lips to his, making him exhale a groan as he leaned into me, still holding my wrists above my head as he kissed me back.

I pulled away, staring up at him when I saw the fire light in his eyes.

"Why aren't you satisfied?" he asked me.

I tugged one of my arms out from his hand and reached below the covers, gently playing with him as he tensed.

He caught my arm then and pinned it back above me, the fire in his eyes glowing brighter.

"What are you *doing*?" he questioned me.

I gazed up at him, tipping my head to the side curiously even though I was being held down by him. "I'm not satisfied."

His eyes rounded. "But... why?"

"Put it in me," I told him.

He gazed up. "Huh?"

"Put yourself in me," I repeated.

He just watched me. "Riley."

"Do it," I told him. "I want you in me."

He just leaned down and pressed his lips to mine, his body almost feverish.

I pulled up to meet him, opening my mouth so his tongue could explore me.

And seconds later—without separating our lips—he lifted me up by my hips and I wrapped my legs around his waist, his cock gently brushing against my ass as he carried me back into his sex room.

Seconds later, he placed me on a swing that dangled from the ceiling, separating our lips as he watched me.

And moments later, he started wrapping my legs to the swing with a rope.

Binding them open as he watched the liquid drip off my pussy and onto the ground.

I saw a smile twitch his lips.

After binding my wrists, he looked up at me. "You ready?"

I nodded, sweat sliding down my temples as I worried if this would hurt.

And he slowly—painfully slowly—slid his cock into my tight hole, and I winced at the slight pain of it, but he only thrusted harder, making me throw my head back in pleasure.

"Shhh..." he cooed, "take it like the good girl you are."

"I'm a good girl?" I whispered, gazing up at him as he held still inside me, clearly trying to get me used to his size.

He looked up at me, eyes glowing in amusement. "Do you want me to prove it to you?"

My eyes glistened with his reflection.

"I can prove it to you," he answered, "but I'll be mean about it."

"How can you prove it to me...?" I asked him.

He smirked. "How fast?"

My eyes glittered.

He smiled wickedly. "This?"

I gasped when he started pumping fast.

"This?"

I whimpered when he thrusted hard, and then pulled out slowly, and then trusted hard again.

I could feel his thrusts all the way to my chest.

"Paris..." I whispered. "I'm not used to this."

"What did I say?" he responded, smiling up at me as I tried to breathe. "What did I say?"

"Take it like a good girl," I responded.

"Are you a good girl?" he asked me.

I nodded numbly, trying to keep my composure.

His eyes darkened with mischief. "Then prove it."

And then he started slowly pushing in and out, and I could feel him watching me.

And he started thrusting.

Then moments later pounding.

I cried out, struggling against my bindings as he pumped in and out of me at an alarming rate.

Paris watched my expression the entire time, and finally, when he was fed up with me having my eyes closed, he demanded, "Look at me. Only me."

I raised my head to meet his gaze, still crying out at how good this felt.

"I can't," I said, struggling against my bindings as his heat started pulsing through me. "Oh, God," I moaned. "You're so hard."

He smiled.

"And big," I added, trying to regain my breath. "And... long. Jesus *Christ*!" I threw my head back, crying out as he went faster.

"Are you a good girl?" he asked again.

"Yes, sir," I responded.

"I told you to watch me, Riley," he said then. "Are you watching me?"

"I can't..." I told him.

"Look at me," he said, "and I won't be heartless."

I gazed up at him. "Why?"

"I want to see your expression when I do *this*." He shoved into me, making me gasp as I felt the thrust rattle through me.

Oh, god. This felt so good.

Why wasn't it like this with Ryan?

"There we go," he said, chuckling as he did it again. "Good, huh? Do you like this, Riley?"

I nodded.

He slapped my clit, making me cry out. "Use your words."

"Yes, sir."

He started pounding, making my hands clutch the chains of the swing as I was held helplessly open to him with the bindings.

"Who do you belong to?" he asked me, pounding harder as tears slipped from my eyes.

When I didn't answer, he slapped my clit again, and I cried out.

"*Who* do you belong to?" he repeated. "Answer, Riley."

I murmured his name, and he slapped my clit again.

"Louder," he demanded.

"You, sir," I told him. "I belong to you, sir."

He smiled. "Good girl."

And he pounded faster, making me start sobbing at how good this felt.

Oh... wait...

I felt it.

My orgasm was cresting.

"You're tightening on me," Paris stated. "Are you close?"

"Yes," I responded, "yes, sir."

He pounded me faster, making me throw my head back.

It was coming.

It was *coming*!

I cried out, tightening on him while he pounded harder, the orgasm rattling through me like gold as he tensed too.

He came the moment I tightened on him, letting out a feverish roar as I felt him fill me.

He slowly rode the orgasm out, thrusting in and out of me gently as we both caught out breath.

I smiled when he stopped and pressed his forehead to mine. "Again?" I said.

He gave me an amused look. "Fine, but this time you're going in a *whole* new position."

I nodded without even thinking about it.

I stared up at him when he pressed a kiss to my forehead, his hardened cock still inside me as he pressed his head to mine.

"Riley," he said, "do you love me?"

"I love you times a thousand," I answered, making him smile gently.

He gazed up at me then, untying my bindings. "Round two, you ready?"

I nodded. "Always."

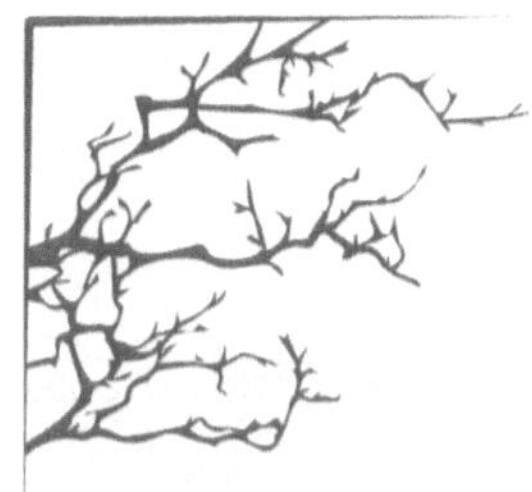

26

Paris

It was around two in the morning, and I smiled as I watched my beautiful girl rest on the bed before me.

Riley was under the silk sheets, back drifting up and down slowly with her soft breaths, and her breasts as well as her stomach were uncovered by the bedding, giving me a sight of her slightly budded nipples.

I liked this... Just sitting here and watching her sleep.

It was a creepy thing to do, but I loved how she looked so gentle and innocent under the moonlight.

Like a goddess, honestly.

But I broke myself out of my trance, pulling out my cellphone as I dialed Veo, pressing the phone to my ear seconds later.

"Yes, sir?" he said, sounding slightly exhausted.

"Sorry for waking you," I told him, "but I wanted to ask you if Julie and Claire were doing alright?"

"Yes, sir," Veo responded. "Julie has been sleeping in Claire's bed for a couple nights, and Claire always reads her bedtime stories before she helps her sleep."

"How's the kiddo doing?"

"Julie's alright…" Veo responded. "I really hope so, she has nightmares almost every night and I walk out of my room to find her hiding under the dining table."

"Night terrors," I responded.

"Yeah," Veo said, yawning. "Yeah, but every night I coax her out and carry her back to bed."

I paused at the warm hint to his voice. "You've grown an attachment to her," I said, "haven't you?"

He was silent for a moment. "I know we're not supposed to grow attachments, sir, but…."

"She reminds you of your daughter," I answered. "I understand, Veo."

The one that my father killed.

"Riley hasn't asked about them," I told Veo then. "I honestly wonder why."

"Maybe she trusts you," he told me.

I remembered our conversation earlier:

Do you need me to show you I'm not bad?

No. I—I trust you, Paris.

"Maybe," I said.

We were both silent for a moment.

"Listen, Veo," I said then, "I want you to try something with her. My mother did this with me when I was a kid. Whenever she has nightmares, do what you do, coax her out of her hiding place, and then sit on the couch with her while reading her a bedtime story, and while you're reading, try rubbing her shoulder."

"Do you think that Riley would be okay with that?"

"I think so," I responded, "I honestly think so. I also think that Julie needs a father-figure because both her parents were taken from her, and Riley is too traumatized to care for her the right way, she needs someone older, someone she can trust. You, Veo."

He was silent for a moment. "Thank you, sir. I—I'll spend more time with her. Thank you."

And he hung up.

I smiled down at my phone at his enthusiasm.

Glad I could boost *someone's* mood.

I stared at Riley's blissful state for another minute before getting up and making my way into the kitchen to get a snack.

I was halfway through making my PBJ sandwich before I heard a, *Thump*!

My heart stopped and I darted straight into the bedroom, throwing open the door.

When I saw the bed empty, my blood ran cold.

I searched the room for her, the walls, the desks.

When my eyes met the floor, my panic cooled when I saw Riley on the carpet, still asleep and breathing under the freed blanket.

"Did you just fucking *fall off the bed*?" I asked her in amusement, stepping over to the girl as I lifted her limp body in my arms.

But as I walked back to the bed, I noticed she clung to me slightly, and when I gazed down at her to find her eyes closed, I realized something.

She wanted me to hold her. She felt my presence fade when I went to the kitchen and fell off the bed because she was searching for me.

I then decided to carry her to the couch in my living room, settling down on it with her in my lap as I switched on the TV while draping a blanket over her.

My neighbors had probably seen her naked more than once, but I didn't really care, and eventually, neither did she.

I gazed back down at her when the commercials switched on, and she was still asleep, cuddled in with me.

I ran my fingers through her brown curls. "You're so beautiful," I whispered to her.

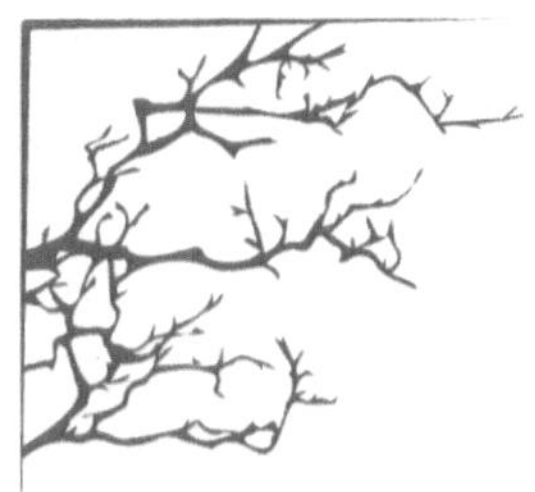

27

Riley

The next morning, I woke up in Paris's empty bed, and I stared up at the ceiling for a moment, watching the sunlight beam through the window before I pushed myself to finally get up.

I was in my panties and bra still, but I didn't really care because his neighbors had seen their share of me and him naked.

As I walked out of his bedroom and into the living room, I searched the couch, the kitchen, and the dining table for Paris.

He was gone.

My brows drew together, and I turned, going back into the bedroom and into his sex room.

He wasn't there either.

Scratching a little itch on the back of my neck, I then decided to walk over to his bathroom.

Nope.

But I squinted my eyes when I found a little note taped to the mirror.

I picked it off, reading it.

Hey, Sweets,

I had to take care of something.

I left some new clothes I bought for you on the toilet. Get dressed, okay? I don't feel like my neighbors watching you walk around naked when I'm not there.

I smiled.

I'll be back soon. Veo's coming over to check on you, so make sure you're clothed when he comes in.

I wondered what he would do if I wasn't.

And, Riley, the next line said, *if you're not clothed, I'm going to teach you a valuable lesson that you won't forget. And if you're wondering "what's the worst I could do?" just remember a couple nights ago when I strapped you down to the bed and tortured your clit for ten minutes, Kay?*

Oh, right.

Also, he knew me well, didn't he?

I'll see you soon, okay?

P.S. STAY IN THE HOUSE, AND DON'T LET ANY-ONE IN. I don't want to find you dead when I get home. Veo has a key, so don't worry about that.

See you soon.

Paris.

I squinted my eyes down at the paper.

But... there was no "I love you" anywhere. Was he ashamed to say it?

Also, why did he just up and *leave* without telling me where he was going?

What was he doing? Did he regret last night?

I shook my head.

No, stop thinking this way. Just... don't get so many doubts. He's not Ryan, so chill, okay?

I still felt something cold swarm in my stomach.

But I walked over to the toilet, finding a silk, blue dress and some leggings resting on the ceramic.

Wha...?

Wow... he bought me expensive stuff.

I wasn't really sure if I liked this, honestly. It was nice, yeah, but... I didn't want to be wearing this.

It felt too fancy. I was afraid to ruin it.

But I slipped it on over my head and pulled on the leggings after.

It would've been easier to do the leggings first, but whatever.

I walked out to his bedroom and stepped in front of the full length mirror, turning my body so I could see my full form.

I blinked.

Wow. Perfect cut. Perfect size.

Was this handmade? Why would he buy this?

Also, did he just measure me in my sleep? That's creepy.

Wait... when did he have time to buy this? Did he leave before I woke up, got this, and then came home to put it on the toilet and left again?

Why didn't he wake me up? I would've loved to say goodbye to him or something.

I didn't want to wake up all alone.

I slapped my cheeks.

You're thinking too much. Stop it.

It was hard, honestly. I started feeling this way with Ryan, and found out I was right. He didn't really love me.

But Paris...? I didn't know why I felt this way. He made me come for the first time and such, and he had so much patience when it came to me.

I knew he wanted to protect me, but... if he did... why would he just... leave?

I started wondering if he'd come back. I started worrying that he was out drinking somewhere to avoid me.

I slapped my cheeks again.

Stop it.

But I heard the front door unlock, and it creaked open seconds later.

I hid behind the bed despite suspecting it was Veo.

I needed to be safe.

"Miss Princes?" he called. "Come on, it's time to go."

Oh, cool, it was him.

I stood, staring at the door in confusion.

But what did he mean... *time to go*? Where were we going?

I walked out of the bedroom then, finding him searching the living room for me.

He looked up at my movement and paused. "Oh, Miss Princes. A lovely dress."

"Uh," I said, "thanks. Where are we going? Paris told me you were only checking on me."

Veo stood fully, clearing his throat as he spoke, "Uhm, actually, Mr. Lucan told me to escort you to school."

I blinked. "Huh?"

"He said—"

"I know..." I responded quickly, "but is it safe? I mean... he's been keeping me here for a reason, hasn't he?"

My heart started pounding ice into my veins.

Was he trying to ease me back into my life to get rid of me?

"There's no need to be frightened, Miss Princes," Veo said. "Paris told me that the school is a safe place for you today, and that he would rather you stay there than here."

I paused.

He didn't want me here?

"O—okay," I responded, trying not to cry as my doubts settled in. "I'll go get my shoes."

I walked off to the bedroom, hurriedly shuffled through my old clothes, and pulled out my shoes while slipping them on without socks.

I was too occupied mentally, though.

Did he not like last night? Did I do bad? Was I too passive? Was I a bad time?

"Miss Princes," Veo said, standing at the door. "Come on, you're going to be late."

"Oh, yeah, uhm, do you know where my backpack is?"

"It's in my car," Veo responded.

Wow... Paris made sure he was ready, didn't he?

Why was I hurting? This hurt; the doubt.

Did he want me out as soon as possible?

I nodded then, and stood, grabbing my phone and purse and walking off to the front door.

I waited while Veo followed.

"You look troubled," he stated. "Is something wrong?"

I shook my head, forcing a smile. "No, I'm okay."

He watched me for a moment and I turned away, hoping he didn't see the tears in my eyes.

He opened the front door then and I walked through, and we both walked down to his car in silence.

The drive to my school, too, was silent, and I stared out the window while playing with my fingers.

Paris didn't even say goodbye.

Was the night before the last time I'd see him?

Did he finally catch the bad guy and thought that he was done with me?

"Miss Princes," Veo said, staring at me through the rear view mirror, "you're safe. The school is safe."

He had the wrong idea of why I was upset, but I didn't feel like telling him, so I nodded. "I know."

He watched me for a moment before going back to the road.

Twenty minutes later, Veo stopped in front of my school, and I didn't even wait for him to open my door, I just grabbed my backpack and got out of the car, walking in the school seconds later.

I felt him watching me through the car window, but he didn't make a move to follow me.

This hurt.

This really hurt.

I didn't like this. I never did.

I made it to my Algebra class two minutes before the bell rang, secretly wondering if Paris was here.

His seat was empty, so I just sat down next to it, watching the table as my teacher fumbled with something on her desk.

"Oh!" she said, looking up at me. "Riley! There you are! How have you been doing? I heard about Claire. Is she alright?"

I nodded. "Yeah."

"You've been gone for a while, too," she stated. "How are you feeling?"

Horrible, currently.

"I'm alright," I responded, not wanting to talk anymore. "A lot's been happening."

"I bet," she responded. "If you need anything," she told me, "feel free to reach out."

"Thanks," I breathed.

Paris wasn't at Algebra.

Paris wasn't at Biology.

Paris was nowhere to be found.

I eventually accepted that he didn't want to be near me right now, so the fact that I was hoping he'd show up to one of my classes was pure idiocy.

He was twenty.

He was a millionaire.

He didn't need to be here.

But I just wanted to see him. I just wanted to see him and ask him, why?

Why did I end up not being good enough for him?

I got the hint eventually.

He was happy last night, but...

Really? This morning did he just have his doubts and scurry off like a pussy?

I fucking hated myself.

What was it about me that had guys first want to fuck me, and then go, *nope*?

I walked outside during passing block before lunch and stared at the sky for a full on ten minutes, and I was wondering what I was going to do with my life.

I felt myself wanting to die suddenly.

I honestly did.

Would anyone miss me? Violet wasn't my real mother, and Julie would be happy with Claire.

If everyone I loved was being taken from me, and it was impossible to *be* loved, then why was I here?

My life was a mistake, anyway.

I wasn't supposed to be born.

I slapped myself internally.

Just because Paris was being a jackass didn't mean I had to go kill myself.

I stared back up at the sky.

But... honestly... I was going to die anyway, wasn't I?

I was going to be murdered anyway.

I wasn't supposed to be born.

No one would miss me because everyone else was dead.

Why not?

All this emotional torment would vanish, and I bet hell was a better place than here.

But how would I do it painlessly? Stabbing myself would hurt, jumping off a building would be agonizing and terrifying, honestly, and... taking pills would suck.

How did people do these things when they didn't want pain?

"Hey, babe," someone said from behind me, and I spun around to find Ryan there.

I sighed, turning back to the sky. "What?"

He wouldn't miss me either. He wouldn't miss his mother if she was murdered.

He'd only pretend to feel bad because it gave him attention.

He walked over to me. "What are you doing out here? You look like you're planning your own demise."

Really? Was it that obvious?

"I don't know," I stated then; the only thing I could respond with right now.

"You wanna come inside with me?" Ryan said. "They got burgers today. The best food the school can make."

"No," I responded, "I'm not hungry."

"Alright," he answered, and then stopped. "Riley," he said then, making me look at him, "whatever you're planning. Don't do it. It's not worth it."

And he walked away.

I stared after him.

Huh?

How did he...?

But I looked back ahead, seeing Veo standing next to a tree, watching me with dark eyes.

What the fuck was happening right now? I thought he'd ditch me by now.

Veo stared at me for a moment before speaking into his earpiece.

Who was he talking to?

Also... did he hear me and Ryan's conversation?

I just stared at him before turning and walking back inside.

"Riley," Veo said before I could disappear through the doors.

I turned. "What?"

He stepped up to me, and I remained still as his tall form hovered over me. "Paris is wondering what's going on."

I blinked. "What are you talking about?"

"You're acting weird," Veo said.

I shook my head. "I'm always acting weird, and why does he care? He just left me this morning with a note and now is easing me back into school, tell him I got the hint, okay? I'm going inside now."

And I walked back through the doors.

But something caught my arm, pulling me back outside. "Riley," Veo said, "Riley, what are you *planning*?'"

I stared at him.

"What Ryan said," Veo stated, "Paris is on the phone right now, I told him about your conversation. What are you planning?"

"To destroy the world," I joked.

"Riley," Veo said with more urgency.

I sighed. "Nothing, okay? This happens a lot and I never go through with it, I'm too much of a pussy."

I pulled out of his grip then, throat constricting.

"Tell Paris that I love him," I said, "even if he doubts me, but also tell him that I understand if he's upset with me or something. I know I'm hard to deal with. I don't know what I did, but I accept it, okay? Now leave me alone."

Veo stared at me. "Riley," he tried to reason.

I pulled out of his grip. "I said to leave me alone."

And I walked inside then.

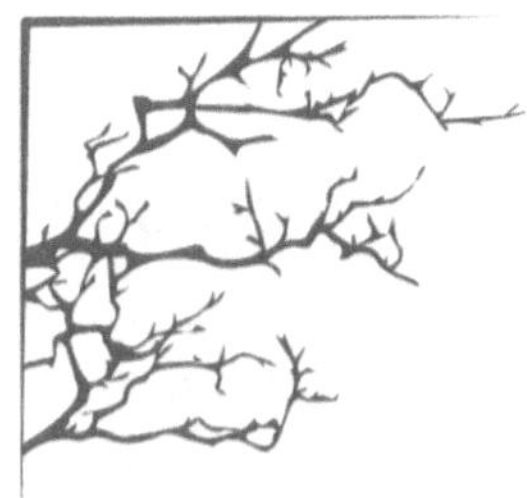

28

Paris

"Where the fuck is she?" I questioned Veo as he stood outside the front door, my blood simmering.

He sighed. "She went inside. I couldn't stop her, sir."

"*Where* inside?" I said.

"I don't know," he said, looking toward the wall. "I'm not allowed in unless I go past the security desk, and even then, I have no parental connection to her, so they wouldn't let me further in the school."

I sighed, running a hand down my face. "Well, technically I'm a student, so I'm going in. Stay out here," I ordered him, "and make sure no one *suspicious* comes in, got it?"

"Yes, sir," he stated. "But wait."

I cast a look at him.

"She said..." Veo stated, "to tell you that she got the hint."

I gave him a bored look. "I heard, and she has the wrong idea."

"Paris," he stated before I could go inside, and I gazed back at him, eyes burning with anger, "sir..." he corrected, "um. I'm worried that she—"

"I know," I stated, "so let me going fucking inside so I can make sure she doesn't."

He nodded then, stepping back, and I went inside, searching the lobby for her.

But my eyes narrowed when they settled on Ryan.

I walked calmly up to him, seeing him sitting lazily on the lobby floor, one leg kicked up as he stared down at his cellphone, swiping through his shorts or whatever.

I stopped in front of him, and he glanced up at me, rolling his eyes before staring down at his phone.

"Where is she?" I questioned.

He gazed up. "Huh?"

"Where is she?" I repeated.

"Who the fuck is '*she*?'"

Oh, that's right. He didn't know me, did he?

"Riley," I responded then, "Riley Princes. Where is she?"

Ryan put his phone down and gazed up at me fully now. "Why do you want to know?"

I pierced my eyes into his. "My guard heard you and her talking."

"Your *guard*?" he echoed, laughing. "Who are you? Christian Grey?"

I stared down at him. "You told her out of nowhere not do to '*it*' and that it wasn't worth it."

His eyes darkened.

"Want to tell me what *it* was?" I prompted.

Ryan rolled his eyes and leaned against the wall. "Who are you to her anyway? Why should you even care, bro?"

"I care about her," I stated. "I do. So tell me where the fuck she is so I make sure she doesn't *kill* herself, Ryan."

"Woah, there," Ryan said, throwing his hands up. "Who said anything about death?"

"Ryan," I hissed, "you told her not to kill herself and then left her alone. Do you know how stupid that is? If you really don't want your best friend to die, then tell me where she is."

He sighed and gazed up at me. "She usually wants to be left alone," he stated, making my teeth clench before he added, "but during that time, she usually goes to the library."

I unclenched my teeth. "Thank you."

And I walked off without another word.

I basically darted down the hall and ran up the stairs at the end, going to the top floor and spinning around until I met the double doors of the library.

I walked in, scanning the desks and group tables for her form, but I couldn't find her.

So I walked over to the front desk, locking eyes with the librarian until I faked a smile.

"Hi," I said kindly despite simmering inside, "do you know where Riley Princes is?"

"Oh, Rye?" She smiled and gestured to a corner hidden behind a bunch of separate cubicles. "She usually takes a nap over there."

The fuck? A *nap*?

"*Usually*?"

"Thank you," I said, stepping over to the cubicles.

There were a couple students working on their computers there, but I ignored them, circling around the last one to the corner.

And there she was, curled up into the fetal position.

And she was asleep, breathing softly.

My heart melted slightly at the sight of her vulnerable self.

If she was falling asleep constantly like this... "usually," that meant she had been spiraling into depression for a while.

I kneeled down beside her, gently shaking her to wake her up.

"Riley," I whispered, "wake up. Come on, Sweetheart. Get up."

She rolled over, groaning in annoyance as she faced away from me and to the wall.

"Riley," I said, "come on, Sweets. Get up. Geeet up."

"Stop," she moaned. "I'm trying to sleep."

"I don't fucking care," I told her. "Get up. Right now."

Her eyes opened a slit at my stern tone. "Paris...?"

I was silent, just watched her expression darken.

"What are you doing here?" she said. "I thought you were busy."

I sat criss-cross in front of her and set my hands on my knees. "You thought I wouldn't come back. Don't lie to me."

She sighed, putting a hand over her face. "There are people studying for finals, Paris. I don't want to do this here."

"Then let's go somewhere else," I told her, "come on."

She shook her head.

A sudden annoyance washed over me. "Riley, get up. Go outside. Or I'll carry you out. Your choice."

She glared at me before getting up, clearly not waiting for me, and stepped out of the library.

I followed her then, brows raising when she just turned right and continued down the hall.

"Riley," I said when she continued, not stopping, "where the fuck are you going?"

She never answered, just continued walking.

"Riley," I urged.

She never stopped.

I caught her arm then, pulling her toward me and she let out a grunt of annoyance, but didn't resist when I stopped her.

There were tears in her eyes, and I could tell she was slowly breaking inside.

"Honey," I whispered, searching her gaze before she moved it to the floor, "can you talk to me?"

She was silent.

"Riley," I urged.

"You left," she stated.

"I never—"

"You left this morning," she told me, "you didn't bother to wake me up to say goodbye, and then you had one of your *men* take me to school which I haven't been to in a *week*. You didn't bother to call me to check up on me, and I was almost *wishing* and *pleading* to see you in my classes. I thought that you were mad or something. Last night... when we did that thing for the first time ever... I was scared. I was scared I wasn't good enough. I'm not good with these things, Paris! I thought you were done with me because I finally let you in!" Her voice lowered. "Like... like Ryan."

I felt my eyes soften. "I'm not like Ryan."

"I thought..." she whispered, "that you didn't like me anymore... and... you got me back here because... because you were trying to get me out of your life and back in my own."

My heart started shattering. "I would never think that, Honey."

She shook her head. "It always happens, Paris. I'm a handful, I know that. I have so much stuff going on and it's hard to live with me, I've been told that by Bella and Ryan and everyone in my classes. I get it, okay?"

"That doesn't mean," I said, "that you don't deserve to live."

She froze, and closed her eyes as if in pain.

"Come here," I said, pulling her toward me so I could wrap my arms around her. When I started rubbing her back, she turned further into me, burying her face in my neck while I soothed her. "You're going to be okay," I promised her. "You'll get through this, okay? I love you, Riley."

She shook her head.

"Yes, I do," I told her, "and I wasn't pushing you away, you have the wrong idea. You have the wrong idea, Sweetheart." I pulled her away then, smiling softly down at her while brushing some tears away. "Shhh... don't cry. Don't cry."

She covered her face in her hands. "I'm sorry... I'm...."

"Hurting," I finished, "I know."

She gazed at my chest then, eyes still glistening.

I felt myself slowly start tearing apart inside.

"Let's go back down to the lobby," I told her. "Down to the lobby, and we can go get some burgers, yeah?"

She shook her head. "I'm not hungry."

"Riley," I said, brushing my finger along her cheek. "Just... come on."

I caught her arm and pulled her down the hall.

And surprisingly, she followed.

We went the way I came, down the stairs, through the hall, and to the lobby.

The lunch room was across the hall and through another pair of double doors, but I stopped in the middle of the lobby, and she did, too, looking at me with her glistening eyes when I pulled my hand out of her grip.

Confusion washed through her expression, and I noticed Ryan look up at us from the corner of my eye.

Good. I wanted everyone to see this.

"Paris...?" she whispered.

"Knees," I said.

Her brows pinched together. "What?"

"Get on your knees, Riley," I stated.

After glancing around nervously, she listened, kneeling down until she got down on her knees, keeping her eyes on me when I stood tall above her.

Everyone was watching us, and I wanted them to.

I could tell the security guards were also staring at us cautiously, unsure if I was going to do something bad or not.

Ryan shifted his position, staring at us fully now.

The whole room was silent.

Her silver eyes glistened as she stated at me, clearly still unsure of this situation.

"Paris?" she asked me. "Did I do something?"

"Yes," I stated, watching a flash of hurt go through her eyes.

I shook my head then, indicating she got the wrong idea.

"Yes, you did something unforgivable." I smiled. "You stole my heart, Riley."

Ryan was *defiantly* watching now.

The hurt in her eyes vanished and replaced with confusion.

I got down onto my knee in front of her, making her catch her breath along with everyone in the lobby.

Her eyes started clouding with tears.

I pulled my mother's diamond ring out of my pocket, and she started breathing shallowly. "Riley Princes," I asked her, the entire school gone silent, "marry me?"

I could see her eyes glistening more, and her chest was rising and falling rapidly when she gazed up at me.

She was going to cry, I could tell.

"This is sudden," I told her, "I understand. But I love you so much. I also understand that you feel as if you can't be loved because so many people have hurt you," I glanced at Ryan and then moved my gaze back to her, "but I also want you to know that it's possible. You don't have to hate yourself. Everything you've been going through is not your fault, and I don't blame you. I love you even though you're broken, I'm broken, too, you know. And I know we've only known each other for such a small amount of time, but you are the love of my life." I smiled when I saw tears flood her eyes. "So, Riley... will you marry me?"

She nodded slightly, and I felt my smile tilt.

"Say it aloud like a good girl, Riley."

She glanced at Ryan.

I shook my head and moved her head so she looked back at me. "No, Honey. Me. Look at me. Say yes or no."

I glanced at him to find him seething.

He doesn't control you, I thought. *You make your own decisions.*

"Yes," she whispered.

I smiled. "Louder."

"Yes," she choked, but everyone in the lobby still heard it.

And cheering scattered through the room, and screaming and laughing.

I smiled as I slid the ring on her finger.

She threw her arms around me, burying her face in my neck as she started crying softly.

I rubbed her back in long, soothing gestures and kissed the top of her head.

"I'll treat you good," I promised her. "For the rest of our lives."

"Yaaaaaay!" a childish voice said, and I smiled as I let Riley go.

Her eyes widened when she took in Julie's form along with Claire who was still in a wheelchair.

Veo was standing next to them, smiling, as well.

Claire wheeled over to us. "Congratulations, Riley and Paris."

Ryan still remained in his position.

"Yeah!" a bunch of teen men said, stepping over to me and wrapped their arm around my shoulders. "Congrats, bro!"

They were my pseudo friends. I just got them to look normal, but it still felt good to be congratulated.

Claire, Riley, and Julie all exchanged hugs, and I also gave them hugs, as well.

Everyone was so happy.

"So, Riley," I told her, making her glance up at me.

"Yeah?"

"I talked with the school board," I stated, making her brows draw together. "They made a deal with good 'ol me and said that since you have all straight A's for your whole high school carrier and that you have over ninety percent on all your tests in each class, they're going to graduate you without finals. It's the end of the school year, anyway."

She looked concerned. "Is that even legal? Are they allowed to do that?"

I smiled wickedly. "They are now."

She looked down to her niece. "I'm not going to ask who convinced them or *how you did it*, but thanks, I guess."

"Eh," I said, "you were going to graduate anyway if you got a zero on all your finals, so... You're good."

I saw a smile peak through her lips.

Twenty minutes later, I basically dragged her out the front door and almost to my car when we stopped at an irate voice.

"*What*?" a guy said, stepping outside after us. "Riley, WHAT?"

We both turned to find Ryan standing at the doors to the cafeteria, where no one else was.

It was just me, him, and Riley.

Veo took Julie and Claire home, and it was class time now.

"Ryan," Riley said, "please understand."

He shook his head, eyes burning with rage and hatred. A type of vengeance and anger I had never seen in him before.

He looked rattled, and startled, and... *pissed off.*

I was starting to wonder if he hit her or not.

He was seething. I could tell his teeth were clenching, and his eyes were burning with rage.

"Riley," Ryan said, eyes glimmering with tears.

It wasn't tears, though, he was manipulating her.

"Riley," he said again when she didn't move from my side, "I thought...." He looked back to me, eyes darkening in anger. "She's mine, you fucker."

And he pulled a pistol out of his pocket, making Riley scream as I immediately threw her behind me, holding an arm out to her so she could grasp something.

"Paris!" she cried, trying to get in the way so I wouldn't be shot but I held her in place. "Paris, no!"

I knew what she was afraid of. I knew she was terrified of losing me.

But I wasn't losing her, either. I'd find a way for us both to win this twisted game.

"Ryan," she cried from behind me, "what are you *doing*?"

He only pointed the gun at me, making my breathing sharpen when I pierced a glare at him.

"Do you think..." Ryan said curiously, "that if I shot you through the neck, it would hit her in the head?"

I heard Riley start to breathe shallowly.

"So you want to kill *her* now?" I questioned, rage boiling inside me. "What the fuck is WRONG with you? You said you *loved* her, you FUCKER."

But two men came through the doors behind Ryan, standing by his side like bodyguards.

"Mr. Raymond," one of them whispered, making my heart still when they whispered something in his ear.

It wasn't the whispering that startled me, it was the name.

My eyes darkened when I pulled my Glock out of my pocket, aiming it at him. "You fucker. You MOTHER FUCKER."

"Paris!" Riley cried, but I kept her in place.

Ryan gazed back at me, eyes dimming in boredom. "Paris? So you had one this entire time, haven't you?" His eyes darkened. "So *you're* the reason she'd been gone, aren't you, Paris? She's been hiding with you."

"You fucker," I repeated, anger boiling me inside as I felt myself start sweating, "it's *you*. It's been YOU. I knew it. I fucking KNEW IT."

"What's him, Paris?" Riley said, pulling at my arm. "Paris, what are you talking about?"

"Mr. Raymond," I stated, teeth clenching, "*you're* the copycat, Ryan. I knew it. I *knew* it was you."

He stayed silent, but I felt Riley start shaking from behind me.

"Why?" I said, waving my gun around while his two men pulled out theirs, clearly stupid enough to just notice I had one. "Why would you put her through this? You killed her best friend. *Your* friend, Ryan. You fucking KILLED her. And then Claire? You tried, but you failed. You killed Riley's aunt and uncle, and left her little niece alone. You murdered every person she could love, and then she was the final target, wasn't she?"

"Actually," Ryan stated, "that's not true, Paris."

I narrowed my eyes.

"I never wanted her *dead*," Ryan told me. "I wanted *her*. I wanted everyone out of her life because she was supposed to me MINE. I took everything she could love and I was honestly heading for her mother next, who..." he gazed up at me with his cold, hardened eyes, "magically disappeared after Riley did. She never liked me, Paris—her mother. Everyone told Riley that I wasn't good enough, so I thought if I took everyone she trusted away from her, then she'd have no doubts about me."

"You sick *fuck*," I snapped.

Riley was still shaking behind me, clearly frozen in fear.

"But now," Ryan stated, "I know for a fact by your secretive *BDSM* play that you've fucked her, haven't you? I can tell you're a dom, Paris. The way you talked to her during the lovey-dovey engagement was clear enough. But what I didn't know," he glanced at her behind my back, "is that she was a submissive. That's curious. I honestly didn't see that in her. And the fact that she could date someone as sick and twisted as you," he glanced at me, "and fuck you with no hesitation. Well that's a clear sign that," his eyes grew colder, "that bitch betrayed me."

All the sudden, I heard Riley cry out, and I felt her get ripped away from my hold, screaming.

I reached out for her, but one of Ryan's men pulled her away and wrapped an arm around her throat, pressing a gun to her head seconds later.

My throat constricted as my heart started shattering.

All guns were aimed to me then apart from her captor.

"Paris," she whispered, eyes glimmering.

I knew she was terrified. I knew she was pleading for me not to do something stupid.

But I was always one step ahead.

Ten shots burst through the courtyard, making Riley scream in fear.

But three of Ryan's men collapsed onto the ground, deceased.

And my own surrounded the area, me smiling menacingly as Veo aimed his gun to Ryan who was the second one standing.

Though, Riley was still restrained by that singular man.

But I could tell by his shivering leg that he was injured.

Ryan glanced around nervously as my men surrounded us.

"Take her out of here," Ryan said.

And I shot my gaze to Riley before—

Before one of my people smacked the butt of his gun to her captor's head, knocking him out.

But I darted to her then, screaming "IDIOT" at the man who knocked him out and right as her captor's knees buckled, his hand fell.

And his finger squeezed the trigger.

A fire echoed through the entire courtyard, and I saw a burst of light come from his gun.

And something pierced through my leg.

I collapsed, Riley screaming as all me and my men remained still in shock.

Ryan started laughing as Riley came toward me, and he started for her and grabbed her by the waist.

I distantly heard her cry out my name before he struck her across the head and threw her over his shoulder when her face fell.

No. No. Fuck. Fuck.

Why weren't my men going after her?

What the fuck?

But all of them came for me, asking me if I was alright and if I needed to call my doctor.

"No, YOU FUCKERS!" I screamed. "WHAT THE FUCK IS WRONG WITH YOU? DON'T LET HIM TAKE HER!"

But when they gazed up, to look for her.

She and Ryan were gone.

I started breathing heavily.

Shit.

Shit.

FUCK.

I forced myself up then, the adrenaline that pumped through my veins currently shoving the pain away.

I felt like I was on drugs.

I was angry. I was pissed.

And I wanted to kill him. I wanted to murder his ass.

When I got onto my feet, I could distantly feel my leg shaking with the agony, but I barely acknowledged it.

"Sir!" one of my men said. "Your leg!"

"Screw my fucking leg," I growled, starting in the direction that he started taking her. "He's going to *kill* her."

"Paris!" Veo said with urgency in his tone.

I turned, seething as my whole body shook with anger. "WHAT?"

He seemed taken aback by my anger, but I didn't really care right now.

"Sir," Veo stated then, "I know where he took her."

I felt my eyes glow with anger. "Where?"

"The forest," Veo stated, stepping toward me.

He clearly knew I wasn't going to back down.

"The forest," he repeated. "It's where your father killed my daughter, and it's where he killed Bella before transporting her to the alleyway for Riley to find."

I started there, and he followed.

My men started following, as well.

"How do you know this?" I questioned.

"I found evidence on one of my lookouts."

"And you never *told me*?"

"No, sir," Veo stated, "I was hoping to find more evidence before... before telling you, sir."

"Why?" I said then, practically running now despite my leg bursting with distinct pain.

"I was hoping to catch him in the act, sir," Veo told me.

I shook my head as we ran into the woods.

"All of you back down," I told my men. "This is *my* job. I don't want you intervening."

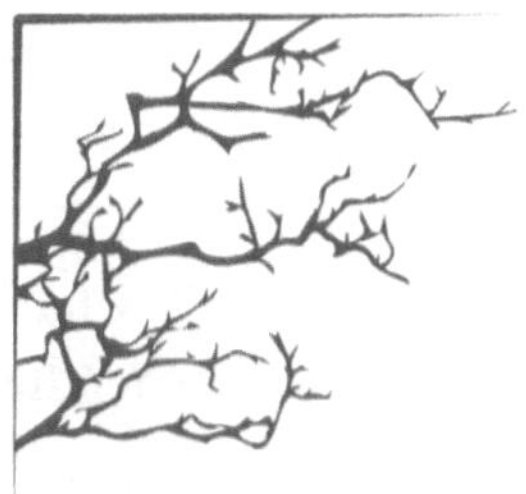

29

Riley

"What did he do to you, huh?" Ryan said as I leaned against a tree, holding me at gunpoint as I stared up at him, cheek throbbing from his punch earlier. "What did Paris do to you that I couldn't have done better?"

He kneeled down beside me.

"Did he fuck you?" Ryan questioned. "Put his dick inside you? I did that. I fucked you to oblivion, you never loved it. Did I really need to grab your hair and shove your head back? Bite your daintily little neck while I thrusted inside you?"

I glared at him despite disgust clogging my airways. "I never loved you."

He shoved my head back against the tree, making me cry out as he threaded his fingers roughly through my hair. "You like playing games, don't you? Like I've been playing your life like a game?"

I never answered, refusing to let him get in my head.

My heart was hammering against my chest when he pulled a knife out from his pocket, making me suck in a breath when he trailed it lightly across my throat.

"You're sick," I spat despite the silent threat. "*You're* the one? YOU'VE BEEN DOING THIS TO ME? What have I done to you, Ryan? What have I DONE?"

He slapped me across the face, making me cry out when he caught my hair and nearly ripped out the strands when he forced me to face him. "What have you done?" he whispered to me. "You're mine, Riley. You always have been."

"I WAS NEVER YOURS!" I screamed. "I NEVER BE-LONGED TO YOU!"

He slapped me across the face again, and pulled me back with the same harsh force. "Don't talk back to me like that," he hissed. "You fucking cunt."

I glared at him then. "I was never yours," I repeated slow-ly, loving how his eyes glowed in anger. "Never," I repeated, "ever. Ever. EVER. All this time," I told him, breath shutter-ing as his previous giving gaze was now replaced with a cold, emotionless one, "all this time it's been *you*? When Bella died you comforted me in your own little way. When Claire al-most died you did the same. You told me today that killing myself wasn't worth it. Was it all an act? Was it all an ACT? And don't give me that, *you loved me* bullshit. You had two men try to *kill me* a day ago."

He stared at me then, and I watched as he moved close to me, whispering menacingly, "Riley—Riley—Riley. You're mine, Riley. You're *mine*. They acted out of line, Riley. I never told them to kill you. And I'm not letting you give yourself to hell, or to your *friends*, or to your *family*. You're mine, Ri-ley. All MINE. Since we were kids you've been mine. Since we started going here, MINE. Now don't you get it?"

"I'm not yours," I told his cold, twisted mind, "I never was. I belong to me, and I belong to Paris."

His eyes darkened at the name of my fiancé. "Well... if you were going to kill yourself, anyway, I'd let you now, but... I don't think so. No. It would be more fun to torture your life out of you, wouldn't it, Riley?" He shoved himself to me. "With all this... EMOTIONAL TORMENT you'd given me."

"That was all YOU," I answered. "I never asked you to BECOME A COLD, HEARTLESS, *PSYCHOPATH*."

He slapped me hard across the face then, and I cried out once more.

But he then glared up at me. "I'm going to love murdering you, Riley."

I stared up at him as he leaned forward to hover his face over mine.

"Slowly," he said, "I'll murder you. I'll slice you open over and over again until you start begging for mercy, and then I won't stop until all of your beautiful blood leaves your body. And then I'll dismember you piece by piece and scatter your entrails all over the city. And then Paris is next. Oh, I'd love killing him. Worse than you, you know."

But I grabbed a loop in his jeans where something stiff stood, pulling him closer as I whispered, "Then do it, pussy."

He glared at me, shoving me away as he reached for his gun.

But the movement of him pulling away made the object I grabbed in his jeans come free, and I smiled as I flipped the pocket knife open and swiped it toward him.

I aimed for his neck, but he flinched.

And I sliced his eye instead, making him scream and fall back.

I kept a hold on the knife as I shot up and darted away from his pained screaming.

I covered my mouth as I gasped for breath, heart pounding wildly against my chest as I watched Ryan hobble through the woods under me.

I was stuck in a tree I climbed what felt like hours ago, though I honestly didn't know I could climb trees that fast, but I didn't put much thought into that.

I went on pure instinct, and still was.

"Riiiiiiley," Ryan sang from below me, scanning the woods with his one good eye, "where arrrrre you?"

I noticed even from up here that he wrapped some kind of white clothing on his eye to stop the bleeding, but I knew I was at an advantage because his depth perception and peripheral vision were gone, but I couldn't find myself running out of here alive still.

He might've been handicapped, but I knew he was smart.

"Where are you, Riley?" he continued singing. "Riley, my Riley. Come out—come out—wherever you arrrrre."

I started breathing shallowly when he stopped right below me, my heart hammering against my ribcage, and the blood roaring through my ears making it hard to focus.

"*Pssst*," someone hissed from above me, making me shoot my head up to find a figure crouching in the trees.

I felt my body warm when I saw his golden hair and sharp blue eyes.

Paris.

He was alright... He survived the gun wound.

I didn't see where it hit him, and I worried that it killed him.

When I snapped back into the real world, I watching him press his finger to his lips, telling me to be silent.

I nodded, knowing he had a plan.

But when I looked down, my heart stopped.

Because Ryan had a smile spread along his lips.

What...?

But he aimed the gun up at me, and I stiffened when I noticed him look up.

"There you are," he said.

And before I could register what was about to happen, a gunshot echoed through the entire forest, and I felt a bullet slice an inch of my shoulder off before flying past my face.

I cried out, the impact loosening my hold on the tree branch.

And I fell, screaming.

When my back met the forest floor, I blacked out for a moment when all air left my lungs.

I came to within seconds, gasping as my hands searched the forest floor for something to hold onto.

I couldn't breathe, and it reminded me of the ocean when I almost drowned.

But I still couldn't breathe.

Ryan laughed when he stood over me, kneeling down to my level when my watery eyes met his single, cold one.

"Did you get the wind knocked out of you?" he asked me as I started getting air to my lungs. "Yeah, sucks, doesn't it? Maybe if you were more quiet up there and not making *psst* noises, you would've escaped."

I blinked away tears when he leveled his emotionless gaze with mine.

He didn't know Paris was here then.

Thank fucking God.

When I gazed back up at the tree, I noticed that the spot where Paris once stood was empty, and I turned my head to the side in hopes to not alert Ryan that someone else was here, finally getting air to my lungs as I tried to roll over.

But Ryan shoved me back to my place, making a *tsk* noise when the movement burned the wound on my shoulder.

"Ooh," he said, looking at the blood blooming through my dress, "ouch. That's gotta hurt, huh?"

He pointed to his bandaged eye. "This feels fucking fantastic, though."

I stared up at him hazily, unable to move out from under him.

Paris had a plan, I hoped.

Or I was going to die.

I didn't know what I could do.

Ryan smiled, slipping his hand inside the collar of my shirt despite me yelling out in protest, and he took the knife that I had from out of my bra without my permission and flipped it open.

How did he know it was there?

"Your body is warm," he stated, running his hands down my wounded arm and knowing I couldn't move it, "I wonder if I could get one more fuck out of you before you die."

I glared at him, trying to look menacing as my face broke out in a sweat.

"You look more ill than scary," he stated, laughing. "Aww, does it hurt?"

And he took the knife, slicing the front of my dress open and making me scream as the tip of the blade lightly slid across my skin.

He pulled the front of my dress open, and I used my free arm to push against his chest but he caught it with his hand and pinned it down, watching my breasts.

"Oh," he said, staring down at the blood blooming along a line down my front, "looks like I cut you a little."

I winced when he ran his finger along the wound, picking up the blood on his skin and took a look at it.

"Red," he stated, making me writhe from under him when he tried to unclip my bra from behind, and he laughed when he finally let go. "So feisty."

But he shoved me down hard, making let out a choked cry as he slipped his hand behind my back again, attempting to unclip my bra one last time.

But a pair of legs crashed down next to us, and I noticed Ryan tense at his presence.

"Leave her alone," Paris growled.

When I gazed up at him, Paris held his Glock, trained to Ryan's forehead.

What took him so long...?

But Ryan smiled, dodging out of Paris's range when he sliced my arm open with the pocket knife.

I cried out at the burning pain.

Paris shot at him, but it only hit the ground next to Ryan, and the psycho only smiled.

"Hold this for me, Honey," Ryan said.

And seconds later, he shoved the tip of the knife into my throbbing gun wound.

I screamed.

I screamed louder, shaking from under him when electricity shot up my body.

He smiled at my pain and he laughed, but I couldn't move.

This pain... was unimaginable.

It burned. It stung. It stabbed. And it struck through my body like lightning.

I heard another gunshot a second later, but this time, it sliced through Ryan's leg, and he yelled out, collapsing beside me.

I didn't realize it, but I was crying. I was unable to move, but I was screaming at this pain, and I didn't have the strength to pull the knife out.

Paris ran over to me when Ryan scrambled away from us, but I couldn't see what he was doing with my vision cracking at the edges like glass.

"Shhh..." Paris soothed, assessing my wound without touching it, "hold on. You'll be okay."

But a low chuckle came from next to us. "Will she?"

And without notice, Ryan's leg came at me.

He shoved the toe of his shoe into the knife, driving it further into me.

I screamed, my vision growing black around the edges as pain coursed through me life waves of electricity.

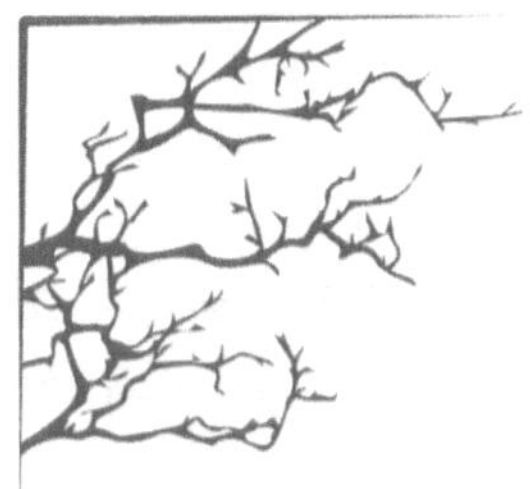

30

Paris

I stood faster than I ever thought I could, storming over to Ryan as he stepped backwards away from me.

I could see the bitterness in his eyes, but I could also see that...

Well... he was terrified of me.

I pulled my gun out of my pocket and backed him against a tree, watching his singular eye beat in fear as I pressed the nose of the Glock to his forehead.

He started laughing despite the fear clearly coursing through him, and I still heard Riley screaming from behind me, clearly unable to get the knife out of herself.

I was originally going to pull it out, but when he kicked it, I wasn't sure how deep it went, so I needed to make sure it was safe to now.

"Paris," Ryan said, eye burning with rage and fear, "all bark, no bite."

And he shoved his wrist against mine, knocking the gun out of my hand as I yelled out.

And he landed a blow to my gut, but I hardened the muscles there so it barely impacted me, and I ended up striking him across the face with my fist.

He yelled out and collapsed to the ground, and I menacingly walked up to him when he shoved his hands to ground to get up.

But I forced my foot into his shoulder, and he screamed as I heard a snap echo through the forest, and he collapsed back onto the ground, gasping.

I then stepped further to him while he tried to scramble away, not stopping when he finally managed to stand, legs shaking with all the pain clearly coursing through him.

He pulled up his gun and aimed it at me shakily.

But I struck his wrist with my fisted hand, knocking it out of his grip.

And I shoved him to a tree, making him yell when his shoulder hit the wood.

But I didn't stop there.

I took my thumb...

And I jabbed it into his wounded eye.

And that's when I heard his gorgeous screech, writhing from under me as the blood bloomed through the fabric faster, and slipped down his cheek like red tears.

I smiled then, pulling some barbed wire I found around here out of my pocket, and I shoved it to his throat, tightening it around the tree trunk as I pinned him to the wood.

His lips opened and closed like a fish, clearly trying to get air to his lungs when I blocked access to them.

"This was how Bella felt, I growled. "This was how Claire felt. Now you'll understand the pain they're in, and what Riley's feeling right now." I narrowed my eyes at him when his face started darkening to purple. "You mother fucker."

He started shoving his hands to my chest, but he was already so weak that it didn't even make me sway.

Blood bloomed from his skin of where the sharp bits of wire cut him, and I noticed his good eye starting to hemorrhage.

I wanted to watch the life drain out of him and I was enjoying it so very—very much.

His iris rolled to the top of his head, and I smiled when I noticed clear liquid pouring from his nose.

Cerebral spinal fluid.

I didn't stop choking him until he went limp under me, and I let go, watching him drop to the ground like a deformed teddy bear.

He was dead, but I still grabbed his gun from the ground next to us.

And I shot him in the head three times.

Riley was still crying next to me.

When his body lay limp under me, I immediately dropped the gun and ran over to her.

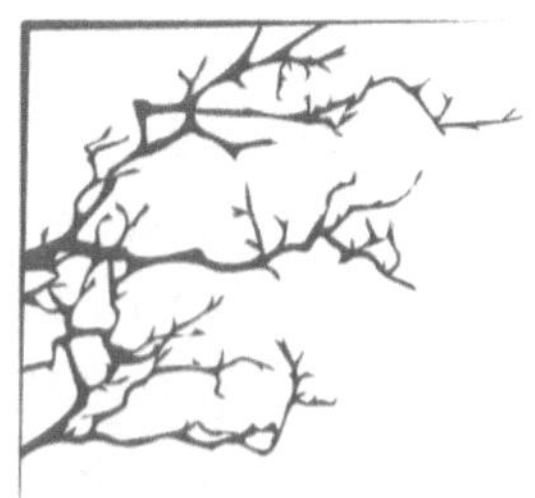

31

Riley

I woke at a start, gasping as the burning pain consumed me.

"Shhh..." someone breathed next to me, "it's alright. Don't be afraid. You're safe now, my love."

I turned my head to find Paris lying on the other side of the bed, watching me softly as he gave me an assuring smile.

"Don't worry," he told me, pulling some hair out of my lashes and tucking it behind my ear. "The doctor said you'll be okay."

My lashes fluttered at the calmness washing through me at his gesture.

"How long have I been asleep...?" I asked him gently, still feeling the wound on my shoulder burn, but it wasn't as painful as I remember.

"A couple days," he said, giving me a sad smile as he tucked more hair away from my face. "You had some brain trauma when you fell off the tree."

I stared at the ceiling then, blood running cold. "Oh...."

"My doctor had to put some meds in you to help you sleep off your concussion. Brain rest, I think. And he checked out your wounds, as well."

"Do I have brain damage?" I asked him carefully.

Paris shook his head, making me exhale a long breath.

"Also," he stated, running his fingers gently down my arm, "the wound that he caused?" He gently touched the bandage on my shoulder. "It's not fatal. The bullet grazed it, and the knife didn't go *too* deep. So it should heal like a bit of a deep wound. The bleeding stopped two days ago, and good old doc said I could give you a shower when you wake up. Do you want to now?"

I nodded, feeling sticky and crusty with all the dried blood and sweat stuck to me.

"Here," Paris said, sliding off the bed as he made it to me, "do you need help up?"

I nodded, and he slipped his hand under my back, making me exhale a groan due to me lying here for a couple days. My muscles needed a workout.

"Did you know I'd wake up today?" I asked him as he guided my feet off the bed.

"It was either today or tomorrow," he answered, holding my arm as I tried to get up.

The moment my knees buckled, he caught me and held my waist as we walked to the bathroom.

"Have you been lying next to me all day?" I asked him then.

"I had nothing else to do," Paris answered.

I smiled at his kindness. "I love you, Paris."

He gazed at me and returned the grin. "I love you, too."

And halfway to the bathroom, I felt my leg muscles start working now, and he released me a little as we walked in.

I still felt faint and weak, but I could walk.

I wasn't *too* high in the tree, so I didn't think I broke my spine or anything. And I didn't injure any limbs because I landed on my back.

Except for my shoulder that Ryan shot.

I winced.

The thought of him made my stomach turn.

Paris turned the nob of his luxury shower and let it heat up while I sat on the toilet.

"Here," he whispered, pulling the straps of my bra down. "Sorry about stripping you while you were sleeping. We needed to make sure you had no other wounds."

I let him gently unclip my bra and pull it off my front.

The wound from Ryan's knife was now scabbed over on my front; like a line of red crust.

Paris ran his thumb gently on it, and I gasped when he leaned forward and pressed his lips to the wound, all the way down to my stomach where it ended.

I smiled at the tingles running through me, and the burning that started coiling in my stomach.

"I have another wound for you to kiss," I told him as he ran his thumb gently on the scab.

He gazed up at me in response.

I turned my head away to expose my neck, and pushed my hair to my other shoulder. "My muscles hurt here."

His eyes glimmered with amusement as he leaned up and set his lips on my neck.

I gasped as he gently suckled and bit, and moved down until he kissed my nipple lightly.

I threaded my fingers in his hair when he sucked the bud into his mouth.

"Paris…" I murmured.

He drew back and smiled up at me, though I could see the fire burning in his eyes. "Let's get you clean first."

I let him pull my panties down, take off all his clothes, and he later guided me into the shower.

He had a bandage wrapped around his leg, but he was walking fine, so I assumed the bullet grazed him as well.

I set my head on his shoulder when the water hit me. "That feels good…."

"I'll make you feel *better*," he promised. "But you have to sit down first."

I looked to the floor of the shower, lashes lowering as the warmth of the water consumed me, but I listened, legs shaking as I attempted to sit, but Paris eventually caught me.

"Here, baby girl. Let me help."

I let him wrap an arm around me and lower to the ground with me basically using him as a crutch.

I collapsed toward the very end, but he caught me and let me rest in between his legs while we both faced forward.

"Lean back," he told me, guiding my head to his chest. "Good girl. Now I want you to focus on me."

I watched his bright blue eyes as he gazed down at me, and I felt his arm snake around me and his hand gently cupped the spot in between my legs.

I tensed, and immediately cried out when the wound on my shoulder burned with the movement.

Paris kept still there, but his other hand gently moved to my head and stroked my hair softly. "Shhh…" he murmured, "this is why we're going slow, angel. *Slow.* I need you to work on your tensing, okay? Don't be afraid. I won't hurt you."

He started moving his hand in between my thighs, making me suck in a breath.

He also stroked my hair to calm me, but I was too focused on the other movement.

"Relax," he whispered, "be a good girl and listen for once, okay?"

"Paris...?" I asked while he kept doing what he was doing.

"Hmm?"

"Was Ryan right...?" I questioned him softly as he kept a slow pace on his stroking. "Am I a submissive?"

"Yes," Paris responded, "you are, but that doesn't mean anything on the outside world."

"What do you mean...?"

He chuckled. "You know that thing in TV shows now-a-days like Criminal Minds and such?"

My eyes glistened with his reflection.

"There was this one episode where there was the big buff and fat businessmen guy," Paris explained, "complete asshole and such. And he clearly is a billionaire and is overly powerful."

I nodded.

"This big and powerful man was in his house," Paris continued, "and he ordered a fucking *prostitute* that was a BDSM play girl to be a dom on him." Paris waved his hands then. "And you know Criminal Minds, she became a serial killer or something."

A smile peaked through my lips.

"What?" he said.

"I think that was *Blacklist*," I told him, "not Criminal Minds."

He rolled his eyes. "Whatever. My point is that even big buff powerful men are submissives," he smiled softly at me, "and it's a trope, you know. Because sometimes, we're *way* different outside the bedroom. Which I guess was why Ryan was surprised by how you were a submissive. He doesn't know that factor about BDSM or S and M relationships."

I gazed up at him as he kept stroking me down there softly. "Paris...?"

"Yes, Honey?"

"Am I a good person?" I asked him.

He smiled. "An amazing person," and he poked my nose, "but such a pain in my ass."

I giggled.

But I gasped when he slipped two fingers inside me, pumping slowly.

"Did I surprise you?" he asked.

I nodded.

"I would apologize," he told me, "but, *nah*."

Despite his rudeness, he pressed the palm of his free hand to my injured shoulder.

"Relax, baby," he told me. "Don't hurt yourself."

"I'm sensitive there," I told him as he pumped.

"I know." He found the rough spot inside me and pressed down, stroking my G-spot roughly as he continued pumping.

I cried out, arching my back.

He kept his hold on my shoulder, hovering the warmth of his hand on my wound as he kept pumping. "Relax, baby. Listen to me for once. Relax."

I listened, easing the top half of my body into him as my lower started unconsciously riding his fingers.

I moaned softly as the heel of his hand started massaging my clit, and he smiled and kissed my neck.

"There you go," he said, "you're getting the hang of it."

The fire was building inside me.

No. No. I couldn't do this.

I needed...

I stopped then, and shoved my hand to his arms so his fingers would slip out.

I needed more.

He gazed at me as I attempted to climb off his lap and turned around, straddling him as he held still against the wall.

He smiled when I positioned his cock at my entrance.

But he dropped his head to the wall when I sank down on him, both of us groaning at the feeling.

And I rode him slowly, making him exhale a curse as I rested my palm on his shoulder, the injured one lacing its fingers through his.

I felt his other hand set on my waist, controlling my pace so I wouldn't go to far.

"Fuck," he whispered, throwing his head back. "Fuck, Riley. Go faster."

I felt like teasing him, so I went slower despite my body burning with him inside me.

He opened his eyes a slit to glare at me.

I giggled, but it faltered when he dropped his hand from my waist and gently stroked my clit.

I felt all my senses flood then.

I went faster without another thought, loving how he felt inside me.

So warm and hot and... *big.*

"Fuck," I whimpered then, going faster.

"Are you close?" he asked me.

I nodded. "So very—very close. You?"

He smiled. "I guarantee when you tighten on me, it's coming."

I kept our pace when the orgasm crested, and I rode him a little faster. "Fuck," I whispered. "Why do you feel so good?"

He never answered, just ran his thumb along the wound leading down my front, and he smiled. "So beautiful."

That was it.

I came, screaming and crying, and he pulled me to his chest so I wouldn't hurt myself tensing.

But he came, too.

Loudly.

I sank into his form when both our orgasms eased, and he ran his fingers through my hair as we caught our breath.

Without another word, he stood, holding me up while keeping himself inside me.

I wrapped my legs around his waist as he turned off the shower and carried me back to his room.

I wasn't sure if I was strong enough for another round, honestly.

"Paris..." I protested when he lowered my wet body on the bed.

"I know..." he responded, slipping out of me. "I can't either. You just feel so warm in there."

I smiled. "Have you gone flaccid...?"

"Yeah," he answered. "That's how hard I came."

I laughed softly when he picked up a towel from the side of his bed and dried both of us off.

"I have a question," he asked me as I lay beneath him, shuttering at the sudden cold.

"Yeah?" I said.

"I feel like..." he said, "that you like soft things, am I wrong?"

I shook my head. "I always have."

He smiled. "That's what I thought, so... I found this at a retail store near here and..." he pulled a large, feathery blanket from a bag next to the bed, "tell me what you think."

He draped it over me.

I nearly fell asleep just then.

As the softness brushed over me, I felt all pain—all fears—vanish, and I sank further into the bed, holding the blanket to my nose so I could feel it on my cheeks and inhale his beautiful lavender detergent.

"Riley approved?" he said.

I nodded.

He smiled then and lay down next to me, getting under the covers seconds later. "Good. I'm glad."

I let him brush his fingers through my brown locks while I kept the blanket to my nose, currently too comfy to acknowledge my damp pillow from my soaked hair.

"So..." Paris whispered, tucking a strand away from my face as I opened my eyes to look at him, "about that marriage thing...."

I smiled under the covers. "I said, yes. Still do."

His eyes lit up at my words. "Good. I'll prove to you for these next few months that saying yes was worth it. I hope tonight was a good start."

"It was," I told him. "It is. I love you."

"I love you, too," he responded, running a thumb along my cheekbone. "Just stay beautiful, Sweetheart."

I giggled. "I'm not wearing any makeup or hair product."

"Exactly," he responded. "Just stay beautiful. Stay yourself."

My cheeks glowed as I lowered my face further into the covers to hide it. "Thank you."

He only smiled. "Go to sleep, okay? I love you. I'll be here when you wake up this time."

I rested my forehead on his chest while closing my eyes, but while I was drifting, I distantly felt him wrap my shoulder with fresh bandages.

Yeah... this was nice.

I'd love this every day for the rest of my life.

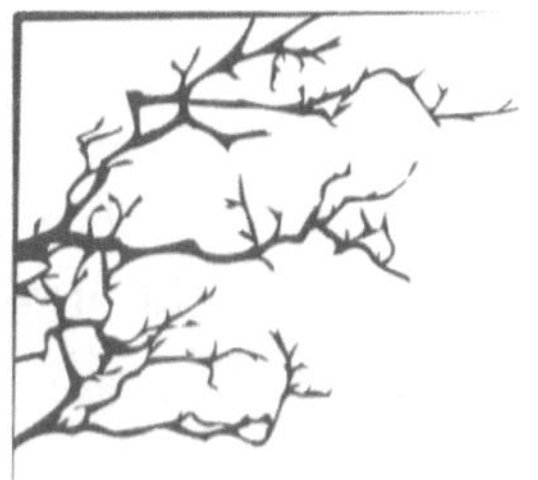

Epilogue

Paris
A YEAR LATER...

I woke up early the next morning, but when I turned over to check to see if Riley was alright, the left side of the bed was empty.

I looked up then, seeing the door to my bathroom wide open and hearing the shower running.

When I stepped over to the bathroom, I found Riley washing off her body under the water, gently rubbing her skin with the loofa I bought her the first time we met.

She glanced at me when I stood at the entrance to the bathroom, and I watched her smile.

She turned toward me and leaned against the shower wall, exposing her pussy while she lightly ran the loofa on her clit, moaning softly as she tipped her head back.

I stepped over to her then, closing the bathroom door behind me as she smiled, watching me open the shower door to join her.

I clasped our mouths together, grabbing her bottom lip and letting it drag out through my teeth.

"Our wedding's in five hours and you're *already* testing me, huh?" I asked her.

She smiled up at me, lightly trailing her finger down my stomach and along my length. "You need a release, don't you? So you don't run at the alter."

I smiled down at her, leaning forward so I could press her to the wall. "You're going to be the death of me."

"I could say the same," she responded.

And I touched our lips together, hearing her moan softly when I pressed her to the wall, kissing down her neck until I sucked her hardened nipple into my mouth, feeling her thread her fingers through my hair.

"Paris..." she moaned, "Paris, oh, god."

I drew back, and she gasped as she looked up to me.

And I slowly slid my dick in her entrance, making her press her head to the wall while I pumped in and out of her.

"Fuck, Riley," I groaned as her heat swarmed me. "Fuck, you make me so crazy."

She whimpered, gasping as she grasped onto the railing on my shower wall.

In and out... in and out... Jesus, she felt so good...

I fucked her for almost twenty minutes, the warm water raining down on us the entire time.

And when she hadn't come at the twenty minute mark, I thrusted hard into her, making her cry out.

I always had a plan for these types of occasions.

I leaned back, still inside her, and slid open a little drawer beside the shower, pulling out a long, vibrator as she looked up to me wide-eyed.

"Hold it," I demanded, pressing it to her clit while I guided her fingers around it.

When I turned it on, she gasped, shaking from under me.

But I only started thrusting again, making her throw her head back in pleasure.

"Fuck..." I growled when she tightened slightly on me, "you like that?"

She cried out again when I pounded in her, massaging the vibe on her clit when she started shaking more.

The moment she tensed and screamed...

I knew she came, and I did with her.

I pounded harder despite my entire body rattling with the gorgeous orgasm, making her sob and catch my shoulders.

But when the orgasm eased, I slowed my pace, letting us both catch our breaths when she took the vibe off herself, resting her forehead on my shoulder.

"Wedding first," I told her breathlessly, "and then I teach you a lesson."

She nodded, smiling softly. "Okay."

"**O**h, my gooooosh!" Claire said, wheeling up to us while she laughed happily. "I'm so proud of you guys!"

"Yeah," her boyfriend, Josh, said, "you guys look so nice together."

Riley laughed nervously next to me, holding her wine in her hand while I wrapped my arm around her shoulder, rubbing her arm unconsciously.

"So, how old are you?" Claire asked her, staring down at Riley's wine as an indication.

"Oh," Riley responded, "I turned twenty-one at the end of May."

"Oh!" Claire said then. "That's right! I forgot we had your twentieth birthday party at the end of the school year! I feel like you were the oldest girl there."

"Did you get held back?" Josh asked her.

Riley shook her head. "No, just started *really* late."

"Yeah," Claire said, "I get it. It happens a lot, Josh."

He nodded his head to the side, looking up at me, then. "So, you must be Paris."

I nodded. "Yep. And you're Josh?"

He returned a nod.

While Riley and Claire immersed in conversation, both of us stared at them in response.

"Thank you," I told Josh.

He gazed at me. "Huh?"

"Thank you for taking care of Claire," I explained. "Riley's been worried about her for years—kind of like a mother—and it seemed very unhealthy. She's very eased up now that the killer's gone, but... She seems more happy that Claire has someone to depend on."

"Yeah," Josh responded, "Claire has her hard moments, too. She's told me that Riley depends on herself most of the time, and Claire blames herself for a lot of Riley's problems. I think Claire told me that when that guy stabbed her, she honestly thought of dying because she worried that Riley would find her first, but then Claire realized that she would've been *less* traumatized if she fought the pain."

I nodded. "I've forced Riley in therapy. She fought *hard*, but I managed to get her into it. It's been a year since she's been seeing the therapist, and she's getting *so much* better."

"Claire, too," Josh said, "I forced her into therapy. The same outcome, honestly."

"Hey, sir!" Veo said, running up to us with Julie holding his hand and giggling. "Sorry for being so late."

"What's the verdict?" Riley asked him, eyes glittering with excitement.

All of us watched him scratch the back of his neck.

"They ruled, yes. Julie's now my daughter."

Everyone screamed and cheered, Julie jumping in the air happily when Veo gazed down at her, picking her up by her armpits while she hugged him back.

"Everyone!" I said, feeling warmth consume me. "Drinks on me!"

More cheering.

Riley gazed up at me when everyone rushed to the bar, and she stepped up, lightly kissing my lips before drawing back.

"Paris...?" she said, lacing our fingers together. "I love you."

"I love you, too."

"When we get home," she said, "we're binging Criminal Minds."

I laughed. "Not before I teach you a lesson."

She pouted, sticking her bottom lip out. "I thought you were joking."

"I never joke," I responded. "Right when we get home, your on your knees, got it?"

She smiled and rested her head on my shoulder. "Yes, sir."

I smiled, kissing her neck. "I love you."

"I love you, too."

Jesus... I would long to hear her say that over and over again.

"Hey, Paris?" she turned to me. "I wanted to tell you something."

"Yeah?"

"Remember a year ago when you told me I had an unhealthy obsession of finding the killer?"

I nodded. "Yeah."

"Well..." she smiled up at me, "I have a new one, now."

My heart stopped at her evil look. "Oh, no. What?"

She leaned up, whispering against my lips. "You, Paris. You're my obsession."

"Are you teasing me?" I asked her playfully. "Because you already know I'm fucking you *hard* tonight."

She smiled up at me. "You better."

"I *better*?" I echoed. "Mmm... are you hinting something?"

"No," she responded, "just saying that... well... maybe we could go to the bathroom for a little. Let out a little steam?"

My smile widened when her lips twitched. "You're asking for it."

"I am," she said.

"Fine," I said, setting my glass on the counter as she did the same, "garden, go."

She smiled and let go, starting off before I caught her arm and pulled her back.

She gave me a confused look.

"You're mine, too," I told her honestly. "Riley Princes," I whispered, "my ultimate obsession."

She giggled happily and ran off seconds later, and I smiled as I watched her exit through the back doors.

Wow, I made her come this morning and she *still* needed me.

I chuckled, starting after her.

This girl was going to be the death of me.

When I made it outside to the back porch, I walked a bit into the forest where no one really went during parties, and I made it into a secret area, finding a girl sitting on the garden floor, the flowers lightly brushing the bare small of her back as she faced away from me, her dress settled next to her.

The wind blew her hair suddenly, and she tipped her head back as if it felt good.

I smiled and walked up to her, running my hand gently down her spine and she looked up at me with a small smile.

Turning as she exposed her full breasts, I ran my hand over them, watching her lashes flutter as I gently tortured her nipple.

"That feels good," she whispered, setting her forehead on my shoulder.

I smiled, pulling away and lying her on the flowerbed.

She was so beautiful naked here... it looked like she was Mother Nature herself.

"You're so beautiful," I told her, gently running my hands down her sides.

She arched her back in response, nipples hardening at my touch while I trailed my palms down her legs.

I smiled up at her, loving how quiet it was out here.

How the birds were singing and how the wind blew gently against us, and how she looked so sweet and beautiful under the sunlight.

I ran my thumb over her cheekbone while my other hand started lightly rubbing her clit.

She arched her back, moaning softly.

I didn't speak the entire time, and neither did she, I just watched her as she let out little whimpers and moans, her skin glistening under the sunlight that beamed down on us.

I ran my hand down her breast as my other massaged her sensitive button a little more, and she turned her face into the flowers as she arched her back.

I never knew that something so quiet and peaceful could be so beautiful and sensual.

I pulled away then, whispering, "Open your legs."

She listened, and I didn't pull my cock out like it was screaming at me to, I just crawled over her bare form and set myself between her thighs.

And I drank.

She moaned softly, threading her fingers in my hair as my broad shoulders kept her open.

"You taste good," I whispered. "So good, my beautiful."

"Paris…" she moaned. "Oh, God… Paris…."

I kept drinking, pulling her clit into my lips and gently suckling it, swirling my tongue around her aching core while she arched her back under me.

I was planning on teaching her a lesson again, but…

She was so beautiful under all this nature and sunlight… I just wanted to please her the entire time and I didn't know why.

Her moans were so quiet while she turned her face into the petals under her, and I gazed up at her gently while she controlled her moans and gasps.

"Good?" I asked her gently.

She nodded into the dirt, still moaning as I continued to please her.

But I let her go, then deciding to rise up and hover over her while she gazed up at me curiously.

I didn't open my slacks, and I didn't care how wet she was going to make me.

We want what we want.

I came over her and leaned slightly down, making her still when my cock lightly brushed her clit.

And I started massaging it over her, and she moaned, turning her face into the petals again when I ground her a little faster.

"Paris…" she cried softly. "Paris, that feels so good…."

I smiled when I continued, setting my forehead on hers while gazing into her slightly glazed eyes. "I wanted to teach you a lesson for teasing me this morning," I told her while she smiled up at me, "but you're too Goodman beautiful. I need to fuck you in flowers more."

She giggled, closing her eyes while I ground my cock on her clit, feeling my orgasm cresting.

"Do you remember," I asked her softly, "the first time we had sex? You couldn't come this way, could you?"

She shook her head, still smiling at me.

"But now..." I said, locking eyes with her, "it's coming, isn't it?"

She nodded.

"So, sweetheart," I told her, grinding faster, "come. Come, my beautiful girl. You have my permission."

She dropped her head back and moaned, riding me faster, and the act forced me to start orgasming, but I urged myself forward, wanting—no *needing*—to please her.

She started shaking from under me. "Paris, I'm coming. I'm coming."

I smiled as she shook, dropping her head back as I rode out her orgasm, and her moan was so silent and peaceful.

And when she dropped back in the flowers, her eyes were hooded with a sudden exhaustion and peacefulness.

I couldn't help but lay next to her and hold her to me, and she smiled and she hugged me back.

She was completely naked, and I was fully clothed.

But neither of us seemed to care.

She laughed when she turned further into me. "That felt *really* good."

"I'm glad," I responded, stroking her hair.

I felt like I needed to do that more often.

She snuggled up with me as I lightly rubbed her back, but I felt her tense when I teased my fingers down her spine.

And eased them into her slick hole.

She covered her face in my shoulder, moaning softly.

I pushed her away from me and straddled her. "Can you sit up for me, Sweetheart?"

She listened, using her hands to push herself up, and I wrapped a single arm around her while the other pumped gently.

"Wrap your arms around me," I told her, and she listened, giving me a bear hug while I rubbed her back softly.

Jesus... her skin was so soft... and *warm*.

"I'm going to make you feel good..." I promised her again. "Really good."

She laughed softly while nuzzling her face into my neck. "I already came, Paris."

I knew, but I didn't care.

I wanted her to come again.

"Hold onto me," I told her, and she gasped when I started pumping my fingers in and out faster.

"I feel—like ever since—the night—I almost died," she told me through gasps, "that—you act like this—at abnormal—times."

I kept the pace. "What do you mean?"

"Plea—sing me," she responded, starting to ride my fingers, "only—me."

She was wrong. "It feels good to please you," I said to her. "Really good. Before I was being a jackass and only caring about myself."

"That's—not—true," she told me, tensing on my fingers as she hugged me tighter. "That first night—you were really—nice to me."

I went faster, making her let out a choked cry.

"That first night," I told her, "I wanted you to see how good it felt to come. All the times after that, I was being selfish." I lay her down on the ground, letting her keep a hold of me while I fucked her with my fingers. "I realized that at any moment I could lose you, Riley. *Any moment.* When Ryan ripped open your dress, it angered me... How my men didn't go after you when he shot me, it pissed me off. All those times where you needed me most, and I yelled at you for being clingy... when I made you feel so horrible that day you almost died. I realized how selfish I am." I kept pounding in her when I lightly kissed her neck, hearing her moan. "Riley," I whispered, my fingers keeping the pace, "I can make sex all about me, and I can make it all about you, too. And I can make it all about *both* of us." I watched her close her eyes while riding my fingers. "And, Riley," I told her, seeing her gaze up at me, "right now, I promise I'm satisfied. I just want to show you how happy I am that you didn't run at the alter."

She laughed and turned her head into my shoulder. "Is it Riley Lucan...?" she asked me. "Or Paris Princes?"

I gazed down at her while I continued the act. "What do you think? We sign the marriage documents in two hours. When we drive off, so what do you think?"

"Well," she said, easing when I slowed my pace, "Paris Princes can make you sound like royalty."

"Yes," I responded, "and Riley Lucan can make you sound badass."

She tipped her head back and grinned while I continued pumping in her.

"I think..." she whispered, "I like Riley Lucan. Not because I'm going with societal terms," she gazed up at me, smiling, "it just makes me sound like I'm a werewolf."

I laughed and leaned over her, kissing her and pulled back while she held onto me. "Riley Lucan it is."

She wrapped her arms around my back tighter, burying her head in my shoulder as she started shuttering.

"Paris..." she whispered, "please, can I...? Can I please...?"

"Yes, Riley," I responded, "you can come."

She cried out, burying her head in my shoulder when her body rattled with her release, and I smiled as she gasped, lowering herself into the flowers as her eyes hooded more.

I ran my hands along her bare body, loving how beautiful she looked under the beaming sunlight.

She turned her face toward me, smiling as I admired her form.

I smirked when she gave me the satisfaction and arched her back so I could see how good this felt.

"You're being so gentle," she told me, giggling while I continued the act. "I'm not a fragile flower."

"You look so good *on* them," I responded. "Naked and all."

She laughed even though I was being serious.

"Paris?" she asked me. "Do you think we could keep up all this passion for the rest of our lives? All the teasing and the fucking and such? Does it ever run out?"

I shook my head. "We could be decrepit old people and I'd fuck you."

She stuck her tongue out. "Gross. I don't want to think of that right now."

I chuckled.

"But, Paris," she argued this time, "I'm nervous, really. You know that couples usually go out on dates and then cuddle on their couch while they watch action movies, right?"

I gazed up at her then, still feeling her up while I watched her eyes glisten uneasily while waiting my response. "Riley," I told her, "we can still do those things."

Her eyes lit up. "Really?"

"Yes," I responded, "and when we watch the action movies, we can cuddle," and I smirked, "and then I can fuck you in front of the TV."

She laughed, a sound that could echo through the world endless times, and I would never get sick of it.

Her laugh was so different from other girls. It was so loud and obnoxious, but it sounded so light and airy.

I loved it.

I rested my forehead on hers while lightly tracing my fingers up and down her thigh.

"I could fuck you a thousand times in a year," I told her, "and I would *never* get sick of how you feel." I ran my thumb along her lip. "Never get sick of your smile."

She tipped her head back as I clasped our lips together, and I kissed the corners and let go, wrapping my arms around her body.

She was so warm... I could feel it through my clothes.

I remembered a year ago of how I wanted to understand everything about her. I was so fucking curious that it nearly drove me mad.

I watched her close her eyes as the sun beamed down on us.

Riley Princes... I thought, *my ultimate obsession.*

The End

Also by Aspen Wolff

Obsession

Also by Arianna Courson

Chronicles of the Enchanted
The Silent Kiss
The Silent Kiss
Lullaby: A Book of Enchanted Shorts

The Bane Saga
Alpha Bane

The Chained Saga
Quiet, Now
Quiet, Now
Be Still
Be Still

The Crave Saga
Crave

Chains
Secrets
Bloodless: The Entire Crave Saga

The Fallen Shadow Saga
Lily's Fallen Shadow
Jason's Angel of Storms
Silence Me
Silence Me

The Switched Chronicles
Switched
Twisted
Deviant
Hush, Little Angel: The Entire Switched Chronicles

The Vendetta Saga
The Demon's Duchess
The Shattered Carnival
City of the Dead
The Wonderland Show
A Song of Darkness
Duchess of Death
Vendetta

About the Author

Aspen Wolff is an adult romance author who lives in Colorado. She enjoys living with her four dogs and three cats, and also enjoys listening to music endlessly for hours. Her favorite hobbies are writing, drawing, and watching anime. In the future, her dream is to be a famous author for years to come.

www.ingramcontent.com/pod-product-compliance
Lightning Source LLC
Chambersburg PA
CBHW031439160726
47994CB00005B/1801